THE GIANT SMUGGLERS

Chris Pauls & Matt Solomon

FEIWEL AND FRIENDS | NEW YORK

A FEIWEL AND FRIENDS BOOK

An Imprint of Macmillan

Our books may be purchased in bulk for promotional, educational, or business use. Please contact your local bookseller or the Macmillan Corporate and Premium Sales Department at (800) 221-7945 ext. 5442 or by e-mail at MacmillanSpecialMarkets@macmillan.com.

Library of Congress Cataloging-in-Publication Data Available

ISBN: 978-1-250-06652-7 (hardcover) / 978-1-250-06653-4 (ebook)

Book design by April Ward

Feiwel and Friends logo designed by Filomena Tuosto

First Edition: 2016

2 4 6 8 10 9 7 5 3 1

mackids.com

FOR OUR PARENTS,
DALE & SUSAN PAULS AND CONNIE & JERRY SOLOMON,
THE GIANTS IN OUR LIVES

1

A slew of newly crowned seniors gathered to celebrate finally becoming the ruling party of Richland Center High School in the darkened rock quarry just outside of town. The sun had been down for hours. No parents, neighbors, or teachers were around to break up the party, safely hidden in the open space between hulking piles of crushed rock. The closest building was an abandoned silo out past the end of the gravel pit.

The kids didn't hear the silo's dome creak as it rose up a couple of feet. An enormous hand reached out and wrapped its fingers over the edge of the forty-foot structure, propping up the top. Huge eyes blinked and watched from inside.

The eyes darted left and right to make sure the coast was clear. Then a mammoth leg swung out over the side of the silo, and without a sound, a twenty-five-foot-tall giant emerged.

This giant was no monster. His youthful, dark-skinned

face was huge, but otherwise it looked like that of any teenager. He wore nothing but a brown canvas tunic, and his long black hair swirled in the breeze against the cloudy night sky.

The music got louder, and the kids got rowdier, dancing to heavy beats in the headlights of their cars.

The giant folded, unseen, into the darkness at the edge of the quarry. The thumping music confused him—he recognized the beating of drums bouncing off the quarry walls, but where was it coming from? He studied the teens thrashing to the beat, and soon his head bobbed in unison with theirs. He thrust his right hand in the air, almost perfectly imitating their dance.

At the point where the headlights dimmed and night began lay a pile of four signs that read SPRING GREEN CITY LIMITS. Valley High, Spring Green's high school, was Richland Center's chief rival. Swiping the signs was the seniors' first jab in what promised to be a yearlong contest for local supremacy. A kid wearing a letterman's jacket snapped a picture of them with his phone, proof of their plunder. The giant blinked in disbelief. He'd seen it for only an instant, but somehow an image of the signs glowed on the box in the kid's hand. The giant had seen a few strange things on his trip so far, but if he could trust his own eyes, this was magic.

A growling bass line kicked in, and the kid in the jacket hurried to join the throng by the cars. The giant edged closer to the sign pile, curious.

"This is epic!" another guy shouted with a fist bump to a fellow partyer. He jumped onto the hood of a car. "Let's not wait until Homecoming to burn their stupid signs. Valley sucks! Let's do it now!"

All the other kids threw up the chant. "Bonfire! B

They didn't see giant hands reach out from the the darkness and snatch the signs away. A colossal, curious finger traced the strange letters as the giant tried to make sense of the weird wooden placards. How had they duplicated themselves inside the kid's glowing box?

"People in Spring Green won't know if they're coming or going," yelled the guy on the car, slipping and landing on the hood with a thud. The kids all laughed, except the one who owned the dented car. The guy rolled off the hood and lumbered toward where the signs had been. "Hey, what the heck?" The other partyers gathered around, some confused and some downright angry. Cutting down the signs had been risky. "Where'd they go?"

Then a truck pulled into the quarry, heading straight for the party. The kids winced at the bright headlights as the vehicle skidded to a stop. A silver-whiskered man, old enough to be everyone's grandfather, leaned out the driver's-side window.

"Get out of here right now!" His voice boomed through a cloud of gravel dust, rising above the music. "All of you! This is private property. You got three minutes before I call the cops."

"Cops!" shouted the ringleader. He dove into the passenger seat of a buddy's car. "Adler! Let's go!"

The giant hightailed it back into the silo unseen, accidentally pinching the tip of his right index finger when he lowered the top. He dropped the signs and bit his lower lip, muffling a scream that would have been heard all the way into town.

The old man favored his right hip as he got out of the truck. A German shepherd bounded from the cab behind him. Between the old man punching numbers into his cell phone and the mean-looking dog snarling at everyone, the party broke up in well less than the man's threatened three minutes. Soon the last cars were peeling away, racing back toward Richland Center.

"Powder, that's enough," said the old man, swinging aside his long leather duster coat and slapping his thigh. The dog stopped barking at the escaping cars and heeled. The man peered over at the silo. "You can come out of there now."

The giant threw the top off again and vaulted out of the silo, landing as quietly as a cat on the ground. He looked as disappointed as the other kids that the party was over.

"I know, I know," grumbled the old man. "The music was loud, and everything is new and interesting."

The old man had that right. The giant pointed to the phone that the old man had threatened to use to call the cops—did it work like the kid's had?

"You stay away from phones. If someone sees you or snaps a decent picture, we're finished. You're a secret. You have to stay that way. We've been through this before." The old man spat on the ground. "I should have moved you sooner. Kids hang out in quarries—always have." He kicked a stone and looked up at the giant. "Well, you can't stay here. Let's get moving."

The giant stayed in place, sucking the tip of the finger he'd pinched on the silo top.

"What are you standing around for? Let's go," he repeated. "We're heading to a new hiding spot. It's an old warehouse, and the place is falling apart, so take it easy climbing up. Once you're on the roof, don't dally—get your big butt down the hole and quick. You got it?"

The giant nodded. Long black bangs drooped in his face.

The old man's whiskered cheeks billowed as he pointed toward a large dump truck. "You know what to do. Get moving."

The giant bounded to the truck in one leap. The truck's suspension groaned as he hopped into the bed and lay down on his side. He had to work hard to scrunch his huge frame into the uncomfortably tight space.

The old man yanked a lever on the side of the truck. A motor pulled a canvas tarp along a metal track, sealing up the giant in the back. The old man stopped the cover short of the giant's head. "So we're straight," he said, "this is town we're talking about now. That means people, so no screwing around. I can only keep you safe if you stay out of sight."

The old man started the tarp back up. As the cover reached the end of its track, he missed the giant's mischievous grin.

Charlie Lawson saw his opening. He spun the steering wheel, and his white Lamborghini wailed past *99NInʒas*'s lame Dodge Charger. Charlie's *Total Turbo* alter ego, *CUGoneByeBye*, was back in the lead.

Charlie checked the map at the top of the screen for the other racers. He was scorching *SpeedDealer* from Spring Green; *Rocket2Ride*, the Viroqua motormouth; *DaleEarnhardtʒr.ʒr.*, from Muscoda; and *Adelicious*, a girl from his school. Man, he loved beating these guys.

His best and only real friend, Trenton Mullins, had moved to Germany at the beginning of summer. He joined Charlie's dad and brother on the list of people who'd split and left Charlie alone in boring Richland Center. His only escape from the monotony of small-town life was *Total Turbo 4: Danger Ahead*. He dominated the game and had spent the whole summer racing online instead of hanging out at the pool like everyone else. Now that school had started, he'd already gotten in trouble a couple of times for being late because he had a good race going.

"Looks like you got another one, *CUGoneByeBye*," chirped *Adelicious* in Charlie's headset.

"The only thing he's got," hissed an obnoxious new voice, "is a major problem. Me."

Charlie checked the map again. A new car had entered the race. A pitch-black Porsche driven by someone with the boring username *Fitz* was bullying its way through the field and coming up fast.

Fitz roared unscathed through police gunfire on an airport runway, muscling *Rocket2Ride* right off the course with a nasty bump move before settling in behind Charlie's Lamborghini. The two cars were locked in a battle for the finish line with one turn remaining: a hard ninety-degree corner. Charlie laughed at *Fitz*'s audacity. "Bring it, buddy!" He took the turn low, jumping his foot from the brake to the accelerator to put this new guy in his place.

The Porsche zipped right around him. Charlie cringed as *Fitz* flew first across the finish line, shouting "Game over!" through the headset.

Charlie threw down the wheel onto his unmade bed and kicked the foot controls away. He shook his shaggy, ash-blond hair in disbelief. *Fitz* had stolen the race, handing Charlie his first loss in months. It was even more humiliating than the time in fifth grade when Mrs. Hendricks got on the loudspeaker to call him to the office because his mom had brought his snow pants.

On-screen, "Another race?" blinked in taunting red letters. *Absolutely!* Charlie fired up the next course. He'd been playing for five hours, even skipped dinner, but that didn't matter. He wanted revenge, to kick this guy's butt and prove the win had been a fluke, especially as he heard *Fitz*'s voice crackle through the headset:

"Let's do this thing again, *CUGoneByeBye*—unless you're scared?"

Charlie toggled a button on his headset, switching to audible disguise mode to make his voice deeper, mechanical, and menacing. "Scared they're going to have to scrape you off the pavement," he shot back.

Then Charlie heard a stern man bark through the static. "Jamie, I told you to shut that off. You've got work to do!"

"Bye-bye, *Jamie*," Charlie mocked in a singsong tone, which sounded even more condescending with his voice buzzing way down low. "Daddy says you gotta go."

"You better hope I never get my hands on you."

Fitz disappeared before Charlie could snap back a reply. One by one, the other drivers signed off. Charlie could imagine parents yelling to knock it off with the games. No one would yell at him tonight—his mom was out with DJ, her boyfriend. Charlie shuddered. He hated thinking about his mom dating. It was just one more way real life in Richland Center continued to suck. He powered down the game and heard muffled screeching from the apartment below.

Uh-oh.

Charlie had been playing *Total Turbo* for so long that he'd forgotten all about Pansy, the cat downstairs. He'd promised Mrs. Lundstrom that he'd feed her nasty beast by six at the latest. It was nearly eleven. With no more roar from the game, he heard the cat yowling like crazy.

He kicked his way through the moving boxes on the floor of his new room, which was even worse than the one in their last crummy apartment. He and his mom had been in this cramped place for only a week, their third home in the past two years. Rita Lawson had made Charlie promise to finish unpacking before she got home. What was the point? The boxes would just have to be loaded up again, dragged around to wherever they were going to live next.

More caterwauling told him that chore would have to wait. He threw a hooded sweatshirt over his scrawny frame, went out the back door, and bounced down the wooden stairs from his second-floor apartment.

"Hang on, Pansy." Charlie turned a key that Mrs. Lundstrom had left for him under the mat. He seethed as he remembered how the old lady had thought he was eleven (not his actual thirteen going on fourteen) when she asked him to feed her cat while she was on a bus trip to the Indian casino. He pushed the door open.

Pansy, all black and all business, dashed right between his legs and out into the night. Charlie yanked the door shut with an angry bang. He wasn't in the mood for stupid games.

The cat postured on the sidewalk, taunting him, her eerie yellow eyes glowing in the night. "You want to get fed or not?" Charlie took only two steps toward her before she dashed toward the old warehouse across Church Street.

He chased Pansy to the back of the building and down a murky alley, finally cornering the cat by some trash cans. "C'mon, cat," he said. "I got better things to do."

But Pansy had other ideas. She jumped through a shattered ground-floor window and into the old building.

Charlie hesitated. Chasing her into an alley was one thing; following her into the creepiest building in town was another. The AD German Warehouse, built by the famous architect Frank Lloyd Wright around 100 years ago, had been abandoned for as long as Charlie could remember. In fact, it reminded him of Wonka's chocolate factory: Nobody ever went in and nobody ever came out. The warehouse stood about four stories high, with huge, casted-concrete Mayan hieroglyphics etched into its roofline. It seemed weird and otherworldly, as if a UFO had swung by and dropped an ancient ruin into the middle of town.

Taking care not to cut his hands, he pulled the biggest shards of glass from the shattered window pane. Then he crouched down and peered inside, finding only darkness.

"Pansy?" he called. There was no response.

Cursing the cat, Charlie contorted his body and squeezed through the opening. There wasn't enough of a gap for a normal-size eighth-grader to wedge through, so for once being a shrimp played in his favor.

He swore that the temperature fell fifteen degrees as soon as he dropped out of the window onto a cold concrete floor in a small room. No cat in sight. He went through a stout metal door into a short hallway.

"Pansy?" he called, with not so much as a meow in response.

Charlie breathed in the dank air, which became mustier as he passed out of the hallway into an enormous room. The skeletons of small birds and rats littered the cement floor. The warehouse was even spookier on the inside, if that was possible.

Rough, jagged concrete ran along the walls where the building's floors had once been. The place had been hollowed out. It was more a four-story cave than building now.

"C'mon, you stupid cat," he shouted.

The moon cast eerie shapes through the slit windows that ran near the ceiling, creating just enough light to see by. Charlie crept in farther, the sound of his footsteps echoing off the concrete. The cavernous room was empty except for a few odds and ends: a rickety-looking table with a single chair; two stacks of crates balanced on wooden pallets; a large wooden box with a hinged lid—man, did it stink; and, for some reason, an old bathtub.

A muffled noise froze him.

He peeked in the direction of the sound. It had come from the crates. He crept over and inspected the nearest stack, hunting for cat hiding spots. The lid of one of the boxes was askew. Maybe Pansy was holed up inside. He slid the top all the way off, finding a bunch of fat cylinders wrapped in brown paper and tied up with rough twine in bundles of six. Charlie lifted out a pack and grunted—the mystery bundle was a lot heavier than it looked. As he turned it over, moonlight caught the side of a crate. It read DANGER: EXPLOSIVES.

Dynamite!

Had someone blasted out all the floors inside the warehouse? That would explain a lot, though Charlie couldn't figure out how it could have been done without alerting the entire town. He eased the deadly weight back into the carton.

"Pansy?" he called, hoping she'd just pop out from wherever, and they could leave. No response.

He investigated a metal accordion door that hung off the side of a large, square opening jutting out of the wall. It was way too big to be a chimney. Charlie guessed it could have been an elevator shaft at one time, but there was no car inside. He slipped his head into the cavity, half expecting to get a face full of bats. No bats—but no Pansy, either. He looked up the shaft and saw stars in the night sky. It was open at the top.

Then the floor shook and little hunks of concrete rained down all around. He gave a yelp and stumbled back away from the shaft. Out of the corner of his eye, he saw Pansy dart out of the dark with a frightened mewl and hightail it down the hallway.

Two huge, bare feet landed in the elevator shaft, kicking up a cloud of cement dust. Despite their size, the feet barely made a sound as they hit the ground.

Charlie's instinct was to run from whoever or whatever those huge feet belonged to, but fear nailed his own feet to the floor. It was the most inconceivable, unbelievable, utterly incredible thing he'd ever seen in his life. Charlie tried to will himself to run, but then there was a rush of air. Something grabbed him and thrust him up, up, up into the moonlight.

He found himself face to face with the impossible.

The only word to describe his captor was *giant*. The behemoth had no trouble holding Charlie's entire body in his fist. The giant pushed his face, big as a tractor tire, toward Charlie's and examined the boy like a jeweler who'd just come into possession of an unusual gem.

Charlie finally found his breath and let out a high-pitched yell.

The giant put his free index finger over his lips in the universal sign to "keep quiet." The gesture, surprisingly human, shocked Charlie into silence.

He still was desperate to escape. But pushing against the monstrous fingers was useless. His captor had to be at least twenty feet tall and probably twenty times as strong as Charlie. He forced himself to check out the giant's face, which was dotted with the soft black stubble of a guy who was old enough to shave but hadn't gotten around to it yet. His wild hair was pretty crazy-looking, thrusting every which way. Was he wearing a toga? He looked like an overgrown, emo caveman.

The giant cocked his head to the side. "Hi."

The greeting surprised Charlie almost as much as the fact that he was being held in a huge fist. Whatever the giant was up to, he didn't seem threatening. "Hi?" Charlie responded. "You . . . speak English?"

The giant's lips parted into a smile, revealing an unattractive set of yellowed, neglected teeth. His breath smelled like a combination of fish and oatmeal.

Charlie had taken a trip to Crazytown. Giants didn't exist, let alone live across the street. He spat over the side of the giant's hand, just to test reality. *Splat.* Yep, it sounded real. There he was, twenty feet in the air.

"Think you could put me down?"

The giant lowered Charlie to the floor and loosened his grip. Charlie's first instinct was to run, but just as he hit the floor, his phone went off. The ring tone, thumping dance music, echoed in the warehouse. Charlie did a double-take as the giant pumped his fist in the air and bobbed his head to the beat.

The screen said the call was from Charlie's mom, probably checking in on him. Charlie silenced it, and the giant held out his hands as if to say, "You just killed my jam!"

"Who are you?"

The giant stared back, unwilling or unable to give an answer. Apparently, the English only went so far.

"I'm Charlie," the boy managed, now 90 percent convinced that the giant wasn't going to eat him.

"Ch-ch-charlie?" the giant stuttered, trying to pronounce the unfamiliar name.

"That's right, Charlie."

Then both their heads jerked in the direction of a loud crack from out in the hallway. Someone was coming.

A beam of bright light snapped on in the hallway. The giant nudged Charlie into the dark of the elevator shaft. The giant held his index finger to his lips once more and signaled for the boy to stay put. Sounds of heavy footsteps mixed with an accelerating skitter of claws on concrete as the ominous light bounced toward them. A German shepherd bounded into the main room of the warehouse, tail wagging.

"Powder!" chuckled the giant. Shielding Charlie's position in the elevator shaft, the giant bent down low and held out his enormous right hand. Powder licked the tip of his huge finger, still red and sore from the pinch at the silo.

The beam of light disappeared just before a flashlight clanked on the old table. The silver-bearded old man in his leather duster coat hobbled into the moonlight. Charlie edged deeper into the darkness of the elevator shaft.

"Welcome to your new digs," said the old man. "For a little while anyway." He pulled up the splintery chair and collapsed into it. "People in town couldn't care less about this place, but don't push it. I can't be around all the time, and there's not much I can do to keep you in here. But remember, this isn't just about you—there's your family and others to think about. You'll see them soon. Sitting around in here's no picnic, but you'll just have to make the best of it."

Powder raised her nose in the air and sniffed. Then she turned toward the elevator shaft and seemed to stare right at Charlie in the darkness. He thought he was a goner for sure and held his breath.

The giant intervened. He bent down to one knee and scratched her head with a colossal finger. The dog flopped onto her back so her belly could be rubbed. "Powder stay?"

"You two, together? No thanks," the man grumbled. "Best thing you could do during your time here is rest up. You'll need it for the next leg of your trip."

The giant nodded his head and yawned an outsize yawn, letting the old man know it was time to go. Charlie smirked. It sure looked like the giant was playing the guy, the same way Charlie played his mom when he wanted to sneak in a few more *Total Turbo* races.

"All right, we're taking the dump truck back. Don't expect to see much of us when it's light out. Not worth the risk." The old man hobbled away, dog at his heel. "We'll be back with some breakfast before the sun comes up."

"Okay, Hank."

The giant waited until the sound of a door shutting echoed down the long hallway outside the room. "Charlie!" The boy tiptoed out of his hiding spot—the coast was clear. "Secret!"

"Dude." Charlie held up his fist for the giant to bump. The big guy looked down, confused by the gesture. Charlie bumped his own two fists together to show him how, then offered his up again. The giant grinned and dropped his huge paw down in front of Charlie, who bumped it hard. "Yeah! Like that! That means we're cool."

"Cool?" the giant said, trying out the expression.

Charlie's phone buzzed again. This time, there was a text from his mom:

Be home in 5. Expecting to see some empty boxes.

He knew she wasn't kidding. There'd be heck to pay if he hadn't touched the boxes, and he was off somewhere else on a school night. It wasn't like he could tell her about the giant—she'd think he was nuts. Or worse, she'd want to come over and investigate. He had to go—he didn't have a choice. Finally something had happened in Richland Center. He'd just stumbled into the weirdest, most fantastic thing of his life, and he had to unpack moving boxes.

Unbelievable.

The giant was on his hands and knees, trying to get a better look at Charlie's glowing phone. The boy stuffed it into his pocket. "I'm really sorry, but I got to go."

The giant's face sagged.

"But I live right across the street." He gestured toward the apartment. "So I'll be back. Tomorrow. First thing."

The giant sat back against the wall. "Cool," he said, showing off his new word.

Charlie took one last look at the most unbelievable person he'd ever met and waved. Then he ran as fast as he could back down the hallway, squirted through the window, and dashed back across Church Street. His mom's boyfriend's truck was nowhere to be seen, which meant she wasn't home yet. Pansy was back on her stoop, like nothing unusual had happened. Charlie let her in, threw some food in her bowl, and rocketed up the steps to his apartment.

He just got the back door open when the headlights of DJ's Hummer curved into the driveway. He rushed into his room, hit the lights, and hightailed it under the covers, clothes still on.

It wasn't long before, predictably, his mom peered around the door to check on him. Charlie's eyes were closed in his best imitation of deep sleep.

"Charlie." She sighed, disappointed. Boxes were still all over the floor. He'd hear about it in the morning.

But it didn't matter. The moment he fist-bumped *an actual freaking giant* was burned into his brain.

His mom closed his door for the night.

Charlie slid off the bed and over to his bedroom window. From there, he could see the top of the warehouse. An approaching truck's lights climbed up the front of the building, illuminating the slit windows near the roofline.

That's when Charlie saw the giant staring at him. The big guy winked. And even though the boy was pretty sure the giant couldn't see him, Charlie winked back.

Now that he was over the initial shock of what he'd seen, questions raced in Charlie's mind like speeding cars in *Total Turbo*. What was a giant doing in Richland Center, of all places? Were there more out there like him? And who was the old man with the dog? The giant had called him Hank.

Charlie was going back in that warehouse first thing the next morning to find some answers.

The sun peeked over the vast gravel pit atop Quarry Hill as a piercing siren wailed. The surrounding hillsides were still green, but it was green on the run. In another month the trees would explode with fall colors before every trace of foliage fell and was lost until spring.

Below, at the base of the steep hill, an industrial white van sped toward the rock-strewn pit. The two scientists inside the vehicle ignored the dying siren.

A battered tin sign stood at the entrance to the quarry: ALL VISITORS MUST CHECK IN AT OFFICE. "Head for the silo," said Dr. Sean Fitzgibbons, ignoring the warning. It had been a long time since he had allowed rules to get in the way of what he wanted.

The doctor was about forty years old, with broad shoulders and a strong, arrogant chin. He double-checked their position using a GPS app on his phone, then leaned out his window to survey the quarry. It looked deserted, just as he'd hoped. "Let's go over this one more time. If we find our giant, we tag it and get out of here. No engagement. That's not our area of expertise, and we don't want to attract attention. The Stick will handle the rough stuff."

The driver, Neil Barton, was younger than Fitzgibbons by ten years and heavier by at least thirty pounds. Squinting in the early morning sun through a pair of smudged, wire-rimmed glasses, Barton zipped the van right past a rusting office trailer, a weigh scale, and additional warning signs. "Why is he called the Stick, anyway?"

"He's the kind of man who solves problems one way. And talking isn't the way."

Atop a blasted-away section of hillside across the quarry, the old man in the leather duster frowned. He watched the van snake around the gravel piles, crushing red plastic cups from the previous night's party. Powder stood at his heel. She followed the van's journey with wary eyes.

Reaching into his duster with a steady left hand, the old man pulled out a detonator. The dull metallic trim was scuffed and scratched. He rested his thumb on a lone toggle switch, mostly bronze because all the chrome had long since worn away. It sat in the middle of the controls beneath a stub antenna and red button.

He squinted to make out a green logo imprinted on the van's rear doors. Everyone in town knew the Accelerton symbol, a double helix that formed the stem of a leaf. The multinational conglomerate had an agribusiness arm that controlled nearly all of the local fertilizer and seed market.

The van continued toward the vine-covered silo. Powder let out a low growl. The old man's thumb twitched against the detonator's switch, but he pulled it back, spitting into the dirt and slipping the metal box back inside his waist pocket. He turned to his dog. Her black ears shot up.

"Powder," he commanded. "Go say 'Hi.'"

Powder didn't need to be told twice. She exploded from her perch on the hilltop, kicking up a cloud of dust as she darted toward the silo. The old man winced as he began the rocky descent toward the quarry's trailer office.

The van pulled up next to the silo. Barton grabbed a metal case off the seat and hurried out of the vehicle, his shirt already wet with anxious sweat. He peered up at the battered old building's dome.

Fitzgibbons swiped his phone to call up a grainy, black-and-white satellite photo. He compared it side by side with the actual silo, weather-beaten and leaning just a bit to the right. It was the same building, but there was a crucial difference: in the picture, four huge, oblong shapes pushed up the silo's dome. They looked like immense fingers.

"The place is sure big enough," Barton said. He couldn't wait to see a giant up close for the first time but was a little frightened by the idea as well. He dropped the metal case on the ground, opened it, and reached for the custom rifle inside. It fired a tiny device that could be tracked anywhere in the world.

"Hold on," commanded Fitzgibbons, peering over his shoulder back toward the office trailer. "Let me scan it before you bring that out into the open." He closed the photo app with a finger swipe, then opened another labeled *WiVi*. He held up his phone as if he were shooting video of the silo. Using a satellite signal, the app penetrated the walls and allowed a blurry view of the structure's interior, like an ultra-sound searching for an unborn baby. Fitzgibbons let loose a frustrated sigh. "There's nothing here. It's empty. We're late again."

"You've got to be kidding me. That picture is from ten forty-two last night!" Barton slammed the case shut. "It was just here! Where could it go?"

"Whoever's helping the giants is shrewd." Fitzgibbons drew in a breath of the country air, heavy with the earthy smell of manure. He took in the small, tilled field a short distance away. "We already knew they're moved all the time. We just need to find where." He circled the silo's exterior. "Chin up. You were right about Richland Center; it appears to be on the giants' route, and that's something."

"What will we tell Gourmand?"

"I'm not concerned about her right now." Fitzgibbons pulled a small flashlight from his pocket. "I'm going to take a look inside the silo. And you," he said, pointing to the field, "put that case away and grab some soil samples."

"What good is dirt?" Barton grumbled. He returned the metallic case to the van and grabbed two soil collectors. Then he trod out to the field with the vials and pushed them into the black, fertile earth.

Ten yards away, Fitzgibbons inspected a small, ground-level discharge door at the base of the silo. He donned a pair of latex gloves, got down on his knees, and pushed his flash-light through the swinging door. After he squeezed through the opening, the steel door clanked shut behind him.

Fitzgibbons stood and brushed decades-old silage from his knees. He shined his light here and there, finding nothing but dust floating in the air. A careful sweep of the ground revealed four Spring Green city limit signs, dented and discarded. The signs were too big to have come in through the silage door.

His flashlight explored the walls, finding mossy growth on the mortar where water had seeped in between concrete blocks. Then he noticed an uneven spot at the edge of the silo's half-cylinder dome.

The block had been chipped and torn away. Fitzgibbons called up the aerial photo on his phone again; the damaged area corresponded with the location of the giant fingers in the picture. He searched along the walls for a ladder to get a better look. No luck. Not done yet, Fitzgibbons probed further with his flashlight.

The light settled on a small pile of chipped concrete that had fallen from the top edge of the silo. He got on his knees, sorting and sifting through the rubble before coming across a crescent-moon sliver of opaque, colorless material. The discovery measured about six inches long and perhaps three quarters of an inch at its widest point. Its lead edge was rounded, relatively smooth and uniform, while the opposite side was jagged in spots, as if it had been torn off. It appeared to Fitzgibbons that he had found a very large piece of fingernail. He pumped his fist, an old gesture of triumph from his track-and-field days. Then he removed tweezers from a kit in his jacket, gripped the discovery, and dropped it into a sample bag.

The swinging door made a rusty squeak, and Fitzgibbons spun around. The beam of his flashlight met the hostile eyes of a German shepherd. The beast snarled, exposing a mouthful of sharp teeth. A deep, throaty growl swirled in the silo as she advanced.

Fitzgibbons put the sample ahead of his own safety, securing the bag in his jacket before retreating to his left. The menacing dog closed the distance between the two of them. He put his back to the silo wall and slid along, block by block, toward the door.

When he arrived, Fitzgibbons couldn't bring himself to get down on the ground to scuttle through the door. He'd be defenseless. But then reason stepped in, and he chided himself. The dog hadn't attacked because she wasn't supposed to. Fitzgibbons was relieved—he was being herded. It was time to find the dog's master.

"Have it your way," he said, dropping to his knees and passing through the opening. As he did, he felt the German shepherd clack her teeth at his heels for good measure.

Outside, his eyes strained against the bright September morning before he saw Barton cowering inside the van. Evidently, the dog had done her job with him as well. Fitzgibbons was calm and deliberate as he made his way to the vehicle, despite the aggressive snout prodding at his ankles. When Fitzgibbons reached the van and opened the passenger door, the animal barked twice and bolted past him inside.

Barton panicked, slamming up hard against the driver's-side door. But the dog didn't attack. She settled between the two front seats and narrowed her eyes at Barton, who fumbled for the door handle.

"I'm certain if that dog meant you harm, she would have torn your leg off by now," Fitzgibbons said, though the words did little to reassure his partner. The scientist checked the inside pocket of his jacket to make sure the sample he'd collected remained secure then hoisted himself up into the passenger seat. With an emphatic slam of the door, he trapped the dog inside the van. "Let's go."

Barton's hand shook as he found the ignition key and turned it. He pulled away from the silo, his eyes bouncing from the road to the dog, which was poking a suspicious snout into his right leg. When the van hit a bump and lurched, the dog gave a sharp bark. Barton recoiled, jerking his foot off the accelerator.

"Keep your foot steady on the gas. Head back the way we came."

Barton retraced the route he had taken through the quarry. As the van turned past the office trailer, an old man in a duster jacket strode into its path. He held up his hand for the van to stop, glaring into the cab through the dusty windshield. The dog recognized her master, and her tail smacked Barton's thigh with a steady *thump-thump-thump*.

Barton's fingers twitched on the steering wheel. "Should I go around him?"

"This is where the dog gets off," said Fitzgibbons. "Let's have a word."

Barton brought the van to a stop. The old man approached the passenger side and slid open the side cargo door.

"Powder, out!"

The dog bounded through the opening. The old man slammed the door shut and rapped the passenger window twice. Fitzgibbons slid it down. "I see Powder introduced herself," said the silver-haired man.

"Beautiful dog," said Fitzgibbons, his follow-up smile closed and brief.

The old man fumed. "This is private property. What's your business?"

"I'm Dr. Sean Fitzgibbons and this is my associate Mr. Barton." Fitzgibbons extended a firm hand. The old man took it, returning the show of strength.

Barton offered an anxious smile and a small wave. "How's it going?"

"Fitzgibbons," said the old man. "Should I know that name from somewhere?"

"Perhaps you remember him from the sprinting trials a few Olympics ago?" offered Barton.

"No, that's not it," said the old man, unimpressed.

"We're with Accelerton," Fitzgibbons said, waving off his partner. "We're out doing routine sweeps to determine if there's been any spread of our seed from one farm to another. It happens all the time, you know."

"Your genetically modified seed?"

"Yes."

"You won't find any of your stuff back there. That land's organic."

"Yes," said Dr. Fitzgibbons, wrinkling his nose. "I smelled the manure."

"Funny," returned the old man. "I didn't smell any until now." He made no effort to disguise his sarcasm.

"Our apologies, Mr. . . . I'm sorry. I didn't get your name?"

"Hank Pulvermacher. Didn't you hear the warning siren?

That ridge you drove under is rigged to blow. You're damned lucky I saw you when I did."

"Mr. Pulvermacher, we're sorry to start your day this way. We didn't hear any siren. But now that we have our soil samples . . ." Fitzgibbons reached between the seats and held up the containers Barton had collected back at the farm.

Hank squinted at the vials, dubious. "You can tell what's what from that little bit of dirt?"

"Your dog persuaded us to stop our canvass. Powder, is it?"

A wry grin crossed Hank's face, signaling acceptance of a stalemate. "You want to dig around back there, call the main office. Otherwise, you're trespassing. That's how it is, so get on your way." He gave the side of the van a smack to hurry it along.

"Of course, Mr. Pulvermacher. Once again, my apologies." Fitzgibbons slid the window up. Barton, the armpits of his shirt now dark half-moons of sweat, took the cue to hit the gas and drive away.

Hank watched the van pull off and slapped his thigh twice. Powder followed as he hobbled toward the trailer. He reached into his pocket, withdrew the detonator, toggled the main switch up, and pressed the red button.

Across the quarry at the ridge, a small puff of dust jumped from the rock face. Then a series of thundering explosions ripped through the pit. Tons of rock dutifully and dreadfully crashed to the ground, sending a chalky cloud into the air.

Inside the van, Barton jumped in his seat at the sound of the detonation. He checked the rearview mirror and hit the gas. A maelstrom of dust showered down on the vehicle. "Did he just try to bury us?" exclaimed Barton.

"It doesn't matter. The visit was a success, and we're on our way."

"You're satisfied with soil samples? Gourmand won't be, and you know it."

"No, we didn't find a giant," Fitzgibbons said, reaching into his jacket and pulling out the fingernail sample he'd collected in the silo. "But we didn't come up empty."

"What the heck is that?" asked Barton, sneaking a sideways look while maneuvering the van through the cloud of dust and back onto the main road.

"This," said Fitzgibbons, "might just be the break we need."

The last thing Charlie wanted to do was unload moving boxes, but his mom had insisted. He'd woken up early to sneak across the street and get some answers to the questions that had rattled around his skull all night long, but she'd gotten up earlier and cornered him before he could slip away. Now he had to wait. If only the giant had a phone!

Charlie kicked the carton marked *Tim* in fat marker. His mom had dragged the box of his brother's stuff around to the last three apartments, always stowing it in Charlie's room. She wouldn't throw it out.

To make matters worse, it was time again for the Richland County Fair, which meant his older brother would roll back into Charlie's life for a few days. Tim had dropped out of high school a few years back and joined Tip Top Shows, a traveling carnival that set up at county fairgrounds all over the country. He'd left home just into his senior year, leaving behind a note that essentially said, "Sorry. I have to do this."

It took his mom a couple of years, but she was sort of over the whole thing now. Charlie, not so much. He was still plenty ticked at Tim for abandoning them, right on the heels of their dad leaving for some woman he met on a sales trip. And now Charlie was stuffing Tim's box of crap into a closet that was already way too small for his own things.

The box was heavy with an old-school film projector and a bunch of other useless garbage: an empty black liquor flask with the initials *TL* engraved in gold; a silver, refillable lighter (no fluid, no wick); random poker chips; a pen featuring a girl in a bikini that got naked when you turned it upside down; a miniature Swiss Army knife with the toothpick missing; and an old pair of field glasses. Pressed up against the side of the box were old-timey film reels, ancient kung fu movies with corny names like *Game of Death* and *Enter the Dragon*.

Charlie couldn't figure out why Tim kept the old junk. "It's not old, Charlie," he'd argue. "It's vintage."

Whatever.

Then Charlie saw something under the film reels that sparked an idea: a pair of oversize walkie-talkies. They looked like they still worked. He grabbed the walkies and stuffed them in his backpack. With school starting in forty minutes and a long bike ride still ahead of him, he was nearly out of time to visit the giant. He had to get across the street, like now. Charlie hustled out to the kitchen just as his mom opened the oven door, filling the room with stifling heat.

"Finished already?"

He hesitated. "Nearly. Almost. I'll finish after school,

okay? If I don't get going, I'll be late." Charlie knew the excuse was golden—he'd received a couple tardies already by finishing *Total Turbo* races when he should have been biking off to school.

"You better not be. If I get another call from the school . . ." Rita Lawson let the threat linger in the air as the oven timer went off. She pulled her famous rhubarb crisp out of the oven and set the hot pan on top of the stove.

He grabbed a frozen waffle from the freezer, resisting the delicious smell drifting from the pan. Charlie held the entire waffle in his mouth as he grabbed a couple of nine-volt batteries from a kitchen drawer, slipped past his mom, and made for the back door. It stuck, and he forced it open with his hip.

"Don't forget—I want the rest of those boxes unpacked before we go to the fair tonight!"

"Got it," he managed to say through a mouthful of waffle. He bounced down the wooden stairs and scattered a few colorful butterflies, residents of his mom's monarch way station. She (and often, Charlie) tended to their temporary roost and even glued little tags to their wings so her Save the Monarchs group could track the butterflies' annual migration to Mexico. His mom did stuff like that.

He hauled his old twenty-inch BMX bike from under the stairs, shook the morning dew off, and rode to the intersection. He waited out the morning traffic to cross Church Street. It seemed like there were more cars than ever in town for the fair.

The traffic finally cleared, and Charlie pedaled across the street. He hurried the bike into the alley next to the warehouse, remembering that the old man had said he wouldn't come back when the sun was up. Charlie figured the coast was clear, but he hid his bike away deep in a patch of overgrown weeds just in case. Then he squeezed through the window he'd used to get in the night before.

Charlie dashed down the hallway into the huge room. The giant was lounging in the middle of the floor, grinning. Sprawled out like that, he wouldn't have fit in Charlie's apartment.

"Charlie," the giant exclaimed, and sprang to his feet. He held out his fist.

The big guy caught on fast. Charlie bumped it. "The old man's not around, right?"

"Gone."

"Sorry it took me so long to get . . ."

The giant didn't wait to hear the end of the sentence. He grabbed Charlie and hoisted him up to the high windows, giving them a bird's-eye view of the Richland Center downtown. The giant pointed. "What's that?"

Charlie looked at the tall county courthouse spire, a dull brick structure he'd seen pretty much every day of his life. "It's a clock. Supposed to keep time, but it doesn't even work," he said. "You don't know what a clock is?"

The giant turned toward Tower Hill and gestured toward the blinking antenna jutting skyward. "That?"

"A tower for sending out radio signals, I think." Charlie wasn't sure how to begin to explain radio.

The giant's ignorance didn't make him self-conscious about asking questions, which meant Charlie spent the next several minutes trying to explain mundane stuff like paint stores and school buses. It was as if the giant had never even been in a city before. The boy checked his phone and groaned. He had like three minutes left in the warehouse, max, or he'd be late for school—and Principal Dobbs had made it clear that was a big deal. Enough with describing gas stations and mail boxes. He had to get some answers of his own. "What's your name?"

The giant shrugged.

"You don't know your own name?"

The big guy shook his head. "No name."

"Weird! Do you even know why you're here?"

The giant chewed on his bottom lip. "Secret."

"You're just stuck in here the whole time? You can't get out and look around?"

"Secret," the giant repeated, and he didn't look very happy about it.

"That sucks!"

"Sucks?"

"Sucks. That means it's bad. Like you wish things could be different." Charlie wanted to press further, but he was out of time. "You got to put me down, man. I have to split!"

The giant blinked his eyes. He had no idea what Charlie was talking about.

"That means I have to leave. Got to go."

"No!"

"I have to! I'm going to be late to school."

"School?" The giant lowered Charlie to the warehouse floor.

"Be glad you don't have to go. It sucks."

The giant gestured around the warehouse. "Sucks!"

Charlie felt for the giant, but he just couldn't get away

with skipping. "I'll get in trouble," he explained. "With my mom."

The giant seemed to get that part. He gave a reluctant nod.

"I'll come back when I'm done," Charlie said. "But I've got something for you in the meantime." He dug in his backpack and pulled out the walkie-talkies.

"Phone?"

"Kind of, but not as cool." Charlie turned one on and handed it to the giant, who gave it a curious sniff. Charlie depressed the Talk switch. "Hey, can you hear me?"

The giant's face lit up, and he nudged his own talk button. "Yep."

"I just put in fresh batteries. Keep that on, and I'll call at lunch." Charlie held out his fist. The giant bumped it. "And I'll be back right after school, okay?"

"Okay."

Charlie busted out of the warehouse and fetched his bike out of the weeds. He pedaled hard out of the alley and down the block, determined to beat the bell. But more traffic for the fair stopped him at an intersection where a group of kids were circled up. Something was going on.

Fight!

Charlie wheeled up to the edge of the mob and waited out the traffic. He saw two guys squaring off in the middle, each waiting for the other to make the first move.

Brent Frawley, a running back on the high school's junior varsity football team, had a stupid grin on his broad, ruddy face. His long-sleeve T-shirt was pushed up around his massive forearms. He took a half-step into the other guy's space so that they were practically nose to nose.

Charlie didn't recognize this new kid, who showed no signs of backing down. Shorter but stockier than Frawley, his red hair was shaved tight down to a bumpy scalp, accentuating his square jaw. Thick crimson eyebrows furrowed into a *V*, creasing a pimpled forehead that shone with oily perspiration. "Say it again," he snarled.

Charlie heard a girl whisper "Fitz," and the name clicked in his head: *That's the guy from* Total Turbo*!* He remembered hearing the kid's menacing voice in his headset the night before. Fitz sounded nuts then, and he looked nuts now.

"Say it again." Fitz didn't appear to be breathing.

The students were dead silent, waiting in anticipation as the threat of violence filled the air.

Frawley smirked to a couple of buddies, wrestler types in vinyl jackets with spark plug insignias that advertised a custom car shop. He leaned in toward Fitz with a grin. "I wish I was blind," Frawley said, "so I could read the bumps on your face."

Charlie chuckled out loud, then stopped himself. Nobody else had laughed. He raised his hand to his mouth like he was trying to cover an errant cough, but it was too late for that. The insult echoed in the silence. His heart pounded up into his throat, and his face got hotter than July.

Fitz turned. His eyes narrowed even further, zeroing in on Charlie. Fitz almost seemed to be memorizing him, cataloguing every physical detail for future reference. After what felt like an eternity, Fitz pointed an angry finger at Charlie.

"Big mistake."

Then Fitz spun around. With unimaginable speed, he landed a devastating upper cut to Frawley's chin that sent the taller boy to the ground. He hit the pavement with a stomach-turning *thunk*. Blood gathered in the corners of his mouth like he'd chomped his tongue in two. Frawley tried to get up, but Fitz planted his right foot hard in the fallen boy's rib cage.

"Got anything else to say?" Fitz asked, punctuating his question with a stomp.

"Stop it!" screamed a pony-tailed girl wearing an orange and black *It's an RC Thing* T-shirt. "What's wrong with you? It was a freaking joke!"

Charlie didn't wait for traffic any longer. He darted out into the busy street, and a car horn blared. He tore across the intersection but couldn't help looking back.

Fitz stood at the edge of the circle of kids. He pointed at Charlie. "I owe you," Fitz shouted. "You're dead meat!"

Surveillance cameras atop iron masts glared down as a white van drove past an understated Accelerton sign on a manicured patch of lawn. The grass was pristine despite not having been mowed in a month. The blades of grass (a test product, specifically Accelerlawn #5) were genetically modified to reach a predetermined, perfect height of precisely two inches.

Dr. Fitzgibbons stood outside the main campus building on his phone, negotiating with a junior varsity football coach. His son's misbehavior at the bus stop was costing him precious time. The coach wanted to suspend Jamie for knocking his starting tailback out of the next game. A few calm, well-chosen words kept Jamie on the team for now.

Fitzgibbons put his phone away and stormed inside. He hurried down a long corridor where his fellow scientists were hard at work. Digital signage described research projects such as *Citrus Augmentation Trials* and *Biofuel Crops*. Each lab had a steel door with a rectangular reinforced window that allowed views of the research being conducted inside.

All the labs, except the new one.

Fitzgibbons held his palm to an ID scanner next to the nameless, windowless door at the end of the hall. With a click, the digital lock released, and he entered a research space unlike any other in the Accelerton facility.

At the back of the lab was a large, mostly bare room filled with natural light courtesy of a ceiling made up of interlocking glass hexagons. The concrete floor was empty except for four winches, positioned at regular intervals. Each was wound with aircraft control cable strong enough to hold down a giant. A tranquilizer gun rested on a ledge next to a control panel that regulated an overhead gas delivery system. Two gas masks hung on hooks nearby.

In contrast, the front half of the lab was dominated by galaxies of glass tubing and droning centrifuges. High-resolution screens mounted above the equipment depicted wire-frame models of human bodies, each one bigger and better than the one before it. Barton was hunched over a digital readout, working to extract DNA from the thumbnail sample they'd found that morning.

Dr. Fitzgibbons remembered the nervous, overweight graduate student who had approached him with an outrageous idea not that many years ago. At the time, Fitzgibbons was well known as one of the world's foremost authorities on human growth hormone. He knew HGH could provide only so much benefit for antiaging, injury recovery, and physical performance. Fitzgibbons wanted more. He needed a game changer. A giant discovery.

Even so, he couldn't believe he'd given Barton the time of day. The young man had e-mailed his research about the existence of giant creatures. He'd mapped all reported sightings, including every single blurry cell-phone picture and nut-job blog post. His hypothesis was that the sightings formed a complex pattern, starting in Alaska, stretching east across Canada, then dropping south through the United States straight down into Mexico via a variety of routes. According to his theory, giants not only existed but were migrating as well. The difficulty of concealing and transporting something that size suggested to Barton that the giants weren't working alone. It was almost as if they were being smuggled through some kind of underground railroad.

Fitzgibbons was understandably skeptical of all of it, starting with the premise that giants existed in the first place. But because Barton was an alumnus of his university, Fitzgibbons had agreed to see the young man.

During their interview, Barton had told a crazy story about a promising lead in Saskatchewan, a location on his giant smuggling route. A local news station had reported a giant sighting by a veteran fishing guide. Barton played the news report for Fitzgibbons on his laptop.

The Northern Lights had been brilliant green that night, and from his boat on Deschambault Lake, the guide claimed to have seen an honest-to-God giant standing on the beach, staring at the bright flickers in the night sky.

"Sure it was dark, but believe me, that was no Sasquatch,"

the guide in the video insisted. "As big as five men, looking right at me! Then he was gone in a flash back into the woods. People can say what they want, but I know what I saw. He was a giant man, not a monster." The news reporter confirmed that the guide had passed a polygraph test.

The guide didn't strike Barton as either a crackpot or an opportunist, so he'd followed up on the story. He got in his car and drove two days to Deschambault Lake. When he found no snapped tree branches or other obvious traces of giant activity, he searched the surrounding countryside, looking for a place where a giant might seek shelter. Four miles away, Barton discovered an abandoned church just tall enough.

He told Fitzgibbons how he had made his way inside the dark, hollowed-out shell of a church. The pews and altar were long gone, leaving more than enough space to hide a giant. Yearning for a bird's-eye view, Barton had climbed up the creaky steps to the bell tower. The bell's frayed rope dangled down. He examined the dusty bell and discovered a pattern that made his heart explode with joy.

In Fitzgibbons's office, Barton had carefully unzipped an ungainly canvas bag and unveiled the bell itself. Fitzgibbons remembered his reaction when presented with the evidence: "What does a bell prove? Even if I set aside the comic-book nature of this, you have nothing to back up these claims but a lot of sketchy accounts from country yokels. The migration angle is interesting, but it's not enough. I'd need something big to convince me."

In response, Barton had only smiled and pulled a small

penlight from his jacket. A blue beam bathed the bell. The dust in one area of the bell had been carefully brushed away. The light revealed long, wavy red lines swirling in symmetry. They comprised a thumbprint, enormous and unmistakable. "Is that big enough?"

It was. Lab analysis confirmed the thumbprint's authenticity; it was even enough to convince Fitzgibbons's old colleague, Gretchen Gourmand, to approve funding for their research. Her company, Accelerton, saw the potential for incalculable profits if the scientists were able to develop a giant growth hormone. GGH would yield revolutionary—even evolutionary—biotech advances with both civilian and military applications.

All of Barton's crazy stories led Fitzgibbons to where he was today, an unlikely Accelerton lab in Richland Center, Wisconsin. He moved to his desk and switched the signal on the monitors, pulling up flickering aerial views of farm fields, tree tops, and, most important, the silo he had visited that morning. Nothing out of the ordinary appeared.

A centrifuge dinged.

"How long?" asked Fitzgibbons.

Barton checked a program on his computer and sighed. "A few hours for preliminary results. If there's enough viable tissue, I can start synthesizing a biologic immediately."

Fitzgibbons nodded. The thumbnail was an exciting but limited find—best-case scenarios indicated Barton could produce only a limited amount of GGH. He looked up at the satellite images, serene aerial views of rural Wisconsin.

Barton stepped away from a centrifuge to join his boss.

He studied the farms and surrounding countryside and let out a frustrated sigh. "Just a bunch of cows doing cow stuff."

"Let's stay on it. In fact, I'd like you to task another bird or two. Whoever's helping these giants clearly has more than one location to hide them. There must be something we're missing."

harlie stood on his pedals and pumped like crazy to make it to school on time. He was more scared about being tardy again than of Fitz's threats. His principal, Mr. Dobbs, would call his mom, his mom would ground him for a month, and that meant seeing the giant again would get a lot more difficult.

Charlie threw his bike on the rack and sprinted through the front doors of Richland Center Middle School. There was Dobbs, standing outside the office, just waiting to catch the late kids. He looked at his watch and raised an eyebrow as the first bell rang. Charlie had made it just in time!

He hustled to his locker to stash his backpack and then off to class, plopping down in his seat way before the second bell. He saw a bunch of the jocks arguing about fantasy football like it was the most important thing in the world. Like usual, they didn't notice Charlie, even though he was sitting on bigger news than any football score. Of course Charlie wasn't about to spill—if he said anything about the giant, the whole town would be all over the warehouse. He was going to keep the secret to himself, at least for a while.

"Crazy loss last night, *CUGoneByeBye*."

Charlie turned around.

There was Adele Hawkins, *Adelicious* from *Total Turbo*, in the seat behind him. She was scrolling through some text-heavy message board on a handheld tablet—she'd always been the class computer dork, a distinction she wore as a badge of honor. But something weird had happened to her over the summer. Her hair, which had been in braids for as long as he'd known her, was down now. He thought it looked kind of awesome. She got tired of waiting for Charlie to respond and started talking again.

"Fitz just got lucky. He's weird."

The name *Fitz* brought fresh reminders of the bigger kid's threats. Charlie tried to play it casual. "You know him?"

"I babysit for his next-door neighbors. He just moved here. Jamie Fitzgibbons is his real name, but he hates being called Jamie."

Charlie thought back to *Total Turbo* the night before, when he'd mocked the bully's name. He was glad Fitz had no idea who *CUGoneByeBye* really was. "Prefers Fitz, I guess," Charlie nodded. "As in 'fits of rage.'"

Adele giggled, and Charlie felt his cheeks turn red. He never knew what to say when girls laughed at his jokes. Which, if he was being honest, didn't happen too often.

"I know how you can do better in the corners," Adele said, her voice dropping to a whisper. She looked around to make sure no one was listening and leaned in close to Charlie. "I found this message board, totally underground, nobody knows about it. You can't even Google it. There's a bunch of hardcore *Turbo* freaks on there. If you're cool, they'll share lots of game secrets with you."

"What, like codes?"

"Codes, cheats, driving techniques," Adele whispered. "Walk-throughs, hints, even backdoor hacks! It's a gold mine. Check it out." She spun her tablet around, and Charlie leaned in closer. Adele was right: The site was crazy. There was insider information on everything from acceleration mods to tire saturation. She paged through to a thread on cornering, his Achilles' heel in the race he lost to Fitz.

Sure enough, there was a technique called "heel-toe braking," a way to brake though a corner while still revving the engine. To pull it off, you controlled both the accelerator and brake with your right foot and the clutch with your left. With toes on the gas and heel on the brake, you could come out of the turn like a bullet. An online video showed just how effective the move could be.

"Sweet—I'll try it tonight," said Charlie.

"Wish I could see how it works. I got a bunch of new tricks I wanted to try myself, stuff even you haven't thought of."

"Why can't you?"

Her voice sagged. "I'm taking Doug and Dennis to the fair."

"Oh man." Charlie knew all about Doug and Dennis Perry, nine-year-old twins who lived about three blocks over from his apartment. A month earlier, the two of them had holed up in their tree fort with a water-balloon launcher and conducted a fierce assault on Seminary Street traffic. It took two squad cars to get them to stop and come down.

"I swore I wouldn't sit for them again," sighed Adele. "Then their parents offered to pay me double because everybody's so afraid of what the monsters will do."

Charlie winced. The Perry twins had twice the mischief-making power of his brother, Tim, and he'd destroyed sitters when he was their age.

The second bell rang, signaling the start of class.

"You going to the fair?" Adele whispered.

"Yep. My brother works out there," Charlie griped. "I *have* to go."

"Maybe I'll see you?"

Charlie tried to untie his uncooperative tongue. "S-s-sure," he stammered, sounding like the giant trying out an unfamiliar phrase. The teacher began talking, giving him an excuse to turn around.

The rest of the morning crawled by as he waited for a chance to test the range of the walkie-talkies. Finally, lunch arrived. Charlie took his backpack into the cafeteria, slammed his crummy sandwich, and split for outside.

The usual game of touch football was under way on the grassy field behind the school. All-time quarterback Mr. Spees, the math teacher, shouted the snap count "Go nuts" to send eager receivers out for passes. Charlie played it cool as he slid by. His plan was to hide out behind the equipment shed. If somebody saw him talking on an overgrown walkie-talkie, the ridicule would be endless.

He made it to the secret spot in no time, then peered around the shed to make sure no one had followed. He unzipped his backpack, pulled the antenna up on the walkie, and turned it on.

"Check one, check one. You there?"

"Charlie?" The giant's voice crackled through almost immediately.

Charlie hit the Talk button. "Yep, man, it's me. This works awesome!"

"Smell!"

So much for formalities, Charlie thought. "Something smells?"

"Bad."

Charlie remembered the smelly box in a corner of the warehouse, but he didn't think that was what the giant meant. "Is the smell coming from outside?"

"Yep."

Charlie chuckled. "I know, right? That's Donovan Dairies." The dairies emptied some kind of steam into the air every day and it stank like crazy. Since they moved close by, Charlie smelled it all the time. It was even worse in the summer, when it got hot. "Has something to do with making cheese. You know what cheese is?"

"Nope."

"You're in Wisconsin, dude. I'll have to get you some." He looked around the corner and saw a group of kids chasing a kickball in the shed's direction. "I gotta go. Somebody's coming."

The giant understood. "Secret."

"I'll be there soon." Charlie clicked off, pushed the antenna down, and stuffed the walkie into his backpack. The bell rang, and Charlie followed the kids back into the school.

Next was sixth-hour study hall. Mr. Bachman, the monitor, sat at the front of the room behind an old wooden desk. He had three rules, which were written on a sign hanging on the wall above his head: *No talking, no gum, no phones.* He started every period by pointing at the sign, then scribbling in a Sudoku book.

Charlie didn't have any homework, so he eased his phone out of his pocket. On a whim, he searched "giants" on the Internet, expecting to find some Jack and the Beanstalk fairy tales. Instead, he uncovered centuries' worth of people claiming that they had had encounters with giants. How had he not known this before? In the 1600s, thirty-foot-tall giants supposedly stomped around Australia. Others claimed a race of giants lived in the wild outside Chile during the eighteenth century. Giant kings ruled Peru, according to some stories.

Even today, there were plenty of people claiming to see giants. Giants in Kentucky. Giants in Mexico. Even giants in Wisconsin! Many of the stories sounded sort of crazy, but Charlie had a pretty big reason to believe them now.

"Rule three, no phones," warned Mr. Bachman in a stern voice. Charlie wasn't the only kid who had snuck his out, and they all rushed them back into their pockets. Mr. Bachman hadn't looked up from his Sudoku puzzle.

The rest of the day passed by slowly, but finally the bell rang. Charlie sprinted to his locker, grabbed his backpack, and tore out of the school. It was giant time. Charlie pedaled as fast as he ever had. Adrenaline drove his legs, and his bike sped along streets like never before. He was just about to cross over to Hillside Drive.

And that's when he saw him.

Their eyes met. His only hope was if Fitz didn't recognize . . .

But Fitz started his chrome-frame racing bike up the hill, his powerful legs pumping with purpose. White-knuckled fists gripped the handlebars, eyes locked on Charlie.

"Hey! Hey, you!" Fitz pointed his meaty index finger. "Game over!"

7

Panic had Charlie by the throat as he pedaled up Hillside Drive. The street was steep and the incline wore on his legs. He stood to push harder as his bike lurched up the tough grade in spurts. His lead over Fitz was evaporating by the second, and it didn't take long for him to come to a realization: *There's no way I can outrun him! He'll catch me before I can even get to the Siefkes' house.*

Across the street, Charlie spotted a poorly paved path that ran down the hill's front face to the Pine River. A wooden-planked suspension footbridge with rope webbing on the sides spanned the black water. Years of cycling around Richland Center had taught Charlie that the footbridge was a lousy place for a bike, but it was especially difficult for one bike to trail another. The lead bike shook the rickety suspension bridge, causing the boards behind to hop up and down. Fitz's bike wouldn't handle a rough ride as well as smooth pavement. *It's my only chance!* He launched the BMX onto the path.

Only twenty feet down the trail, Charlie found himself going too fast for pedaling to do any good. He held the pedals even and just concentrated on coasting. The bike staggered when his front tire collided with a stray hunk of asphalt broken up from the trail. The chunk went sailing. His front tire veered to the right, but Charlie went with the motion instead of over-steering.

His BMX shuddered as Charlie eased the bike back on the trail, and it smoothed out again. He took the opportunity to look over his shoulder. Fitz had just plunged his racer down the path.

Charlie hit the bridge and pedaled hard, building maximum speed and timing his next move. About one-third of the way across, he leaned ahead on his BMX, gripped the handlebars tight, and lifted the back tire up in the air in a donkey kick. Then he brought the back of the bike down as hard as he could. It cost him a lot of speed, but he was willing to sacrifice it.

Fitz was riding all-out as his bike hit the bridge. His front tire jumped all over the place, trying to stay true on the herky-jerky boards that Charlie's ploy had set in motion. Fitz couldn't hold the thin tire straight, and Charlie heard a yell.

He glanced back to see Fitz's bike lying on the boards, its front wheel spinning in the air. He skidded to a halt, raised his fists to the sky, and let out a triumphant "Yeah!"

He stood on the pedals, ready to ride again, when his nagging conscience made him look back one more time. Fitz was nowhere near the bike. Then Charlie heard a shout from the underside of the bridge.

"Help!"

Filled with a new kind of dread, Charlie pedaled over to the edge. Dark water swirled below as a dam loomed in the distance. Its concrete cap was crumbling at the edges from years of holding back the Pine River. He leaned out and peered down alongside the bridge.

There was Fitz, hanging from the boards on the other side of the torn rope. He'd wiped out and crashed through the webbing. "You gotta help me," Fitz pleaded. "I can't hold on much longer."

Charlie couldn't just leave. He rode over to the ripped-up webbing, jumped off his bike, and threw off his backpack. Kneeling down, he extended his arm. "Give me your hand," he said, not even sure he could pull up the bigger Fitz without being dragged over the side. Charlie could smell the kid's sweaty Hornets Football T-shirt.

"You did that on purpose," Fitz accused, his strained, pimpled face turning crimson as he stared up.

"Of course," Charlie admitted. "You were going to kill me." He stretched his hand out farther to the struggling boy.

Fitz coughed and spat from the back of his throat in Charlie's face.

Charlie recoiled in disgust and landed on his behind. He wiped away thick saliva that smelled like grapes, but grapes that had been in somebody's mouth. Fitz's meaty fingers strained white as they gripped the edge of the bridge. Charlie heard laughing. He watched in horror as Fitz's head began to rise.

"You believed I needed *your* help?" Fitz exclaimed. Then he let out a roar and heaved himself belly-first back up onto the footbridge. "Big mistake!"

Charlie's heart sledgehammered in his chest as he grabbed his backpack, jerked his BMX off the ground, and hurtled his leg over the seat. He burned away, standing tall on the pedals. The BMX sailed along the concrete sidewalk that led from the bridge, off the curb, and down Congress Street.

Fitz cleared the bridge. He had an easy, eerie smile on his face that said, "Nothing can save you now."

Charlie eyed construction equipment up ahead, part of the city's massive dike-building program to remedy a flooding problem. Charlie knew he couldn't outrun Fitz, but hoped to use the construction mess to slow him down again.

Adrenaline pumping, Charlie swung at full speed around an orange-striped barricade onto the tough terrain and bunny-hopped the BMX over a pile of metal rebar. He gave the pedals all he had, and the bike's knobby tires gripped the mushy surface. *Let's see how your racing bike handles this, Jamie!* By the time he was well into the heart of the construction, Charlie figured he'd left the bully far behind in the muck.

But when he turned his head, there was Fitz, flying toward him from a cross street. He had not taken the construction zone bait after all.

Fitz had learned his lesson on the footbridge about what his bike could and couldn't do. Playing to its strength—straight-line speed on a good road—he'd headed a longer way around and kept track of Charlie by peeking down side streets. Now Fitz was closing fast. With only the river and little else in front of him, Charlie was running out of room to run.

A massive pile of construction dirt up ahead slanted back toward the road like a huge ramp, practically inviting him to jump the river. He'd try it in a video game, but in real life, there was no way. Especially not on a bike.

Then his rear tire shuddered as Fitz nudged it with his front wheel. Charlie tried to counter steer, but his front wheel jerked sideways, and he went over the handlebars, landing hard on the dirt pile. Fitz skidded to a stop. Charlie scrambled to his feet and dashed up the hill, hoping to escape down the back side. Fitz followed him up the pile, wiggling the fingers of both hands in anticipation of a good beatdown. Charlie reached the top, looked over the edge, and gasped. It was about twenty feet straight down to the jagged rocks on the downriver side of the dam.

He was trapped.

Fitz reached Charlie and grabbed the back of his neck with a strong, hot hand. He grinned. "What are you, scared?"

Charlie's mouth opened, but no sound came out. Fitz was right. Charlie was scared to death.

Fitz tightened his grip and pulled back his other fist. Charlie closed his eyes, but the punch never came as a stern voice burst from below. "Powder, go say 'No!'"

The big German shepherd dashed up the incline, wild barks ringing over the sound of the water. Fitz let go of Charlie and stumbled down the hill, trying to dodge Powder. But the snarling dog drove Fitz back toward her master— Hank, the old man from the warehouse! He hobbled to the base of the hill.

Charlie couldn't believe his good luck, although the old

man didn't look happy to see either one of them. He sized up Fitz. "Looks like I got here just in time. What's your name?"

Fitz was frozen by a growling Powder. "Jamie Fitzgibbons," he groused.

"Fitzgibbons, huh? Sean Fitzgibbons your dad?"

Fitz's face fell, answering Hank's question.

The old man chewed the inside of his cheek. Then he turned to Charlie, who feared being recognized from the warehouse, even though he knew it was impossible. "And who are you?"

"Charlie Lawson."

"And who's your dad?"

"Gone."

Hank's face softened, and he slapped his thigh twice. Powder returned to his side. "Well, I don't care what you two were fighting about. It's done now. You get me, Fitzgibbons?"

"He laughed at me!" said the defiant teen. "No one laughs at me and gets away with it."

"People who worry about being laughed at," said Hank, "often find themselves in laughable situations."

Fitz's eyes burned, and he clenched and unclenched his fists.

"Get out of here," Hank said, "unless you want me to call out to Accelerton and talk to your old man."

Fitz kept an eye on Powder and retrieved his bike. He yanked it off the ground with one hand. Charlie relaxed as his tormentor took off for the other side of town.

"You all right?" Hank asked.

Charlie nodded.

"The last thing I need is kids hanging around and getting hurt. This dam isn't safe. Get on home."

Charlie didn't need to be told twice. He hopped on his bike and rode away as fast as he could. He worked his way through town, beating for the warehouse, and finally flew into the alley. Then his heart and bike skidded to a stop.

The window he'd used to get in earlier was boarded up tight.

r. Fitzgibbons was manipulating a digital simulation of a giant DNA strand when his phone chirped. He'd been expecting the call and transferred it to the lab's largest monitor.

With a flicker, the thin, serious face of Gretchen Gourmand appeared. Her close-cropped hair accentuated the sharp angles of her cheekbones, pinched in an expression that suggested she'd tasted sour milk.

"Good afternoon, doctor," she said in that affected accent Fitzgibbons could never quite place—European, Scandinavian perhaps, though he'd heard from another high-ranking Accelerton executive that she was from Denver.

"You remember Mr. Barton, Gretchen?" said Fitzgibbons, motioning for his colleague to enter the camera's view. Barton, always more comfortable with centrifuges than with executives, slicked back his hair with a sweaty palm and smiled weakly at the screen.

Gourmand ignored him. "I need a status report, gentlemen. I haven't heard anything since you began this current phase in Richland Center."

"My apologies," said Dr. Fitzgibbons. "We've found something promising."

"A giant?"

"Not exactly. It's a piece of giant thumbnail," said Barton. "We're still analyzing but it looks like—"

"Sean?" Gourmand interrupted, her voice sharp with skepticism.

Fitzgibbons took a moment to choose his words. "As I said, we've found *something*, and early analysis indicates the presence of DNA."

"Have the allelic variants been identified? Can you confirm that this is giant DNA?"

"Not conclusively," Fitzgibbons admitted. "At least, not quite yet."

"What about the giant? You have verifiable proof it was there?"

"It was hiding in a silo. I've tasked more satellites to comb the surrounding countryside," returned Barton. "If it's still in the area, we'll find it."

"I'm tired of hearing about 'ifs,'" said Gourmand, seizing on the uncertainty. "I need results. You've delivered for me in the past, Sean—that's why I was willing to pursue this outrageous idea. But there's too much cost here and, so far, no benefit. It's not like I haven't been supportive. I've approved huge expenditures to retrofit labs, task satellites, and I've even authorized you to employ the Stick. Mercenaries aren't cheap, as you know."

"We agreed the Stick was a necessity," argued Fitzgibbons. "When the time comes to bring down a giant, he's our man. And who better to go to the military with product? They all know him. There's plenty of benefit for your cost."

Gourmand sniffed.

"Forget the military," said Barton. "You know the consumer side of GGH alone will be worth billions. Want to be seven feet tall? No problem. Want to be seven foot three? Sorry, that's next generation. We're going to roll out products for decades!"

"There's nothing to roll out," she said. "That's the point."

"You know the process doesn't move that fast," Fitzgibbons said. "But we're on the verge of something that will make our previous military work look like whey powder at the nutrition store. The Stick's abilities are merely amplified. GGH will transform."

Gourmand sighed. "I've heard all the upsides before. I need definitive progress that will yield products, not fairy tales. Soon." She disappeared from the screen.

"Arbitrary deadlines," Barton muttered, adding several expletives about how it was science that bought Gourmand's expensive suit. He stomped back to his workstation and pounded away on his keyboard.

The intercom buzzed. "Dr. Fitzgibbons? Jamie is here."

Fitzgibbons had nearly forgotten. As punishment for that morning's fight, Jamie was "volunteering" with some odd jobs at the lab, including an evening stint at the Accelerton fair booth. The scientist hurried to the lobby to find his son shadow-boxing his own furious reflection in the reception-ist's plate-glass window. His gray Hornets Football T-shirt was wet with sweat around his neck. JoAnne, the anxious receptionist, flinched every time he took an angry swing, punctuating each punch with a powerful grunt.

"Hmph, huh, hmph, yeah!"

"Knock it off, Jamie." Fitzgibbons sighed as his son threw a haymaker uppercut at no one.

"I'm not hitting anybody!"

"You're scaring JoAnne," Fitzgibbons said.

"He's fine, he's fine!" JoAnne insisted with a nervous laugh. She pulled a white Accelerton windbreaker from under her desk. "Jamie! I got you this for the fair tonight."

Jamie held the jacket at arm's length as if it was pink.

"Jamie?" prodded Fitzgibbons.

"Thanks," Jamie grumbled. "It's really cool."

Fitzgibbons reached into his wallet and withdrew a ten-dollar bill. "I'm not a complete tyrant. Play a few of those strongman games and win something."

The boy rolled his eyes. "Right, Dad. Refuse to lose. Got it."

"I love the fair!" JoAnne confided to Fitzgibbons as she slipped on a matching windbreaker. "It's my favorite time of year!"

"JoAnne is your boss tonight, you understand?" said Fitz-gibbons. "You do what she says."

"Sure," Jamie returned in a monotone.

"Then I'll see you back here in the morning at nine o'clock sharp."

"Are you kidding?"

"If you wanted to sleep in this weekend, you shouldn't have acted like an idiot."

With a grunt, Jamie headed out with JoAnne to the parking lot. Fitzgibbons felt one headache begin to subside, at least for a few hours.

"Dr. Fitzgibbons?"

The scientist turned to find Ravi Pradeep, a young agricultural researcher, waving a manila folder.

"Got your soil sample analysis," Pradeep said. "Really weird stuff. Full of fecal matter, which your nose already told you. There's a high concentration of water and a lot of indigestible fiber, oats specifically. But the water content isn't consistent with animal waste. It's way too high. My guess is someone is dumping illegal sewage—and a lot of it. We should report this."

"Hold off on that," said Fitzgibbons as Pradeep handed over the report and returned to his lab. The findings confirmed Fitzgibbons's theory: Someone had been dumping waste by the silo. But was it giant waste?

He checked his watch. It looked to be a long night, and Barton worked better when he was fed. Fitzgibbons sent his partner a text asking what he wanted for takeout, and headed for the parking lot.

A ten-minute ride through town later, his silver BMW pulled into O'Finley's Pub and Grill on Highway 14. Fitzgibbons parked on the far side of the lot to avoid getting the door of his luxury car dinged by one of the trucks up front. He made his way toward the entrance and the smell of fryer grease. Then he heard a familiar growl. There was Powder in a silver pickup, trying to work her angry snout through a partially opened window in the cab.

Fitzgibbons ignored her snarls and walked into O'Finley's, where he was greeted by lime-green walls and sideways glances from regulars sitting at a horseshoe-shaped orange bar. The beer signs were the only thing Irish about the place.

Brandi, a young woman with Chinese symbols on both biceps, greeted him from behind the bar. "What can I getcha?"

"Picking up an order for Fitzgibbons."

"Sure thing, hon. It'll just be five minutes, okay?"

One of the regulars, Gruber, stuffed a twenty-dollar bill into a Cherry Master gambling machine. He wiped his cheek on the shoulder of his fluorescent T-shirt with the sleeves cut off. "Hey, Hank, know my idea of a balanced diet?" he asked.

Hank Pulvermacher didn't even look away from the evening news on one of the bar's TVs. "A burger in each hand."

Gruber cackled. He made eye contact with Fitzgibbons and cocked his head over at Hank. "That guy knows the dang punch line to every joke ever made! Go on, try him!"

Fitzgibbons raised an amused eyebrow and acknowledged Hank.

The old man lifted his bottle in return. "I've been getting acquainted with the whole Fitzgibbons family this week."

"How do you mean?"

"Powder and I met your boy this afternoon. He got into it with one of the local kids. Had to break it up—your boy outweighed the little guy by a good thirty pounds, and I was afraid he was going to end up in the hospital."

Fitzgibbons rubbed his forehead. "Thanks for breaking it up, Hank. I think Jamie's having some trouble adjusting to his new school. New town. You know how it is."

Hank nodded and sipped his beer.

"Can he stop by to see you? Apologize?"

"Not necessary."

"His mother and I are trying to make him take responsibility for this kind of behavior. If you just let me know where he could . . ."

"Hank's right over there by the old warehouse," Gruber called over the *ding ding ding*s of the Cherry Master. "Just down the block. You can't miss it."

Hank shifted on his bar stool and shot Gruber a look.

Fitzgibbons remembered passing by the strange old place, empty and huge. "The Frank Lloyd Wright building?"

"That's the one," Brandi said, returning from the kitchen with a large brown bag, already stained with grease from Barton's double order of onion rings. "Here you go!"

Fitzgibbons threw some bills on the bar. "Well, thanks again for stepping in, Hank."

The old man tipped his glass. The scientist grabbed his bag of food and headed back outside as Gruber resumed his punch-line quiz: "Here's one for you, Hank! What's brown and sticky?"

"A stick."

Fitzgibbons smiled at the irony of the punch line as he walked out the door. Powder barked at him again as he passed by Hank's truck. He ignored her once more, focusing on the dozen fifty-pound bags of feed in the truck bed. The labels read *Oats*.

Oats, just what Pradeep discovered in the soil sample.

Fitzgibbons glanced around the lot to see if anyone was watching him. Then he slid his car keys from his pocket and poked a small hole in one of the feed bags. Powder barked, but trapped in the truck cab, the furious dog was powerless to stop him.

"That's a good girl," said Fitzgibbons. "Bark your heart out."

He sped back through town and stopped in front of the warehouse. The abandoned building, at least forty feet tall, jumped out at him like never before. He pulled out his phone and activated the WiVi application. But the device couldn't produce a single view of what might be concealed inside: The concrete was too thick for the signal to penetrate. Even so, Fitzgibbons concluded that the AD German Warehouse would be a pretty good place to hide a giant—right in plain sight.

And Hank Pulvermacher lived nearby. Hank Pulvermacher, who happened to work at the quarry next to the silo where they'd found the piece of thumbnail. Hank Pulvermacher, who was carrying around a truck full of feed that might just be identical to what was found in the fecal-tainted soil samples.

Fitzgibbons tried the front door, then the one in the alley. The windows were sealed as well. Naturally, the place was locked up tight, but they could watch it better than a hawk. Fitzgibbons punched a name on his phone.

"Barton? I'm on my way back. Listen, I want you to re-task a satellite to 300 Church Street. Yes, that's in town. I don't care what it costs. I want to see who comes and goes from here twenty-four seven."

Hoping to find a tool to help him break into the warehouse, Charlie lifted the door to Mrs. Lundstrom's garage. Tim may have had a box of crap, but she had a whole garageful. It looked like she'd collected every magazine since 1984. There were boxes on top of boxes, some labeled, some not. Two riding lawn mowers dripped oil in the corner, and neither had tires. The garage's crown jewel? A creepy male mannequin wearing nothing but sunglasses.

Frustrated, he raised the walkie to his lips. "Dude, I can't see a toolbox in here, much less a crowbar. I have no idea how to get that board off the window."

"Sucks."

"Sure does, dude. Let me . . ."

"Hey, C-B, what up?"

Charlie didn't even have to turn his head: The unmistakable voice belonged to his mom's boyfriend, DJ Donovan, leaning out the window of his pride and joy, a jet-black

Hummer H2. He could afford it—the man was heir to Donovan Dairies, the largest independent cheese manufacturer in the entire state. He was vice president of Logistics, which involved massive trucks, heavy-duty suspensions, and "the fine art of efficiently moving things around." Everyone in town could see DJ liked Charlie's mom, *really* liked her. Charlie wasn't sure how much his mom liked DJ. It was okay by Charlie, who thought the guy was just too much. He also had a habit of showing up at just the wrong time.

DJ parked the Hummer and jumped out, wearing his "Hey, big guy" grin and the autographed NASCAR jacket he won in some charity auction. "Who you talkin' to on the old squawk box?"

"Dude, I gotta run. Talk to you later," said Charlie into the walkie.

"Later," the giant's voice screeched through the speaker.

Charlie snapped off the walkie and shut the garage door.

"Boy, have I got a surprise for you, C-monster."

"Really," Charlie said, sidestepping DJ and making for the apartment staircase.

"Aw, man, it's the best. Unbelievable, really. But I can't tell you until tomorrow!"

"No problem," sighed Charlie.

"So don't even ask tonight when we're at the fair," DJ said, practically begging Charlie to continue the discussion as he followed the boy up the stairs. When he wouldn't take the bait, DJ changed the subject. "I'm sure excited to meet your brother!"

Charlie grimaced as he pushed his way into the apartment. Even if he could figure out a way into the warehouse, he'd have to burn up most of the night at the fair, just to see dopey Tim. He headed for his room, DJ on his tail. Charlie took one look at the boxes of clothes still on his floor and grimaced again.

DJ looked behind him to make sure the coast was clear. "Looks like you could use a break from unpacking boxes. What do you say—a *Total Turbo* race before your mom gets home?"

It beat unpacking boxes. Besides, Charlie wanted to try the heel-toe maneuver that Adele had shown him. "Sure, okay." DJ wasn't bad at *Turbo*, not for a grown-up anyway, so it would be good practice. The man plopped on the bed and grabbed a controller while Charlie powered up and chose a track with plenty of winding road. How hard could the maneuver be?

Plenty, as it turned out. The first time he tried it, his foot slipped off the brake. His Lamborghini came out of the turn and crashed into a mountain, allowing DJ's Corvette Stingray to take a huge lead.

"Come on, C-Saw, you going to let an old man take you?" DJ had never beat Charlie before, and the boy wasn't ready to lose now.

But every time he tried the heel-toe, he either braked too hard with his heel or gave it too much gas with his toes. He was just about ready to give up when he caught a turn just right. Engine winding out, the Lamborghini ripped out of the tight corner onto a straight stretch. It whizzed past DJ's car just before the two cars crossed the finish line.

"Whoa! What did you just do?" yelled DJ as Charlie whooped in victory.

The kitchen door opened. The two quickly turned off the TV and hid the controllers. When Rita Lawson poked her head in the door, both Charlie and DJ were arranging T-shirts in the top dresser drawer.

"Now that's what I like to see!" She patted her hair, freshly done for the big day. "Let me change my clothes, and then we'll go see your brother!"

Charlie moaned and collapsed on his bed.

"Don't even think about playing sick," said Rita. "You're going to the fair to see your brother, and that's it."

Rita went to her room, and DJ left to load rhubarb crisp into the back of the Hummer.

The boy turned the volume way down on the walkie and clicked it on. "Dude, I don't have much time. I'm sorry, but I got to go see my brother." Charlie was beyond bummed—he was being robbed of a chance to hang out with a giant. And he genuinely felt bad for the big guy, stuck in that empty room with nothing to do. Instead he had to go to the fair to see that delinquent, Tim.

Then again, maybe his brother's dirtbag ways could be put to good use. Before he'd split to join the carnival, he'd broken into the high school library and had a going-away party with about fifty of his best friends. He was an idiot, but if anybody would know how to break into a warehouse, it would be Tim.

"Sucks!"

Charlie's voice picked up. "But here's the upside: I think he'll know how to get in! I'll talk to you when I get back."

"Charlie! Tim's waiting for us!"

He hustled outside to the backseat of DJ's Hummer. He'd

been dreading the fair, but maybe it was the answer to his problems. All he had to do was get Tim alone and pick his brain. DJ helped Rita into the passenger seat, ran around the car, and hopped behind the wheel. He started the noisy engine, and soon the raucous vehicle was turning heads as it rumbled through town.

"Ever tell you about the time the snowplow got stuck out on County Q?" DJ yelled into the backseat.

Charlie nodded. He knew the story well.

"They had to call in the H2 to get that darned thing out! When the chips are down, you play the biggest card you got!"

DJ recounted all of the truck's adventures as they made their way to the fair. Luckily, the ride wasn't long, and soon the heroic H2 pulled into the patchy grass of the fair parking lot. DJ jumped out and ran around to help Charlie's mom to the ground.

Charlie hopped out after her. He kicked up dirt in little clouds as he followed Rita and DJ through the sea of pickup trucks. The setting sun cast a gauzy haze over the white-washed buildings that ringed the fairgrounds, reminding the boy how much he'd loved the fair when he was little. The merry-go-round and Century Wheel flashed brilliant primary colors. Howling rock guitars tangled with thrill-ride screams as the Bullet circled and twisted through its orbit. A shrieking bungee jumper plunged through the sky. A small blimp puttered past overhead, advertising *Duffy Slade's Bar and Grill* on a digital screen.

They made their way past a ticket booth crowned with a ceramic cow and toward their designated meeting place: the red-white-and-blue building where Rita always insisted her sons eat when they were at the fair. She believed the fare sold at carnival trailers was a ticket to food poisoning, only trusting the hand-washing habits of the town veterans who worked the American Legion stand.

Rita looked at her watch. "I wonder where he could be?"

For once Charlie had a reason to see his brother, and the guy was nowhere to be found. *Big surprise*, he thought. Any unexplained absence was classic Tim.

DJ stopped a scraggly-haired carnival worker hurrying toward the midway. "Excuse me, good sir," DJ said. "Do you know Tim Lawson?"

The carny brushed the hair out of his suspicious eyes with a hand that was missing its index finger. Charlie had to look twice—it was one of the creepiest, coolest things he'd ever seen. The four-fingered guy gave DJ a suspicious look. "You a cop?"

"I'm Tim's mother," Rita said with an uneasy smile. "Is he working the midway?"

"That guy could be anywhere," replied the carny, who apparently had no time for more questions about Tim Lawson. He turned and headed off again.

"Do you remember where . . . ?" DJ called after him.

Then Charlie was tackled hard from behind. He hit the grass as a bigger body fell on top of him. The two of them rolled on the lawn, and Charlie heard his brother's signature raspy laugh.

"Get off me, you big idiot!" Charlie hollered, fighting back. Tim pinned his knees on his younger brother's elbows.

Charlie looked up at the ridiculous new sideburns, bushy

and fat, that covered Tim's cheeks. Blue-tinted horn-rimmed glasses hid beneath greasy black bangs.

"You got bigger, Charlie, but not big enough!" Tim cackled.

"Get off!" Charlie squirmed and twisted for all he was worth. He thrashed hard from side to side, which did nothing. He had to try something else. "I threw out your stupid kung fu movies."

"You did *what*?"

It was the opening Charlie needed, and he heaved up with his forearms. The move sent Tim tumbling backward enough for Charlie to squirm free and scramble away. One thing was clear: He was going to have to put up with the usual Tim idiocy all night.

DJ reached down and helped Tim to his feet. "You must be Tim. Heard a lot about you," he said. "Your mom sure is excited to see you—she's been baking up a storm!"

"If you ain't ate it all yet, you're all right with me!" Tim tossed DJ's hand aside, then threw a monster hug around his mom's boyfriend, lifting him off the ground. Tim dropped the embrace and spun back to his brother. "You didn't really pitch *Enter the Dragon*, did you?"

The boy just scowled and dusted the grass off his shirt. Tim would be lucky if Charlie didn't really set the box of crap out with the trash now. Find out how to break in and get home—that was the plan.

Rita got a bear hug from Tim, which for some reason made her laugh and laugh. The stories and giggles and slaps on the back continued throughout their dinner at the American Legion stand, right until the last bits of rhubarb crisp were gone. Charlie kept looking for a moment to take Tim off to one side, but dinner offered no breaks. Soon the entire family was walking toward the midway.

Rita turned to Charlie. "What's first, kid? Maybe take your mom through the Creep Castle? You used to love that one!"

"Whoops! Creep Castle's on the sidelines for maintenance," Tim explained as they worked their way through the crowd. "The mummy unraveled and the fortune teller's head kept coming off. I thought it was scarier that way, but the boss wants it fixed. Should be all patched by the time we split for Illinois."

Charlie kept looking for his moment to ask about the warehouse. But Tim was pretty focused on giving Rita and DJ the royal tour, whispering gossip about the milk can game (you couldn't win) and the attractive young lady running the "Shoot the Star" contest (she turned just so when guys pulled the trigger, distracting them enough to ruin their aim). He even coached up DJ to win Rita a stuffed bear at the basketball game. The trick was a superhigh arc, and DJ dropped one through the narrow hoop on his third try.

"My hero," she said with a twinkle in her eye, giving DJ a quick peck on the cheek. The guy melted like a snow cone. Charlie saw his chance.

"Hey, Tim, can I talk to you about something? In private?"

"Sure. What's up?"

They stepped away from their mom into the chaos of the midway. Charlie pulled close to his brother and talked in a loud whisper.

"I need to know how to do something . . ."

"Hey, Lawson! Your break was over an hour ago!"

The four-fingered guy didn't look happy as he pointed his middle finger at Tim, who gave an unapologetic shrug and hustled over to his game booth on the midway before Charlie could even finish his sentence.

"Later, Charlie! Promise!"

Charlie threw up his hands. There was nothing he could do for now. He grabbed his mom and DJ, and they went to watch his brother work his magic.

Dancing back and forth in front of a large scale, Tim shouted at passersby and offered to guess their age or weight for three bucks a chance. He had to get the weight within three pounds or the age within two years—if he was fooled, he gave out cheap stuffed animals.

"Step riiiight on up!" Tim bellowed into a portable microphone, paying special attention to the young women who smiled at him sideways. "I guess your age, I guess your weight, you take home a prize! Who's it going to be?"

The money kept going in Tim's pockets as he hit guess after guess. The few times he was wrong, Charlie assumed Tim missed on purpose—he always concluded the attractive thirty-five-year-old moms were twenty-three, and from the way they hugged and kissed him after, Charlie figured Tim had won again.

In the past, watching Tim had been kind of fun, but the novelty had worn off. This year, Charlie had other things he needed to do. His eyes wandered the midway, wondering how much longer they were going to stand around listening to people lie about their age. A familiar, cocky voice brought his attention back to Tim's booth.

"Guess my weight!"

Charlie looked twice at the large kid in the white Accelerton jacket. Fitz!

Tim walked around the bulky teen, sizing him up. "That's a lot of muscle, compadre," he said with a grin. "You're one of my heaviest tonight, that's for sure."

"Yeah, yeah."

Charlie slid off to the side and more or less disappeared behind his mom and DJ. Part of him wished Fitz had just slugged him that afternoon—at least then the guy would feel like he'd gotten even and it would be over. Tim looked funny at Charlie crouching behind DJ. Charlie shook his head furiously, mentally telling his brother not to stare! Tim got the hint and worked the crowd on the other side of the midway. The boy exhaled—Fitz was focused on the prizes, and Charlie was pretty sure the bully hadn't seen him.

"Hmmm." Tim surveyed Fitz the way a judge at a dog show might evaluate a Doberman. Finally, he wrote a number on a small notepad and showed it to the crowd. "One hundred and eighty-three pounds! Let's see if I'm right!"

Fitz hopped up on the big scale and the needle twitched before settling in at 181.

"There you go, folks!" crowed Tim. "Within three pounds!"

Fitz fumed. Charlie could see the guy didn't like to lose at *anything*. He kicked off his heavy athletic shoes, and the needle eased down to 180.

"Still within three pounds, pal!" Tim said, slapping Fitz on the back. "Tough luck!"

The Accelerton jacket was next, and then Fitz threw off his T-shirt. The scale still hovered at 180.

A pretty young woman approached. She casually leaned against the guessing booth, and the gold stud in her tongue glinted when she spoke. "Got this under control, Tim?"

Fitz glared at her from the scale. "What's your problem?"

Tim moved himself in between Fitz and the young woman. "Take it easy, big boy," he cautioned. "I see you've been hitting the weights, but believe me, you don't want to make Tiger mad. She's the roughie."

"What's a roughie?" asked Fitz.

"You don't want to find out," she said.

"Tell you what." Tim played to the crowd, rolling his eyes and pulling a fluffy bunny from his prize basket. "Let's call you a winner before we all get to see what color boxer shorts you're wearing! Give him a hand, folks!"

With a smug look of triumph on his face, Fitz took the rabbit and stalked off to the Accelerton booth. Tiger gave Tim a nod and continued walking the midway, looking for signs of trouble. Charlie kept working his way behind other fairgoers so Fitz couldn't see him. It looked like the coast was clear as Tim prepared for another break.

"Um, Mom?" Charlie touched her on the elbow. "Would it be okay if I spent a little one-on-one time with Tim? We don't get to hang out very often."

Rita looked surprised. Usually, Charlie resented having to go see Tim, so this was a welcome development.

"Of course," said Rita, taking DJ by the arm. "It will be nice for DJ and me to have a little alone time, too."

"That's what I'm talking about!" said DJ.

Charlie winced, and she laughed. "You two have fun. But not too much fun." Rita took DJ's arm, and they walked away, stuffed bear in tow.

Tim smacked Charlie in the stomach. "Looks like it's you and me, bro!" He pulled his brother to a beat-up food trailer with *Fried Donuts, Sausages,* and *Taquitos* stenciled across its façade in faded red letters. "I need a couple elephant ears, stat!"

Tim grabbed the food and pulled up two plastic crates from behind the stand. He motioned for Charlie to sit.

"So you're going to think I'm crazy . . ." Charlie began.

"Too late," said Tim, shoving a mouthful of the greasy stuff into his mouth. "Already do."

"Funny," returned Charlie, taking a bite of the crispy fried dough. It was just the kind of forbidden fruit his mom hated.

"Am I right?" Tim asked with an I-knew-you'd-love-it grin on his face.

"S'good."

"Hey, Juice Man," Tim said to a bald, beefy guy walking down the midway. He looked up the entire time, working a remote control. "How about putting a message up on the blimp for my mom?"

"It's not your own personal Jumbotron, Lawson," Juice Man growled back.

"Forget about the blimp," said Charlie. "I really need to talk to you about something."

"Tell me all about it on the Gravitron," Tim yelled, grabbing Charlie's shoulder and running toward the ride. About half of the blue and yellow bulbs spelling out Gravitron were either flickering or snuffed out.

"I need to talk first," shouted Charlie, trying to keep up. But Tim was already up the worn wooden platform and inside the spaceship-looking ride. Charlie found his brother along the padded wall and took the spot next to him.

"What are you doing in here, Wertzie?" Tim hollered to the guy in the center control console, the same four-fingered carny who'd told him to get back to work earlier. "You hate this ride!"

Wertzie crossed his arms over his Buy the Ticket, Take the Ride T-shirt. His bored expression never changed as he leaned on a red button.

"See, Charlie? Any idiot can run the Gravitron."

The ride started spinning and centrifugal force pulled Charlie back into the padded wall. Hip-hop music thumped as the Gravitron spun faster and faster. Conversation was no longer an option as he felt the floor slip away under his feet, his body stuck fast to the wall like he was magnetized. Next to him, Tim screamed along to the music in words that were nowhere close to the actual lyrics.

Finally the ride eased to a stop and the brothers stumbled off, trying to find their balance again.

"No more rides," managed Charlie.

"Okay, okay," Tim said with a friendly grin, holding up his hands to show he didn't want to fight. He led Charlie off behind the carnival games at the edge of the midway, where they could talk in private. "Let me guess—you need to know how to handle the hundred-and-eighty-one-pound tough guy? Mr. Company-Swag Windbreaker?"

Fitz was the last thing Charlie wanted to talk about. "No!"

"C'mon, I saw you hiding from him."

"I wasn't hiding. And that's not what I need to talk to you about."

"You know you can't just keep running away, right?"

"What am I supposed to do, fight him?" Charlie exclaimed, getting caught up in the argument despite himself. "You saw him—he's twice my size! He's a freshman, for God's sake!"

A serene look came over Tim's face. "It's like Bruce Lee once said—practice the art of fighting without fighting."

"Fighting without fighting? What does that even mean?"

"Charlie! *Enter the Dragon!* Come on, you've watched it, right?"

Charlie just stood there and stared at his brother. This was going nowhere. Not only was he not getting the advice he needed, he couldn't even get a word in edgewise. "I haven't watched your stupid movies, Tim. But I do have to haul them around every time we move, which is all the time."

Tim kicked at the ground. "Sorry, man. Thought there might be some stuff in there you'd want."

"Rita!"

The brothers turned their heads in the direction of the man shouting their mom's name. At the end of a bungee line, DJ shot up into the sky again, waving his arms like crazy to show off for his date.

"We so got to do that," said Tim.

"There's no way I'm jumping off that thing," countered Charlie, watching DJ plummet through the air. And then the idea hit him. He had the answer he was looking for, even if he never got to ask the question. It was perfect. He knew how he was going to break back into the warehouse.

Early the next morning, while it was still good and dark, Charlie watched the old man's truck come and go with the giant's breakfast. When the sun came up, it was time to put his scheme into action. He contacted the big guy on the walkie-talkie.

"Okay, I'll be there as soon as my mom leaves for work." The plastic walkie felt greasy in his nervous palm. "Which should be anytime. So be ready. This is going to have to be bang-bang fast. If anyone sees what I'm about to do, they'll call 911 in a second. You got me?"

"Secret," returned the giant in a whisper.

"See you soon. Charlie out." He ditched the walkie under his bed and clomped out to the kitchen to check on his mom's whereabouts.

"Charlie," his mom yelled from outside. "You're up already? Come out here, would you? I need some help."

He headed down the back stairs to find her sitting on a

plastic bench in the grass, a red kerchief tied around her forehead to keep the hair out of her eyes. She held a monarch butterfly by its delicate wings, trying to pick up a sticker sheet full of butterfly tags that she'd set down just out of reach. She didn't want to upset the monarch any more than necessary.

Charlie picked up the slick of paper. He peeled off a small circle that was printed with tiny numbers assigned by some bug professors in Kansas.

Rita took the sticky label and pressed it against the butterfly's fragile black-and-tangerine wing. With the label attached, she opened her hand in a gentle invitation for the creature to take flight. The monarch shuddered and took a moment to recover. She lifted her palm, and the butterfly unfolded into the sky.

Charlie couldn't imagine getting up early on a Saturday morning for volunteer butterfly duty. "Remind me again why you do this?"

Rita looked up and scrunched her face at Charlie. "I like to think I'm helping them on their way. Anything wrong with that?"

Just then the Hummer roared up into their driveway. DJ revved the motor to impress Charlie before killing it. He hopped out of the driver's side with a bag in his hand. "Hey there, C-Squared. I picked up some doughnuts!"

"Cool," Charlie said. He'd take a doughnut.

"For the ride to Madison!" he exclaimed. "Surprise! Let's see what kind of trouble we can get into over at the World of Wheels, then shoot over to the college to get some of those guy-ros with the cucumber sauce and onions. They're Greek, like olives! Madtown, baby!"

As always, DJ's timing was awful. Charlie stammered, "I . . . I can't go."

The man looked like his cable just went out during the Super Bowl.

"Charlie!" exclaimed his mom, with more than a hint of disappointment in her voice. "DJ went to a lot of trouble to plan this trip."

"I'm sure he's got a good reason," offered DJ, looking to Charlie with an expression that pleaded, *It's not me, right?*

Charlie did have a good reason, but he sure couldn't let his mom know what it was. Then, out of nowhere, an excuse popped out of his mouth. "I've got a . . . a date."

Rita's eyebrows arched, crinkling her forehead in doubt. "A *date* date?" she asked. "With a girl?"

The surface temperature of Charlie's cheeks rose a few degrees. He was trying to think fast, but his brain felt like it was stuck in quicksand.

DJ launched into a big grin. "Ten-four, C-B!" He winked at Rita and punched Charlie in the shoulder. "Madison will be there next weekend. But a date with a beautiful girl? You grab those opportunities when they come, am I right?"

"A date at eight in the morning? Sounds fishy to me," argued Rita, hands on her hips.

"We're not supposed to meet until noon, but I wouldn't be back from Madison in time." The excuse sounded pretty good to Charlie.

"Who is this girl, anyway?"

"Adele." Charlie blurted out the first name that came into his head. "Adele Hawkins."

"There you go," said DJ. "Her folks work at the plant. Good people."

But Charlie could tell his mom wasn't quite buying it.

"Adele Hawkins. I suppose I could call her mother and confirm?"

All of a sudden, the excuse didn't feel so good after all. A slick of sweat ran down Charlie's neck. He'd be in a real jam if his mom called, but there was no turning back now. "Sure. Go ahead," he said, trying to sound casual as he leaned against the stairs.

"Another time, C-Horse," said DJ, throwing Charlie the bag of doughnuts. "Have fun today."

"Thanks." Charlie felt kind of bad, but what was he supposed to do?

His mom stood up and brushed the grass from her Ed's Fine Foods shirt. "Well, I need to get to work. I'll see you tonight, Charlie." She raised an eyebrow. "I want to hear more about this girl."

"My plans just got canceled," said DJ with a smile. "How about a ride?" She accepted the offer and they both hopped into the H2. With a wave to Charlie, they were off.

Whew.

Charlie ditched the donuts and hightailed it across Church Street. He looked up to the high windows, flashed an index finger to signal "Just one minute!" and darted into the dark alley.

The plan was simple but terrifying: work his way up to

the warehouse roof and jump down the elevator shaft. The giant would catch him.

Hopefully.

A halo of sunlight glowed around the top of the tree Charlie needed to climb to get up on the roof. He'd imagined the ascent over and over in his head during the night, but the oak was taller and more intimidating when he was standing underneath it. He took a deep breath, reached to grab hold of a low branch, felt the rough bark bite into his palms, and started climbing.

A bigger kid might have weighed too much for some of the more slender branches, but they were sturdy enough to hold Charlie. He climbed like a natural, ascending fifty feet in only a few minutes.

Soon, he arrived at the branch that bridged to the roof. The limb extended well over the top of the warehouse. Charlie straddled the branch and started shinnying across, feeling the substantial bough narrow with each incremental shunt forward. As he crept along, his weight bent the bough, but it still seemed plenty strong for the job. *Piece of cake*, he tried to convince himself. Then about halfway across, he looked down.

In the alley below, broken pieces of glass glittered like they were in a far-off galaxy. Charlie couldn't believe how high he was. His hands slicked with perspiration, and the limb got slippery. He sucked in air as if it could fill him with courage. He pried his eyes off the ground, training them on his destination. An inch at a time, shallow breath by shallow breath, he started forward again. The branch cooperated.

Finally, he dropped down to the roof and approached the elevator shaft.

Soot-stained from decades of absorbing exhaust from passing trucks, the bricked tower jutted skyward ten feet from the roof. A metal ladder ran up the side. Charlie took a quick look out onto the street. A lot of cars were already heading to the fair. Even though the ladder couldn't be seen from the road, he'd have to jump quickly so no one saw him at the top of the elevator shaft. He grabbed hold of the lowest rung embedded into the brick and mortar, and started to climb. The rungs held firm all the way to the top.

From there, he snuck a peek down into the dark shaft. He couldn't even see all the way to the bottom. He swallowed, and the spit balled up in his throat so he had to do it again. For some reason he remembered a story kids told about a girl who ran off Bogus Bluff and fell to her death because Indians were chasing her. If the giant didn't catch him, he'd end the same way. *Splat.*

"Charlie!" The big voice boomed up the elevator shaft.

There was a total break in traffic. The perfect time to jump. He had to go. *C'mon,* CUGoneByeBye—*you can do this.* Charlie tried to harness the fearlessness of his alter ego and pulled himself atop the chimneylike structure, but his legs still shook. It was like being at the end of the springboard on the world's tallest high-dive, except there was a giant waiting below instead of a pool. He wavered. It was now or never.

"Go," said the giant.

"I know, I know," stammered Charlie. "It's just hard."

Faced with a literal leap of faith, Charlie closed his eyes and hopped off the ledge. He plummeted down the shaft for what felt like long enough to die—only he didn't. The giant was as good as his word. He caught the boy right in his fleshy mitt.

The impact was still enough to knock the air from Charlie's lungs. His head swam with stars as the giant pulled him out of the shaft and set him down on the cool concrete. The big guy held out his fist for Charlie to bump, which the boy managed despite his inability to pull in a solid breath.

"Good job!"

"We did it," Charlie said between gasps. "And I don't think anyone even saw me!"

He couldn't have known about the satellite 200 miles above that was sending pictures back to Earth as fast as its digital eye could take them.

11

Jamie Fitzgibbons was facedown on his weight bench, as scheduled, an early Saturday morning ritual in the basement of the Fitzgibbonses' rented house. He lowered his Hornets Football shorts and exposed his bare bottom like it was the most natural thing in the world.

His father inserted a sterile twenty-two-gauge needle into a burnt-orange vial, turned it upside down, and drew out one and a half CCs of a performance enhancer of his own design. It could not be detected by even the most sophisticated test. He could have made a fortune selling it to professional athletes, but he wanted only one person to have the advantage: his son.

Fitzgibbons glanced up at the five framed black-and-white photos hanging on the wall behind his son's weight equipment. The shots provided a time-lapse history of an Olympic sprinting trial held twenty-some years earlier. Sean Fitzgibbons finished fifth in the final heat, behind four men who would go on to represent America at the Games. All of them except Fitzgibbons had used performance enhancers to run faster. He had foolishly thought he could win through training and sheer force of will. Instead, he was beaten by science.

The loss didn't embitter Fitzgibbons. It emboldened him. He returned to school to study performance enhancers, dedicating his life to understanding them, improving them, making them safer. When his young son showed a natural aptitude for sports—and for winning—Fitzgibbons knew why his life had taken this particular path. It was too late for him, but not for Jamie. When the boy's moment came, he would have all the edge he needed.

That was, if Jamie could get stronger. Not just physically but mentally as well.

"I met a man named Hank Pulvermacher yesterday," Fitzgibbons said, tapping the syringe with his finger. Air bubbles rose to the top. "He says he stopped you from beating up a smaller boy."

Jamie scowled. "Guy needs to mind his own business."

"You need to control your temper. We're not doing this so you can be a bully. Think how much a kid like that would want these injections. They're a privilege." He searched for a small area of acne-free skin near the top of his son's gluteus medius muscle, then cleaned it with an alcohol swab.

Pressing the stopper until a bead of fluid appeared at the tip of the needle, the doctor stretched Jamie's skin taut with his free hand. The needle penetrated his son's buttock, plunging deep into the muscle.

"Ow, that hurts!"

"Think about the big picture, Jamie." Fitzgibbons pressed the plunger until the full dose was delivered, then he removed the needle and threw it into a red plastic container marked *Sharps*. "How many times have we talked about this? What do you want?"

Jamie yanked up his shorts, grimacing as he flipped over and sat up. "The Heisman. The NFL. My own shoe deal! I want to be huge!"

"Don't confuse fame with excellence," warned his father, starting up the flight of stairs. "Fame is fleeting. Excellence is forever. If someone hurts your feelings, hit the weights. We're not about getting even in this house. We're about excellence, right?"

"Yes, sir," Jamie said.

"And what do we do to attain excellence?"

"Refuse to lose."

"Can't hear you?"

"Refuse to lose!"

"Playground fights are for losers, Jamie. If you want to be huge, act like it. I'll see you at the lab after you finish your morning workout."

Fitzgibbons left the house and drove to Accelerton. As he worked his way through security, his phone buzzed with an e-mail. He opened the message. Pradeep had analyzed the oats Fitzgibbons found in the back of Hank Pulvermacher's truck—they were an exact match for the fiber material in the manure sample from the silo. The puzzle pieces were coming together.

He entered the lab. Barton was at his desk despite the

early hour. Fitzgibbons doubted the man had gone home to sleep. "What's the latest?"

"Let me show you." Barton finished toggling his keyboard, then wheeled his chair down the counter of whirring lab equipment to a centrifuge. He keyed in a code on the device's beeping interface, which glowed before the front hatch clicked and opened. A silver tray rolled out from its encasement, and the spinning cylinder slowed to a stop.

Barton reached inside, withdrew a small glass vial, and held it up to the light. The container was three-quarters full of fluid, watery and golden. Bubbles bobbed to the top.

"Still need a few hours to replicate vectors," Barton replied. "But all early indicators are promising."

Fitzgibbons pumped his fist. "I know I put you under the gun, but even I didn't expect this kind of progress. Excellent work."

"A combination of no sleep and a certain amount of luck." Barton replaced the vial into the centrifuge and restarted it. "I did call in those new satellite coordinates. Unfortunately, I haven't had a chance to look at surveillance."

"I just received some new information regarding our soil samples. It suggests a few things," said Fitzgibbons. "Let's take a moment to check my warehouse hypothesis. Set a search for any activity."

A real-time satellite view of the warehouse appeared. From an aerial perspective, the AD German Warehouse looked like just another flat-roofed building. The search ended quickly and results populated the screen. It didn't take long before something unusual emerged.

"There!" blurted Fitzgibbons, lurching forward. "At the top of the building!"

Barton halted the images and replayed the series of stills.

"Stop." Fitzgibbons tapped his finger at the elevator shaft on the screen. "Zoom in."

The view leaped forward, revealing someone climbing the rungs that ran up the side of a brick shaft. Barton dialed in the focus. "It's a child," he said with amazement. "What's a kid doing on the roof in broad daylight? This just happened!"

"Facial recognition?"

"Possibly. There's a good view of his face right . . ." Barton punched more keys. "Here. I think there are enough markers." He uploaded the image to a remote mainframe and Accelerton software began comparing the face to millions of others on the web. A handful of pictures populated a queue. The software identified a boy from Richland Center. "His name's Charlie Lawson," Barton said, reading the caption from a picture of Charlie holding a cheap plastic trophy. "He won a video game tournament in somewhere called Boscobel last year."

"Have security run a background check."

Barton resumed his scan of the satellite photos. The sky got darker as the pictures reversed into the night. "Look at this!" He zoomed in on the sidewalk outside the giant warehouse. A truck was backing up into the alley. The time stamp on-screen read 4:35 a.m.

"There's how the waste in the soil samples gets to the quarry," said Fitzgibbons. "And I bet I know who's driving."

Barton ran the images frame by frame. The pictures were dark, but they could make out the silhouettes of a man and a large dog exiting the truck, then disappearing into the warehouse via an alley door.

"We've found the hiding spot," said Fitzgibbons. "Too many things line up. I'm as certain as I can be without breaking in there."

Color flushed Barton's face at the prospect of encountering a giant in the flesh. "Should we try? We could force our way in and tag the thing, just to be sure."

"We'll keep watching. You'll get your specimen," said Fitzgibbons, reaching for his phone. "Now that we're confident where the giant is hiding, it's time to call in the Stick."

12

The giant poked the boy in the chest with a large index finger. He pulled himself up on his elbows.

"See? Told you I'd come back, didn't I?"

"Cool," said the giant.

"Hank said something about 'the next leg of your trip'—you taking off soon?"

"Yep."

"When?"

The giant shrugged. Either he didn't know when he was going or he didn't know how to say it.

"So where are you headed?"

"New . . . home."

"Yeah, I got to move all the time, too. Sucks." Charlie tried to figure out where you'd move a giant. "So where can you go where you can stay secret? In the mountains? Out in a forest somewhere?"

The giant was bored by the questions, like a new kid tired

of telling everyone about his old school. He plopped down on his huge butt and moaned, almost like he was sick or something, and looked at Charlie with pitiful eyes. "Hungry . . ."

Charlie looked at him skeptically. The boy had tried pulling the "I don't feel good" trick on his mom just last night. "I know you just got fed."

"No!"

"Dude. I saw the truck come and go. We talked about it, remember?"

The giant glanced at the ceiling and bit his lip.

He was trying to play Charlie, the same way he'd played Hank! "Come on, man. You don't have to trick me—if you want more, just tell me. I'm not your babysitter."

The giant shrugged and burst out laughing, a long, low chortle that bounced off the bare warehouse walls. He was busted.

"Where does Hank keep the food?"

The giant pointed down the hallway where Charlie had first found his way into the hiding spot. In a dark recess in the passageway, the boy spotted a wooden pallet full of forty-pound bags with red lettering that read *Premium Grains*. Each sack featured a picture of a smiling cartoon horse. Charlie grabbed a bag, which was way heavier than it looked, and dragged it to the happy giant.

The colossus pointed down to the old ceramic bathtub, its tarnished claw feet resting in a rusty puddle. A wooden boat oar sat inside the tub along with the end of a hose that ran from a spigot on the wall. Charlie found an old utility knife lying on the floor near the tub and ripped the bag open.

Smells like the stuff you feed the goats at the petting zoo, he thought as he dumped the bag inside the tub. The oats looked dry and unappetizing. Charlie turned on the spigot, soaked the grains down good, and stirred the whole mess up with the oar. He looked up to the giant, but something was wrong, like Charlie hadn't prepared it right. "What's the problem? I thought you wanted this."

The giant grimaced, then stuck an enormous index finger into the goop. He lifted the viscous slop to his nose and took a tentative sniff. His enormous eyes closed tight as he recoiled from the smell. "Sucks!"

"It can't be that bad." He stuck his own hand into the mushy grain and tried a bit. It was the worst-tasting anything he'd ever eaten.

The giant looked at Charlie as if he was the dumbest guy in the world. "Sugar!"

He looked around. "There's no sugar here."

Trying to squeeze his massive arm back down the narrow hallway, the giant repeated his request. "Sugar."

Charlie squirted past the giant's arm to take another look down the hall. Sure enough, there was a fifty-pound bag of sugar, three-quarters full, set just out of the giant's reach. He dragged it back to the tub.

"Charlie!" The giant rubbed his hands together.

Charlie lifted the bag and drizzled sugar crystals across the top. "This ought to help." The giant snatched the bag. "Hey, what the heck!"

The behemoth dumped the entire contents into the feed, stuck his big paw into the "oatmeal," and plopped a sweet glob into his mouth. He sighed with pleasure—that was more like it.

Charlie stuck in his own hand and tried some. He didn't think the sugar helped much, but the big guy finished the entire tub in about a minute. He picked up the hose between a massive thumb and forefinger, motioning for Charlie to turn on the water. He did, and the giant drank for a good five minutes. Then he got a funny look in his eye and pointed at something back down the hall.

"What?" asked Charlie. "You hear someone coming?"

The giant continued to drink, motioning for Charlie to go ahead and check it out. He turned and looked around the corner. Nothing was there that he hadn't seen before—just the bags of oats and . . .

A hard, cold blast of water hit Charlie in the back of the neck, knocking him forward. He turned and sputtered through the icy spray. The giant was laughing his butt off, working the hose to soak Charlie good. "Knock it off, you big idiot!"

The wetter Charlie got, the more the giant laughed. The big guy was pretty good at forcing the water in Charlie's face, pushing him back. Finally, Charlie managed to get to the spigot and turn it off.

"Come on, man. I didn't jump down an elevator shaft to get soaked."

The giant reached down to turn the spigot back on and broke the entire thing off the wall. Water spurted everywhere, and he danced around like an oversize kid playing in an open fire hydrant. He kicked water in Charlie's direction.

Charlie ran for cover under the table, wishing he had some water balloons or something to fight back with. Giants were definitely fun once they'd had a little sugar. He scrambled for the wooden oar and flicked water that was pooling on the floor at the big guy. The giant stumbled backward and almost knocked over the pallet of dynamite.

"Watch it," warned Charlie, scuttling across the wet floor looking for something else he could fling at the giant.

Bits of oats flew from the giant's teeth with each hysterical guffaw. He scooped up enormous handfuls of water and dropped them on Charlie's head, like the huge buckets at the water park that dumped a thousand gallons at a time. It was the coldest shower of his life, and the giant kept chucking water over and over. Charlie didn't mind—he was having a blast—but he was getting a little worried about all the water. There was a good two inches on the floor now and he was pretty sure it was seeping out the door in the back hall into the alley. It wouldn't be long before someone would wonder where all the water was coming from.

Charlie tracked the copper pipe that ran from the spigot until he saw the rusted master shut-off across the warehouse. He made a break for the handle, put his full body weight behind the effort, and managed to turn off the torrent.

"Water!" shouted the giant, pouncing on and destroying Hank's old chair. Splinters flew everywhere. He reached down to snap the copper pipe and start the fun again.

"Don't break it!" shouted Charlie. He looked around the warehouse—it reminded him of the aftermath of a New Year's Eve party that his brother threw sophomore year when their mom was out of town. In other words, a certifiable disaster zone. Maybe they needed to take it down a notch before someone called the cops. That's what happened to Tim. "I've got something even more fun to do!"

The giant stopped and cocked his head, as if to say, "I'm listening. . . ."

Fun stuff to do. Charlie wracked his brain. What did he do for fun? *Total Turbo*, which was out of the question. The guy's thumbs were way too big to work the controls. Eat stuff, which they'd already done. Watch a movie . . .

Then the boy remembered Tim's box of crap, with the dusty old projector and film reels. A movie! The giant would freak out if Charlie could pull it off. He yelled up at the giant. "Hey, I'll be right back!"

The giant looked dejected, even guilty, like maybe he shouldn't have started the water fight after all. "No," he pleaded. "Stay."

Charlie held up his hands. "I'm not mad or anything," he insisted. "Hang here for a minute and don't break any more water pipes. I just got to go get something—I'm coming back, promise!"

The giant collapsed into an empty corner of the room and put his massive hands on his knees.

In the hallway where he'd found the oats, Charlie discovered the back door that Hank had used a couple of nights before. He was able to unlock it from the inside and most of the water drained into the alleyway and down the sewer. He sprinted back across the street to his apartment. He grabbed the box marked *Tim* and in no time, he was back across Church Street.

The grateful giant offered a fist bump.

He was fascinated by absolutely everything in Tim's box of crap. Charlie showed him the peekaboo pen first. The giant's eyes got big as he held the tiny pen upside down and watched the woman's outdated bikini evaporate like magic. That naughty disappearing trick alone probably could have kept the giant busy for hours—he kept flipping the pen to dress and undress the old-fashioned swimsuit model.

While the giant was occupied, Charlie set the table upright, positioned the projector, and plugged it in. Whew—the old place still had power. He figured out how to thread the reel. Tim had shown him how, but that was a long time ago. After a few false starts, Charlie got it. The warehouse space was perfect. Its huge blank walls were large enough to be real movie screens and a patch of rain clouds had made it just dark enough inside. "You ready?"

The giant looked up, not quite ready to give up the pen but intrigued by the projector.

"Okay, here we go," said Charlie. "Check this out."

With the click of a switch, the projector began to whir. Flickers of light danced forth and then an enormous image of Bruce Lee in black gloves and matching shorts appeared on the far wall. His chubby opponent attacked. Bruce countered with a series of lightning-fast punches and throws that sent his challenger to the ground.

The startled giant backed up against the wall farthest from the projection. "Charlie!"

Charlie turned off the machine, surprised to see the colossus cowering. "Hey, hey, hey!" The boy held up his hands to calm the giant. "It's just a movie!"

The giant scrunched his nose at the word. "M-m-movie?"

"Pictures," Charlie explained. "Pictures that move. They tell a story."

The giant stared down at the projector, then back up at the blank wall. He pointed at the empty space with a tentative finger, inviting Charlie to start the movie again.

Bruce Lee came to life once more, and this time the giant didn't flinch. Instead he edged across the room to try to touch the image. It appeared on the giant's back when he stood between the projector and the wall.

"Come here," said Charlie, grabbing an end of the giant's tunic and tugging him back. "You sit and watch. It's a story."

The giant still was baffled, but he sat against the wall. Charlie plopped down, and the two of them watched the movie together.

Even though Tim was wrong about most things, Charlie couldn't deny that *Enter the Dragon* was pretty great. The giant forgot his initial fear and lost himself in the flickering images on the wall. He was so engrossed, in fact, that when Bruce Lee fought an opponent on a strange island, the giant rose to his feet and began mimicking the martial arts master's moves with surprising grace and dexterity. The giant's punches and kicks mirrored Lee's own.

"Whoa, that's awesome! I think you just got a new name," decided Charlie. "I'm calling you Bruce. You even sort of look like him. Well, a bigger version."

"Bruce," responded the giant, still keeping his eye on the action.

"Right! That's him. And now, that's you. You're Bruce."

13

Jamie coasted to the Accelerton security point. His rear
still smarted from the morning injection, but he'd used
the pain as motivation to push through a tough workout
and make the substantial ride out to his dad's lab.

He pulled his bike up to the intercom and pushed the
buzzer. The gate didn't open right away so he hopped off his
bike, picked up a decent-size rock from the parking lot, and
hurled the stone toward one of the greenhouses. It banged
a pane of glass, cracking it. He was just about to try again
when the security gate buzzed and slid open far enough for
him to walk his bike through.

Jamie eschewed the bike rack at the edge of the parking
lot. He dropped his racer right on the manicured Accelerton
lawn and went through the lobby door, almost colliding with
Neil Barton. The guy, lost in his phone, didn't even say hello.

Jamie noticed how awful the guy looked. Barton's froggy
eyes were swollen and red, and his fat face was even puffier

than usual, which was saying something. A large van checked in at security, and Barton hustled to meet it. Dr. Fitzgibbons called from the lab corridor. "Come on, Jamie, let's go."

His father led Jamie to a room that reeked of acrid chemicals. He groaned when he saw racks of dirty test tubes, beakers, and sample dishes stacked on the stainless-steel counters. Fitzgibbons opened a closet full of long light-blue coats and handed Jamie a pair of safety glasses. "No way," he refused. "These things make me look like a dork."

"I've got no time for the usual nonsense today. Put on the gear and get to work. Glass goes on the trays. You know the drill: Load them in the washer and press *Start*. When the cycle is done, put the clean ones on the drying rack, and start all over again."

Jamie stared at the mountain of dirty glassware. "All of it?"

"For starters," said Fitzgibbons. "Then you can go around to all the open labs and take the trash out back. I'll see you in a couple hours."

Jamie slammed glass into the cleaning trays, and his stomach growled. Morning workouts made him hungry as a bear, so he hurried to the hall to ask his dad for snack machine money. But he was too late. At the end of the corridor, his father was just disappearing inside his top-secret lab, the one Jamie was never allowed inside. The boy watched the door's slow close before it locked tight with a metallic click.

He returned to load trays of dirty test tubes into the industrial washer and start the cycle. He listened to it shoot hot chemical water over the glassware and felt his own blood rushing. Alone in the room with nothing but the mundane task in front of him, Jamie felt like chucking test tubes against the walls, just busting stuff up. He took deep breaths the way his linebackers coach had tried to teach. "Controlled fury" was what he'd called it.

A clatter in the hallway caught his attention. Jamie went to the small square window in the door to see what was going on.

It was tubby Barton, struggling with a wooden crate. Jamie scoffed. It didn't look that heavy, but the guy was huffing and puffing like it was full of cannonballs. He caromed down the corridor, then attempted to rest the crate on his knee so he could press his sweaty palm to open the door.

Jamie did all he could not to bust out laughing. Every time the awkward guy lifted his hand, he lost his balance and almost dropped the crate. After half a dozen tries, Barton managed to both unlock the door and wrangle it open.

He threw the door as wide as he could, then hefted up the box and stumbled through. In a flash, Jamie saw a window of opportunity open. He had like four seconds before the door closed. *One thousand one. One thousand two.*

By *one thousand three*, Jamie slipped out into the hall as quietly as he could and sprinted for the lab. At *one thousand four*, he lunged for the heavy door just as it was about to shut. The steel pinched his fingers, and he bit down hard on his lower lip to keep from yelling in pain. Holding the door open just a hair, he knew he needed to move fast. He pried the door open far enough to slip into the lab and dove under the nearest table.

The door sealed behind him.

Jamie's heart pounded as his dad helped Barton lift the

crate onto a stainless-steel table in the middle of the lab. From his hiding spot, Jamie took in the massive server rows, incredible monitor displays, and mazes of glass tubing that ran throughout the room.

"There's one more box," Barton said, clutching his lower back.

"Let me give you a hand this time." Dr. Fitzgibbons sighed. The two men started for the door, and Jamie slid farther into the shadows under the next lab table, taking care not to get caught in the spider web of cables and wires.

The door opened once again. Conversation faded as the door clicked shut.

He scrambled to his feet, alone at last. Jamie had been to his father's labs in other towns, but none of them looked like this one. There was way more high-tech gear, for one thing, and the weird empty space in the back. He checked out the equipment displays, but they were a mess of math moving at a million miles an hour.

He turned to Barton's computer, which was easy to pick out by the pile of empty takeout bags surrounding it. Jamie knew his dad wouldn't eat that crap, and if he did, he wouldn't have been such a slob about it.

Jamie grabbed Barton's greasy mouse, and the monitor came to life. An animation featured a model that looked quite a bit like Barton—pudgy, balding, and wearing glasses. It stood in the middle of the screen, flanked by digital graph lines. The vertical gradient on the left measured height, and the Barton-model stood a few inches below six feet. A series of tabs labeled *Gen1*, *Gen2*, all the way up to *Gen50*, marked the bottom axis. Jamie clicked on *Gen1*, and the model grew to about six foot two. His features and muscle structure also enlarged to match the model's new size. *Gen2* brought the man to six foot five. Jamie was about to see what *Gen50* yielded when there was a noise in the hall. They were coming back.

He minimized the animation program, which revealed a security profile. Fitz had to look twice. There was a picture of Lawson. Charlie Lawson!

The door clicked open. Fitz ducked out of sight beneath the workstation table. His head spun as he tried to connect growth simulations and *Charlie Lawson*. Had his dad chosen Lawson as a test subject for whatever new growth stuff they were working on? Jamie remembered his father's sermon earlier in the basement, about guys like Lawson killing for the chance to get bigger. The potential betrayal burned.

Barton and Fitzgibbons hauled in the second crate, setting it next to the first and pulling the sides away on both. Inside, rats climbed over one another, complaining in a communal *chee chee chee!*

Fitzgibbons signed a series of release forms and acceptance acknowledgments on a clipboard. "Get JoAnne to file these," he said, handing it to Barton. "And then we'll check the restriction enzymes."

As Barton took the clipboard and hustled to the door, Jamie saw the way to escape. His dad already had turned his attention to calculations at his workstation. Jamie crouched as Barton left, timing the closing of the door.

With his head still reeling from the discoveries he'd made inside the lab, Jamie slipped out behind Barton and back into the utility room like nothing had happened. But now Jamie had a pile of questions.

He dismissed asking his father for answers. If Jamie admitted sneaking into the lab, his punishment would be way worse than washing dirty dishes. He shoved another rack into the washer and started forming a plan to pound the answers out of Lawson.

C harlie shut off the movie projector, despite the giant's protest. The newly christened Bruce continued practicing his new kung fu moves in the musty warehouse air.

"I can't do *Enter the Dragon* again, dude. Twice is enough," Charlie said. Watching Bruce nail move after move with just a little practice was pretty cool, but even that was getting old.

Charlie's phone rang. He expected his mom on the other end. But the glowing screen read *Adele*. At the sound of the musical ring tone, Bruce leaned in. Charlie answered the call.

"Boy," said Adele, "I just got an interesting phone call."

"Huh?"

"We're on a date right now! Didn't you know?" she teased.

Oh no, Mom, you didn't. Charlie closed his eyes in dismay. She'd made good on her threat to double-check his story.

"I hope I'm having a great time!"

"I . . . I . . ." he stammered as his brain spun in its tracks.

"So what's really going on?"

Charlie was busted. All his fibs were coming back to bite him in the butt, so he tried a version of the truth. "See, a friend of mine is in town, but then my mom's boyfriend invited me to go to Madison . . ."

"So, you needed to tell your mom a lie, and you used me as your alibi," Adele concluded. "I don't really mind all that much, but next time you might want to let me in on it so we get our stories straight, you know?"

Charlie flinched. "What did you tell her?"

"Said we were on a date, of course," said Adele, laughing. "You think I was going to rat you out?"

"Thank you, thank you, thank you. I totally should have texted you. I owe you big-time."

Bruce spun and practiced a high kick. The boy turned away so he could talk without distractions.

"Thing is, she talked to my mom, too, and I had to cover," Adele confessed.

"Whoa. What did you say?"

"Told her we're going to the outdoor tonight to see *Total Turbo: The Movie!*"

"A movie?"

"Movie!" exclaimed the giant. Charlie smacked him in the leg to shut him up.

Adele's voice got shy. "So what do you say we go, maybe? Then everything's cool all around."

Did Adele Hawkins just ask me out?

"Charlie? You still there?" Adele asked. "You in or what?"

Bruce had a goofy smirk on his face as he mouthed, "Movie!"

"I . . . do want to go," Charlie managed. "But, I'm kind of hung up with what I got going right now. . . ."

"I thought you owed me big-time," Adele said. "No worries. I'll make up something to tell my mom."

"Go," Bruce urged.

Going to the movie would make things right with both Adele and his mom. He wouldn't have lied after all. And the giant seemed for it. "Wait!" The words tumbled out of Charlie's mouth. "I'd love to go. To the movie. I mean, yeah, I'll go see *Total Turbo* with you."

"Sweet," said Adele, the warmth back in her voice. "I mean, okay. Great."

"I'm . . . going to have to meet you there," Charlie said.

"My mom's headed out that way to the grocery store anyhow. Sure you don't want us to pick you up?"

Charlie turned away from the elated giant. "No, I'll meet you there."

"Awesome. Later."

"Later."

Bruce got loud again as soon as Charlie pocketed his phone. "Movie!"

"Yes, I'm going to a movie," Charlie said. It was a long haul out to the Starlite 14, even on a bike. To make it there before the previews, he needed to get going and soon. "But, don't worry—I'll sneak back in here after it's over."

Bruce thumped his chest with his fist. "Go!"

"Whoa, *you* go to a movie?" asked Charlie. "There's no way. Somebody would see you for sure."

Bruce pointed behind Charlie. The boy spun around. He didn't see anything. When he turned back, the giant was gone. It was impossible!

Charlie searched the shadows. Even though the warehouse had grown dark, it was unimaginable that someone twenty-some feet tall could conceal himself so well. "Okay, okay. You are officially the world's biggest ninja. C'mon, Bruce." But the giant had vanished. Charlie wheeled around.

And there was Bruce, right behind him, smiling like he'd just won a bet.

Charlie jumped. "Holy crap! How'd you learn to do that?"

"Hunting."

"Ah, I get it. If you didn't learn to hide and move quietly, animals would know you were coming from a mile away."

"Movie," Bruce agreed.

"Boy, I don't know." Charlie admitted to himself that the big guy could basically disappear when he needed to, but still. "You could stay hidden the whole time?"

"Yep!"

"I sure wouldn't want to be stuck in here by myself," Charlie said, his voice warming to the idea. Based on the old man's previous visits, Charlie calculated they'd need to be back before eleven. "We should be able to sneak back in here before Hank shows up."

"Go!"

Charlie laughed. "Okay, let's do it."

Bruce crouched down, scooped up the boy, and scooted into the elevator shaft.

"Hold on, big guy. How are you going to climb out while you're holding me?" Charlie asked.

Bruce bent his knees and launched skyward. It took all of Charlie's will not to scream as the bricks of the elevator shaft blurred past. The leap propelled them out the top of the shaft and into the night. They plummeted into the alley, where Bruce landed in nimble silence, his massive frame melting into the shadows of the tall oak Charlie had climbed that morning.

"Wow, you pretty much killed that," he said, swatting a leafy branch away from his face. Charlie took a moment for his stomach to settle—he wasn't used to traveling by giant. Now there were directions to consider. "I'll tell you where to go, okay? When we have to turn, I'll go like this . . ."

Charlie held his right arm out. Bruce turned to the right. Charlie extended his left arm, and Bruce shifted back to his original position. *Well, the turn signals work,* thought Charlie, remembering how DJ showed off the new custom blinkers he installed on the Hummer. His mom's boyfriend would freak if he saw what Charlie was driving.

Charlie's eyebrows knit together as he drew a mental map. He stuck his thumb up and motioned skyward. Bruce held Charlie aloft so that his head peeked just above the warehouse.

The Starlite 14 drive-in theater was on the southeast edge of Richland Center, four or five miles away if they followed Church Street right out of town. That was the most direct way to go, but it would be too strenuous a test of Bruce's ninja skills when the road became Highway 14, with nothing but the stacks of Donovan Dairies and Dewey Zumach's Dugout Bar to shield them from view.

Charlie checked out Tower Hill overlooking the town.

The woods there ran more or less parallel to Highway 14. They would provide a general route that would take them close to the drive-in unseen. "There's where we should start. Can you get us there, you know, secret?"

Bruce lifted his head to get a better look. "Yep."

"Okay, big fella," Charlie said, pounding the giant's fist with his own. "Let's do this thing."

With his back to the warehouse, Bruce edged along in the dark until he came to the front of the building. A big semi rumbled down Church Street toward them. Charlie held his breath. The truck's lights fell just short of Bruce's bare feet. Bruce let the rig thunder a block away before he chanced a peek around the corner. There wasn't a soul in either direction. Bruce winked at Charlie.

And then they were running down Seminary Street— really, really fast.

Charlie had once been dumb enough to ride alone with Tim right after he got his driver's license. He was supposed to be going to Ed's Family Foods for a pound of flour, but Tim had driven to Highway JJ instead, the straightest road in all of Richland County. Out on JJ, Tim got his Thunderbird going 100 miles an hour, laughing his head off the whole time. It felt like warp speed. Charlie couldn't believe they didn't die.

He figured they were going at least that fast as Bruce ate up the first block in two strides. The giant was high-stepping all the way, happy as anything to be out of the dank warehouse. He chose the darkest, most shadowy route possible among the trees, houses, and alleys of Richland Center. Night air rushed past Charlie's face as they took a hard left toward the high bluff. Ahead, the lights on a parked car flashed, and Charlie jerked his arm hard to the right, hoping Bruce was paying attention.

He was.

The giant leaped into the air as the car door opened. An old woman got out, oblivious to the giant soaring high above her in the air. She lit a cigarette and never saw the giant's foot touch down in a dark backyard two houses away. Unfortunately, he landed in a half-full kiddie pool. The giant lost both his balance and his grip on Charlie, whipping the boy high into the night sky.

He reached the apex of his flight against a backdrop of stars and watched as Bruce managed to get a hand down and turn his slide into a miraculous cartwheel that landed him back on his feet. The graceful giant snatched Charlie out of the air before he fell five feet. He hadn't even caught his breath yet when Bruce whispered into his ear, "Fun!"

Charlie could have used a minute to get his stomach out of his throat, but Bruce was just getting started. He hurdled a garage and made another 100-mile-an-hour dash through wooded backyards. They reached Strickland Park at the base of Tower Hill in no time.

"Okay, we'll head for the tower with the blinking light. From there we just have to stay hidden along the tree line until we get to the movie."

Bruce had all the directions he needed. Charlie held on for dear life as the giant zipped across the hills, bounding and bouncing between trees like a halfback eluding tacklers. Whenever Bruce veered in the wrong direction, Charlie pointed him back the right way. They reached the top of the last hill, where the woods ended and the landscape morphed into grassy pasture. Beyond that lay the bright lights of the Starlite 14.

How are we going to get in? wondered Charlie. *It's not like I can go up and pay for a giant.* Then he remembered Tim bragging about sneaking into the drive-in. He'd parked the car on a side road and hopped the fence that surrounded the place. It looked to Charlie like he and Bruce could do the same thing. The hopping part sure wouldn't be a problem.

"Hold up." He scoped out a line of scrubby trees behind the last row of cars and just inside the fence, planted there to keep road noise from interfering with the movies. *Perfect.* Bruce could see the screen from that spot, yet the trees were in a murky netherworld where the lights from cars passing on Highway 14 couldn't reach.

"Okay, that's where you're going to watch the movie. Think you can stay hidden in there?"

"Yep."

"Cool." Charlie pointed out an area in the back by the concession stand. "I'm going to watch from over there with Adele. You stay hidden until I come get you, deal?"

"Deal."

"All right, let's go watch a movie. You're going to love this one."

The two snuck down from the hill, made it over a dark section of the fence, and hid in the trees. Bruce nestled himself in between the poplars so well that Charlie knew where to look and yet still couldn't find him. He was ecstatic—their plan was working. He'd brought a giant to the movies, and no one had any idea. Part of him wanted to brag about it to

Adele. But Bruce was a secret he didn't want to risk telling to anyone.

"Movie!" the giant whispered as pre-movie ads for local nail salons flashed on the screen.

Charlie laughed. "This isn't even the good part yet. I'll meet you right here in a couple hours." The giant held out his fist. Charlie bumped it and took off out of the trees.

The smell of greasy hot dogs wafted through the air, and Bruce sniffed. He saw teenagers flipping burgers and brats at concession stand grills, and his stomach rumbled.

D r. Fitzgibbons tapped the top of a whirring centrifuge, urging the cycle to yield a GGH test sample. Adrenaline and coffee made him sweat. He gave up and returned to his workstation to run another simulation. He leaned back in his chair as the program generated probabilities.

Fitzgibbons closed his eyes and waited for results. Success was perhaps revolutions away. This innovation represented the next evolution of man, a bold new path for humanity to follow, with himself as its architect.

Of course, his work would become that much easier when the Stick arrived to secure the giant and 500 pounds of raw giant growth hormone. The scientist would never again have to go through the machinations of synthesizing from a trace of skin tissue. The closer Fitzgibbons got to an actual giant, the more he wanted it.

His computer chirped, and he checked the results of the latest simulation. Its predictions were discouraging. Even testing a minuscule amount of the GGH on a rat would likely be a waste. Best-case scenarios placed the odds against a rodent surviving at nine to one. Fitzgibbons dropped his head and cursed. He'd hoped to nail this version.

"No improvement?" asked Barton, appearing behind Fitzgibbons.

"Not much. The rat's accelerated physiology is the problem. It won't govern the growth rate."

"What's the projection?"

"Triple before growth becomes unsustainable."

"Well then." Barton tapped his watch. "I say we show Gourmand what triple-size looks like, don't you?"

The doctor agreed. There was little to be gained waiting for the certainty of success. If the rat lived or died, what did they have to lose? Gourmand would see the potential, the rich forest through the trees. "Let's see exactly what we've got."

He put on rubber gloves, then removed the GGH vial from the centrifuge. With a sterile syringe, he punctured the rubber top of the vial, decanting the precise amount. He repeated the process with a bottle of sodium chloride. He tapped the syringe as a shrill sound came from the skittering lab rats.

Chee!

Barton approached the metal cage and hovered over the bedlam. He was drawn to the smallest rodent, a dirty gray fellow only two-thirds the size of his brothers. The runt's fur was tattered and bloody in spots where it had been bitten. Barton watched as a larger rat set its snout in the direction of the smallest one and lashed out.

Chee! Chee! Chee!

"Your runt days are over," Barton said as he thrust his

gloved hand through the top of the cage. He worked his way through the tangled mass and grabbed the abused rat. It didn't make a sound when Barton placed it alone in a second Plexiglas cage. He put the box under his arm and hurried to the greenhouse portion of the lab.

"Looks like your little friend was a goner either way," noted Fitzgibbons as Barton joined him in the open space, the ceiling glowing with afternoon sunlight. Fitzgibbons used a phone app to activate cameras mounted at strategic locations along the ceiling that would capture every aspect of their experiment. "It might as well make history on its way out the door."

Fitzgibbons looked down at the pitiful rat on the bottom of the cage, its chest pumping away at a furious pace. He took hold of the creature, injected its neck, and set it down on the floor. Barton drew up close beside him, careful to not block the camera views. At first, the rat only twitched, its nostrils flaring to pull in as much air as they could. Gurgling sounds came from some haunted place deep within the rodent, and its pupils dilated. It spat a few droplets of blood.

Then the rat started to grow.

"Holy . . ." began Barton.

The rat's snout extended in unison with its extremities, expanding before the scientists' eyes. But its torso lagged far behind. The uneven growth caused the rat considerable pain. It thrashed as the irregular expansion became more rapid.

Cheeeeeeeeeeeee. The cry was lower and more guttural than before.

"Dear God," Barton marveled as the creature contorted and grew. "It's incredible."

The rodent, wheezing in agony, struggled to its feet.

Fitzgibbons readied two pairs of sizable forceps. "If it gets much bigger," said the doctor, handing a tool to Barton, "we may need to restrain it."

The rat continued to grow in herky-jerky fashion, a hind leg expanding here, an ear doubling in size there. Its eyes swelled in their sockets, and the grotesque creature snarled at Barton.

"Grab it!" Both men wielded their instruments to seize the rat, now the size of an angry tomcat, but it evaded them both and dashed for the main lab.

Fitzgibbons and Barton chased after the creature, now flailing on the floor near its original cage. Its long tail lashed back and forth, whipping the men's forearms as they struggled to get a hold on the beast with their forceps.

"Grab it around the middle," Fitzgibbons ordered, "while I get behind its head."

Barton tried his best, but the rat wouldn't surrender. It snapped at him with its sharp mouthful of extended teeth. He brought all his considerable weight on the rat's thick midsection to pin the creature. It resisted with all its might, thrashing side to side as Fitzgibbons struggled to get a better grip on its neck.

The rat tore at Barton's sleeve. He flinched, lost his forceps, then got to his feet and ran.

"Get back here!" shouted Fitzgibbons.

The rats in the first cage raised their snouts, smelling the danger in the air. They cowered in fear.

The vicious giant-rat flipped the steel cage on its side and plunged its snout inside. Frightened *chees* rang out as rat blood splattered everywhere. The giant rodent ravaged all its bullies. Any rat that tried to get away got it even worse.

Barton reappeared with the tranquilizer pistol. He raised the gun to fire, but just as suddenly as the giant-rat had struck, it stopped.

The rodent, now six times its original size, reared up, then floundered to the ground. It battered its head again and again against a leg of the steel table before letting loose a horrific death screech.

Then the rat shut its eyes for good.

The lab, filled with gruesome sounds just moments earlier, was quiet. The scientists stood in the silence after the slaughter. They took in the grisly scene, a giant-rat dead on its back surrounded by the gory remains of a dozen normal-size ones.

"I'll alert Gourmand," Fitzgibbons said, checking his phone to make sure the video cameras had done their job. "You take blood samples so we can start analysis."

His hand shook with exhilaration as he e-mailed Gourmand the video of the test. It had worked far better than his computer's predictions. The analysis would reveal much, and his mind was already bursting with epigenetic modification ideas that could refine and stabilize the GGH.

Someone banged on the steel door to the lab. Muffled, concerned voices called out from the other side. "Dr. Fitzgibbons! Are you men all right?"

"We're fine," Barton shouted back.

"As a matter of fact," Fitzgibbons added, "we're wonderful!"

16

Charlie strolled into the field lined with cars and pickups ready to watch *Total Turbo: The Movie*. He threw one last glance back at the line of trees and saw no sign of Bruce. Previews of coming attractions were just starting, and the crowd was glued to the screen. Charlie wondered if Adele's mom had dropped her off yet. He pulled out his phone and texted her:

where are u?

While he waited for a response, he searched down a row of cars. The concession stand guys were cooking up a storm, and the smell of grilled brats made his mouth water.

ADELE: by the concession stand looking right at u

Charlie laughed. He didn't see how he could have missed her, since she was only about twenty feet away, dressed up in a striped cardigan sweater with a cozy-looking checkered blanket slung over her shoulder. Her hot chocolate whispered curls of steam into the cool night air. It was the first time he had ever seen her wearing lipstick.

"Hey, you," said Adele.

"Hey," he said back. He wasn't sure what to say next. She wasn't saying anything, either. He stuck his hands in his pockets. She shifted her weight and took a sip of her hot cocoa. Finally he spotted a lone picnic table near the tree line. "Want to sit over there?" The two of them hopped up on the top of the table rather than on one of the benches.

"Most of the time, video game movies are stupid, but maybe this one will be different," declared Adele, her fingers crossed.

"Here's hoping." He glanced over his shoulder at the tree line. Still no Bruce. Charlie relaxed. So far, so good.

"You try that move off the *Total Turbo* message board yet?"

"I did. It's tough to nail."

"You'll get it," said Adele with a shiver. "Aren't you freezing?"

Charlie was cold, but he played it off. "Nah, not really."

She spread the blanket across their laps anyway. It helped. "So, who were you hanging out with today?"

"He's sort of like an exchange student."

Charlie was interrupted by people shouting and applauding and honking their horns as the opening credits splashed *Total Turbo: The Movie* on the screen. Adele hollered and tugged Charlie's arm. The car she always drove in the game, a tricked-out Tesla Roadster, scraped an iron guard rail and sent a colorful burst of sparks flying into the air.

The movie started. Charlie wondered if he was on a date

or not. He considered putting his arm around Adele, but where did it go? Over her shoulder? Around her waist? But he knew Bruce could be watching them. Even though the giant was probably paying attention to the movie, Charlie felt weird about it.

Adele shifted her weight to realign the blanket, and her warm hand brushed against Charlie's. He wondered if he should hold it. His was only inches away. Just as he was screwing up the courage to reach over, Adele grabbed Charlie's hand first. Their fingers intertwined.

He completely lost track of the movie's plot after that. There were high-speed chases, good guys who turned out to be bad guys, a beautiful female mechanic, but he was too distracted by holding hands to catch all the details.

Too soon, the credits rolled and people honked their horns in appreciation. Charlie checked the tree line again and like before, there was no sign of Bruce. All he could see was sausage smoke wafting above the picnic tables and a stringy-haired cook getting ready for the intermission rush, slamming brats and dogs on the fire. Charlie's stomach growled so loud that Adele heard it.

"Wow, somebody hungry?"

Charlie was embarrassed. "Not me," he said, even though he was starving.

"Well, I am," she declared, letting go of Charlie's hand and throwing off the blanket. "All I can smell is that grill. You want a brat?"

"Wait!" Charlie reached into his pocket.

"Whatever." Adele smiled, holding up a ten.

"Maybe one."

Adele split for the concession line, leaving Charlie alone. His pocket buzzed and he checked his phone.

MOM: Where are you?

Charlie closed his eyes. He couldn't wait until he was older and his mom would stop checking his every move.

Drive-in.

MOM: How in the world did u get there?

Charlie hesitated before typing. *I told you, I'm with Adele.*

MOM: It's late. I'm sending DJ out 2 pick u 2 up.

2nd movie hasn't even started!

MOM: No arguments. DJ will b there in 20 min.

And that, Charlie knew, was that. When Adele got back, he'd confess that his mom was making him leave. Bruce needed to get back to the warehouse anyway. If they beat it back there, Charlie could get home before DJ even left. He snuck over to the tree line.

"Hey, big guy," Charlie whispered. "We got to split soon."

No response.

"Bruce?"

Charlie went into the trees to investigate. But the giant was gone.

"Bruce!" Charlie called, figuring no one could hear him over the car stereos blasting between movies. "Bruce! Where are you? This isn't funny!"

Charlie spun, expecting Bruce to poke him from behind like he'd done in the warehouse. But he wasn't there. A line of perspiration formed on the back of Charlie's neck and went cold in the night air. He ran along the tree line, searching for any sign of the giant. "Bruce!" he yelled, louder now against the sound of cars rushing by on Highway 14.

His phone buzzed again and just as he pulled it from his pocket, it flew from his hand. A hard blow to the chin sent white-hot pain pulsing through his jaw. He found himself on the grass looking up at the hulking outline of Jamie Fitz-gibbons, wearing a too-tight *Total Turbo* T-shirt.

Fitz stomped on Charlie's phone and snuffed out its glow, leaving them alone in the dark shadows of the tree line. "What are you doing out at Accelerton?" he asked in a scary-calm voice.

Charlie had no idea what Fitz was talking about. "Acceler-what?"

"My dad's lab! Don't lie to me!" Fitz kicked Charlie hard in the ribs. "What are you, his little experiment?"

"I . . . I . . ." Charlie coughed. "I don't know . . . what you're talking about."

"This isn't going to stop"—Fitz gave Charlie another boot to the ribs—"until I get some answers!"

"Stop it!"

Fitz spun as Adele threw herself at him, punching the bigger kid in the chest as hard as she could. "You're hurting him!"

Fitz grabbed Adele by the wrists and threw her hard to the ground. "You sit there," he snarled, "and watch Lawson get his."

Charlie struggled to his knees. "Leave her alone."

"Make me," said Fitz.

Adele backed away from Fitz on her elbows, mouth wide open. Terrified, she raised a trembling hand and pointed up at the bully.

"What's the matter? You scared?" sneered Fitz, right

before giant fingers wrapped around his muscular body and lifted him twenty feet in the air.

Bruce squeezed Fitz, who let out a frightened yelp. The angry giant brought the thrashing boy up to eye level and let loose with a menacing snarl. His enormous yellow teeth were full of hot dog meat. Charlie saw something in Fitz's face that he never thought he'd see: fear.

"Whoever stole all these brats is in really big trouble," someone yelled from the concession building. "I'm calling the cops!"

"Bruce, no!" shouted Charlie, staggering to his feet even though his legs felt like jelly. "People are coming! We got to get you out of here!"

"Let go of me!" howled Fitz.

"Bruce, it's for your own good! Put him down, and let's go."

Bruce didn't listen, disappearing into the trees with Fitz still in hand. The giant was going to teach the bully a lesson. Charlie gave chase through the dark with Adele close on his heels. They followed the sound of snapping tree branches, circling the drive-in lot and catching up with Bruce right behind the Starlite 14 marquee. The giant hoisted Fitz high in the air, the sign shielding them from view. If Bruce wanted to kill him, this was the perfect spot.

"You have to put him down," Charlie yelled. "He's not worth it!"

The muscles in Bruce's brow tensed. The giant looked down at Adele, then at Charlie. Then finally, he grimaced at Fitz. "Bad," Bruce scolded.

He spun Fitz around and tugged the boxer shorts that

stuck out the back of Fitz's low-hanging cargo pants. "Yowwwww!" howled Fitz.

The smirking giant lifted the boy over the sign and hung the waistband of his shorts on the starburst that doubled as the letter *t* in *Starlite*. "Get me down!" Fitz screamed in a high-pitched whine.

Bruce poked his head around the edge of the sign and laughed, long and low. Fitz extended his middle finger. "This isn't over," he said, defiant despite his unfortunate position. "And you reek."

Spotlights below the sign lit Fitz for the world to see, and cars passing on Highway 14 honked at the sight of the humiliated boy sprawling in the air, swinging by his underwear. Red flashing lights spun into the drive. Bruce flinched and stumbled back at the sound of the squad car's wailing siren. He held his hands over his ears and moaned in pain as the piercing cry pounded away at his sensitive eardrums.

A beat-up pickup truck squelched its headlights and pulled through the grass behind the Starlite 14 sign. Charlie pulled Adele into the shadows behind the sign post—they were really in trouble now. At least the sight of Fitz hanging on the sign had everyone's attention. No one saw Hank hobble out into the darkness. "You!" he whispered up at Bruce. "I've been driving all over town looking for you! If I didn't see that kid hanging up on the sign, I would never have found you! You're going to miss your ride. You know where to go, head to the pickup point. Right now!"

"But—" the giant protested.

"Now!" thundered Hank.

The giant made a face, but he turned and dashed unnoticed across the pasture and back toward the woods. Hank hobbled back into his truck and took off for town.

When the old man's truck was gone, Charlie shouted after the giant. "Bruce!" No response. Helpless, he turned back to see DJ's big Hummer pulling into the drive-in lot.

He turned to Adele and gestured helplessly. How could he begin to explain? "I'm really sorry, but I have to go."

She grabbed his arm. "Are you telling me he's the exchange student?"

"Yeah," he admitted.

"Will you tell me what's going on?"

"When I can."

She leaned into him and kissed him softly on the lips. Charlie stood there in the dark with her for a second, paralyzed as the squad car pulled beneath the Starlite 14 sign. Then she shoved him off in the direction of the Hummer. "Go!"

17

Derisive laughter greeted Jamie Fitzgibbons as he hung from the Starlite 14 drive-in sign by his boxer shorts. It was an epic wedgie, but Jamie didn't feel the pain caused by his bunched-up underwear; he was too focused on the fact that there was a *freaking giant* in Richland Center.

He remembered the simulation he'd seen on Barton's screen, the one that grew into "Gen50." Jamie had guessed that his dad was using Charlie Lawson as a guinea pig, but it was clearly his big stinky friend. That overgrown lab rat must have had at least fifty doses of his dad's new growth drug. How else could he have gotten so huge? From the looks of Barton's simulations, the stuff could make Jamie a giant. He'd be famous. The biggest star in the world—literally!

He watched Lawson climb into a black Hummer as swirling red lights from two squad cars spun around the crowd. Was he sneaking off to meet up with his big smelly buddy?

One of the cops silenced the piercing siren, which only

made the kids' laughter easier to hear. A balding officer stood at the base of the Starlite 14 sign and hollered up to Jamie. "You want to explain how you got up there?"

"I slipped," he called down with a sneer. It wasn't like the bald cop would believe what really happened.

"He was rearranging the letters," someone shouted to the officer.

It was Adele Hawkins, the girl who had been hanging out with Lawson. Jamie realized she was covering for him and the giant, too!

"He was bragging about it all night. He was going to switch up the letters in *Total Turbo* to spell . . ." She took a second and focused on the marquee. *"Brutal Toot!"* That brought another round of laughter from the crowd. One of the other officers showed up with a ladder.

"All right, son," said Bald Cop from the top of an aluminum ladder. "I'm helping you down." He wrapped his arms around Jamie's midsection and unhooked him. Jamie felt immediate relief but didn't show his gratitude. He scowled at the officer the whole way down the ladder, just to show all the idiots what was what.

"I was just about to get down."

"Right, right," returned Bald Cop as they reached the ground.

Jamie started after some of the kids who were still laughing, but the officer grabbed his arm. "Hold on. You're not going anywhere until I get some answers. Let's start with an easy one. Name?"

"Fitzgibbons," mumbled Jamie, giving the "this isn't over" look to the kids who were snickering behind Bald Cop.

"Tell me again how you ended up like that?"

Jamie found Adele standing in the crowd, hands defiantly on her hips. "Like she said. Brutal Toot."

"That's real smart, kid. Looks like you bought yourself a ticket and a ride in the squad car. What's your address?"

"My mom's out of town," Jamie lied. "You'll have to take me to my dad's lab."

Twenty minutes and one sore-bottomed ride later, Bald Cop and Jamie arrived at the Accelerton compound. The facility was deserted except for his dad's lab and a sleepy security guard who wasn't used to late-Saturday-night visitors. After a brief explanation over the security intercom, Jamie and the police officer were allowed inside the gates. Dr. Fitzgibbons waited for them in the lobby, looking nearly as angry as Jamie felt.

"Let's hear it, Officer," Fitzgibbons said, though he never took his eyes off his son. "Who did he beat up this time?" For once, Jamie returned his father's angry glare.

"Beat up?" said Bald Cop, puzzled. "You got it wrong, Doc. We got called out to the drive-in about some stolen wieners and saw your son hanging from the sign by his shorts."

Fitzgibbons blinked twice and turned to face the officer. "I'm sorry, what did you say?"

"He claims he was trying to rearrange the letters, but how he hooked his underpants on the marquee is beyond me. All I know is that he's lucky he didn't fall and break his neck."

"I could have jumped from there . . ." Jamie began.

Fitzgibbons held up a hand. "That's enough," he snapped. "I apologize for my son's behavior and even more for his attitude, Officer. Where do we go from here?"

Jamie fumed as Bald Cop tore a pink ticket off a pad. "I'm citing your son with a municipal ordinance violation. Technically the charge is 'disturbing the peace.'"

"More like 'disturbing your doughnut break,'" mumbled Jamie.

"That is enough, Jamie," said Fitzgibbons, taking the ticket and slipping it into his shirt pocket.

Bald Cop rubbed his smooth head, ready to get on his way. "Just pay the fine, Doc. We've never had any trouble with your son in the past, and I expect this'll be the end of it." He gave Jamie a look that said it had better be.

Fitzgibbons held the door for the officer as he exited the building, then took Jamie by his shoulder back through the security door and down the hall to the utility room where he'd washed test tubes earlier in the day. "Okay, let's have it."

"Have what?"

"What in the world were you doing up on a sign?"

"Forget about that! How about you tell me what you're doing in there!" Jamie's head jerked toward the lab that he'd snuck into just hours before. He was so angry that his hands shook.

"Don't you dare try to turn this around, Jamie. This isn't football coaches anymore. It's police officers! And if you think for one moment that your mother and I—"

"A *giant* hung me up there!" Jamie shouted. "Charlie Lawson's smelly, crooked-toothed giant buddy! Gen50! Now do you want to tell me what's going on?"

Fitzgibbons's jaw dropped. "What?"

"A giant, like you don't know," spewed Jamie. "I think

you cooked him up in your top-secret lab with your fat little friend."

The skin on Fitzgibbons's forehead twitched. "This giant—where is it now?"

"You made that guy big instead of me," Jamie seethed, pounding his chest. "Why not me?"

Fitzgibbons put his hands on his son's shoulders. "This is very important, Jamie. After the giant hung you on the sign, where did it go?"

Jamie jerked himself free. "How should I know? Everyone was laughing at me, the cops were shining flashlights in my face, and then it was gone."

"We can't let that giant get away!" Fitzgibbons turned to hurry back to his lab, and Jamie followed.

"I'm coming!"

"I need you here," Fitzgibbons said, spinning Jamie toward a computer terminal on a nearby desk. "Record every single thing you remember about what happened. Do you realize that you're one of the first people in the entire world to make contact? Describe what the giant looked like. Did it talk? What did it say? How did it say it? Don't leave out a single detail."

Fitzgibbons hurried out into the hall and scanned his palm. The laboratory door unlocked. He disappeared inside the lab, leaving his son to watch the door begin to close.

One thousand one . . .

Lightning tore across the sky as an Accelerton company jet soared high over the state of Arkansas. Although the *Fasten Seat Belt* signs were lit, the Stick paid them no attention. He had more important things on his mind, like capturing a giant.

The Stick paced the length of the small cabin, tastefully furnished with four executive-style leather chairs and a marble table. His civilian outfit, as always, was nondescript: a lightweight tan sport coat over a white button-down shirt with matching tan slacks, his impeccably shined shoes black and simple. The black hair atop his head was cut at military length. A little salt and pepper showed on the sides. His build was wiry-strong.

He swallowed hot black coffee in long gulps while checking the windows on both sides of the aircraft. It bounced in the turbulence of a dark storm.

"Please sit down, sir," said the flight's lone cabin attendant,

Lori, a brunette in her late twenties. The lapel of her jacket was embroidered with the Accelerton double helix. She was strapped into her seat near the cockpit.

"No," the Stick said. He was intent on determining the severity of the storm, and the amount of time the weather might delay his arrival in Chicago. Special transport waited there to take him to Richland Center. Any delay was unacceptable.

The attendant pursed her lips. No one had ever told her "no" before when asked to buckle in.

Speakers crackled as the pilot spoke from the cabin in a monotone drawl. "Well, we're in the middle of some weather," he said, stating the obvious. "Doppler's got this front stretching from eastern Minnesota all the way down to Little Rock. Air traffic control isn't going to let us get anywhere near Chicago for now. Looks like we'll be circling St. Louis until she blows through. Just make yourself comfortable. Lori will help you out with anything you need."

The Stick set down the coffee and picked up the black cane that had been resting next to his chair. He turned to the cabin attendant. "Hi, Lori. I need something."

"Sir, I have to ask you again to sit down. It isn't safe."

"No," repeated the Stick. "I need to talk to the captain."

"I'm afraid you can't. Cabin doors are locked. FAA regulations, as I'm sure you know. The only way to reach him is on this intercom." She pointed to a simple handset hooked on the cabin wall next to her seat. "But he's got his hands full at the moment. Is there anything else I can do for you?"

The Stick strode down the center of the plane, heading straight for the intercom.

"Sir!" Lori protested as the Stick reached over her and grabbed the handset.

"Captain," the Stick said. "Circling St. Louis is unacceptable. I need to get to Chicago. I have an important connection to make there."

There was a long silence. Lori frowned at the Stick, who somehow stood stone still despite the plane's violent jitter.

The cabin speaker crackled again. "Unacceptable or not, air traffic control isn't letting us any farther north until this weather breaks. It's spawning tornados all over the place. We do apologize for the inconvenience, but it's out of our hands."

The Stick exhaled. "Fine," he said. "Have it your way." He hung up the handset, then returned to his seat. He set down his cane, peeled off his jacket, and unbuttoned his white shirt.

Embarrassed, Lori turned her head. "Please keep your clothes on, sir."

"Relax." The Stick removed his white button-down to reveal a skin-tight black shirt as sleek as the physique it covered. He took off his pants. Black leggings, made from the same material as the shirt, graced his lower half. He folded his suit coat and pants, depositing them in an overhead bin. Then from the same compartment, he extracted a large black duffle.

He opened the bag, revealing a dozen black sticks, each weapon outfitted with a different high-tech attachment. Many people thought the sticks were the source of his nickname, but they were wrong. President Roosevelt once said "Speak softly and carry a big stick"—the idea that diplomacy was well and good, but only when backed by the threat of massive force. The Stick was that force.

He moved the weapons aside one by one until he found what he was looking for: a compact red-and-white bundle that unwrapped into another body suit. He donned the top.

The flight attendant blinked as she noted the webbing between the arms and torso. After he pulled on the pants, his legs were similarly joined. It made the Stick look like a flying squirrel. He repositioned the duffle's contents and slung the bag across his body. He picked up his cane.

"Sir, I have to ask," said Lori. "What in the world are you wearing?"

"A wingsuit."

"A wing . . . What is it for?"

"Leaving."

"I'm sorry?"

The Stick withdrew his phone and made a call.

"Sir, you cannot turn on portable electronic devices at this . . ." A hard look from the Stick halted Lori's warning.

"Flight scrapped, we're stuck up here. I'll be on the ground in twenty minutes," he said to someone on the other end. "Ping me for the exact location and arrange transport ASAP. There should be something in the area. I'll go off board if necessary. Calculating my departure trajectory now." He ended the call and tapped the screen twice. An app opened and located the plane's current position. The Stick chose a spot on the map and an arc appeared on the screen, tracing a three-dimensional path out of the plane to a landing location. An on-screen clock began counting back from thirty seconds.

Last, he removed a stainless-steel syringe from his bag and tore off the needle cap with his teeth. He plunged the hypodermic straight through the wingsuit and into his thigh, dropping the plunger in a single smooth motion. In moments, his chest and shoulders heaved violently, and his pupils swelled. He yanked out the syringe, dropped it and let it roll down the aisle.

He approached Lori, who had little color left in her face. "Go join the pilots in the cabin."

"Please, sir. You can't jump out of this plane. It's . . . it's not that kind of plane! And the storm . . ." Making her point, an earsplitting clap of thunder shook the aircraft. Lori clutched the armrests of her seat.

He checked the countdown. "I'm leaving in twenty seconds. Once I open that door, the cabin pressure is going to get really uncomfortable. You'll feel much better up front."

"There's only t-t-two chairs in there," Lori protested.

"Then I guess you'll have to stand."

"I . . . I . . . I . . ."

People who were paralyzed with fear often made it easier for the Stick to do his job. This was not one of those times. Lori flinched as he grabbed the handset next to her head.

"Captain, I'm jumping out of your plane. Do the right thing and let Lori up front with you."

He handed the handset back to Lori and donned a pair of goggles. "I'm going in ten," he told her. "Tell him."

"He's opening the door in ten seconds!" Lori screamed into the handset. "He's not kidding! He's dressed like a superhero or something! He's crazy!"

"I've locked the emergency door. You've violated federal law!" said the pilot.

The Stick waved off the accusation with a swipe of his cane. "International law, too—a bunch of times. That door opens in seven seconds. Tell him."

Lori unstrapped herself from her chair and pounded on the door to the cockpit.

"Five seconds," cautioned the Stick.

The cockpit door swung open and Lori darted inside, locking it tight behind her.

The Stick turned to the emergency exit door. Blue electricity crackled out of the business end of his weapon. He aimed it at the hatch lock and fired a cobalt blast. The interior lights dimmed, and the plane dropped in altitude before righting itself. One good kick from the Stick, and the door flung open. He dove out of the plane in a rush of air, his wingsuit gliding through gale-force winds toward the ground.

He wouldn't miss his chance at a giant in Richland Center.

C lear liquid filled the hypodermic as Barton drew back the plunger. His hand trembled from exhaustion or exhilaration—he couldn't tell the difference. Tandem mass spectrometry confirmed what earlier simulations had predicted: The rat's physiology was too accelerated to accept the giant growth hormone. The rodent's internal organs didn't have a prayer of keeping pace.

But now, after several hours of analyzing the dead giant-rat, Barton knew he and Dr. Fitzgibbons were closer to identifying the allelic variant necessary to epigenetically modify, clone, and express the DNA structure to stabilize the GGH. At least, that was what Barton would write in his report to Gourmand. In layman's terms, he was pretty sure he could grow a rat without blowing it up. There were, of course, mountains of tests ahead to confirm his hypothesis.

The door to the lab clicked open, and Fitzgibbons scrambled into the laboratory.

Barton set the hypodermic down, eager to deliver his news. But before he could speak, his mentor shouted about something else entirely.

"We've made contact!" Fitzgibbons's eyes were wild as the door lock sounded. He pulled up the latest satellite images on the bank of monitors. "The giant is on the move. We have to find him before the Stick arrives!"

Barton couldn't quite believe his ears. "We should have gone down to the warehouse with the tracking gun while we had the chance!"

Fitzgibbons ignored the complaint and panned through satellite imagery of the Starlite 14. "It's running around on the edge of town. The thing picked Jamie off the ground and hung him out to dry on a movie marquee."

"But . . . but why would it . . . ?" Barton sputtered, trying to process the strange story.

"It doesn't matter right now. Jamie's detailing the whole encounter for us. How long will it take to access every bird at our disposal?"

"It's the middle of the night on the coast. I'm not sure there's anyone there at this hour."

"We'll have to do it without their consent." He pounded the keyboard. "We need to know the giant's location when the Stick arrives. If we're close, he'll get it." Barton hurried to his workstation and joined the effort. Soon they had retrained every satellite at their disposal and a few more that weren't. It would be a few minutes before they came online and scoured the entire area.

The timing was awkward, but the junior scientist still wanted to share his own news. He retrieved the syringe, holding it up so that its contents glowed with promise in the amber light. "Sean, I have a new version."

"You can't be ready to test again this soon . . ."

"Oh, but I am," said Barton with a wide smile. He handed Fitzgibbons the hypodermic. "Gourmand will double our funding."

Fitzgibbons held the sample up to the light. "This is going to make us giants among men."

The words were barely out of Fitzgibbons's mouth when something rammed him hard in the back, sending the syringe flying into the air. He fell to his hands and knees.

Barton raced Jamie Fitzgibbons for the syringe, sliding across the smooth tile floor, but the pudgy scientist didn't stand a chance. Jamie dove like an All-Pro linebacker pouncing on a fumble. He held the GGH high up above his head, thumb on the plunger.

"Jamie," Fitzgibbons whispered, extending a cautious hand. "What are you doing? Put that down, now."

"You just don't want me to have it!" the angry teenager yelled back, his face red with betrayal. "You made him a giant instead of me."

"Hold on now. We didn't make anything," Fitzgibbons explained as calmly as he could, inching closer to his son. "But that's our goal. And we need the giant you saw to make it happen. I'll explain everything after you put down the syringe. Please. You don't want . . ."

Jamie slammed the needle down into his thigh. "I want to be huge!"

20

The GGH injection immediately sent Jamie into shock, and he thumped his head when he hit the floor. Fitzgibbons and Barton dragged the unconscious teen into the large greenhouse section of the lab, where they did everything in their power to stabilize his vitals. Then Jamie's T-shirt ripped—first the neck, then the shoulders, until the whole thing was rags. When his shoes burst, the laces snapped like overtightened guitar strings. His blue jeans soon were in tatters on the floor.

For modesty's sake, Barton draped Jamie in an absurdly large hospital gown stitched with an Accelerton logo, a garment the scientists had custom-ordered in case they ever secured a live giant.

In twenty minutes' time, Giant Jamie stretched across nearly twenty feet of laboratory. His vein-webbed eyelids twitched, but they didn't open. Fitzgibbons held his palm against the colossal jugular vein in his son's neck and counted out the irregular heartbeats. He thanked the stars for small miracles—Barton's first version of GGH might have caused Jamie's heart to burst out of his chest.

Barton kept his distance, partly out of respect and partly to stay within arm's reach of the tranquilizer gun and security system on the wall. He monitored Jamie's shaky but improving vital systems on a tablet computer. "He's hanging in there," he said, excited that his formula was working but sensitive enough not to show his glee to the boy's father. "There's still a long ways to go, but organ growth has been largely uniform. Vitals are sluggish but continue to function, even as he expands. That's very positive, Sean. When Gourmand sees these results . . ."

"Gourmand is never going to find out about this," said Fitzgibbons, angrily approaching his assistant, "because we're not going to breathe a word about it."

Barton adjusted his glasses and fiddled with the tablet. Then he straightened his shoulders and looked Fitzgibbons in the eye. "Respectfully, I can't promise to keep this between us. It isn't personal . . ."

"Personal is exactly what it is," shouted Fitzgibbons, yanking the tablet from Barton's hands and hurling it to the cement. The screen splintered into a spider's web. "Look at him, Neil. That's my son! And I won't let Accelerton turn him into a huge, walking experiment."

"Accelerton didn't do that to him. He did it to himself." Barton retrieved his tablet, confirmed that it still functioned despite the cracked screen, and tucked it under his arm.

"Look—I didn't plan to test GGH this way. But it happened. And now that it has, no one can help him better than Accelerton."

"That's a lie, and you know it. If Gourmand finds out about Jamie, she'll never let him see the light of day again—he'll be a 'prototype,' for God's sake. Legal will figure out some way to claim him as Accelerton property, mark my words. Is my son still even considered human under the law? You can imagine their arguments."

Barton acknowledged the point. "I can keep things under wraps for a few days, maybe a week, give you an opportunity to come to grips with what's happened," he offered. "During that time, we can track Jamie's progress, monitor his physiology, and take samples of his blood. But I'll only agree to keep quiet if he stays here—and under restraint."

A pitiful moan escaped Giant Jamie's lips. His nostrils spasmed as his skull expanded grotesquely. Fitzgibbons's hands looked tiny as he placed them on the side of his son's enormous forehead.

Barton circled Giant Jamie's hulking body and unwound cable from the winch system on the other side of the room. "This is as much for his protection as it is for ours."

"Neil, come on. He's a kid."

"Not anymore," said Barton, dispensing with politeness. "The fact of the matter is that we don't know what he is now. Whatever performance cocktail you'd been giving him already juiced his temper. You told me about the fights yourself. With the GGH, there's more than a chance that his aggression has grown along with his body. Remember the rat? Now multiply that effect by fifty." Barton set the cracked tablet down and attempted to throw one of the airline cables over Giant Jamie's expanding torso. It took him three tries to get it all the way across.

Just as Barton was about to secure the cable, the tablet came to life and chirped an urgent alert. He picked it up and took in the shuffling images on the screen. "You're going to want to see this." He held out the tablet for Fitzgibbons. The cracked screen displayed four satellite images of a giant— as he approached, climbed up, and dropped into the silo at the quarry. Time stamps at the bottom of each image revealed that the behemoth had returned within the last forty minutes.

The sight gave Fitzgibbons hope that he still might save his son. He turned to Barton. "Here's how this is going to work. Send these coordinates immediately to the Stick. He'll bring down the giant, and we'll have everything we need to synthesize generations of GGH. Jamie can be moved somewhere safe while I evaluate what can be done to help him."

"Jamie's not going anywhere." A defiant Barton picked up the restraining cable to snap it in place.

But he never got the chance.

Giant Jamie's massive right arm whipped the cable aside. He sat up, groggy, the loose blue gown hanging around his midsection.

Barton ran as fast as he could for the tranquilizer gun.

"Jamie!" Fitzgibbons screamed to get his giant son's attention. "Lie back down! You're still growing! You're in no condition to move around!"

Giant Jamie waved his hand back and forth in front of his face as his huge, bleary eyes adjusted. "I've never felt better," he muttered, his newly baritone voice pouring down on the two men from above. "I'm freaking awesome."

A tranquilizer dart whizzed over Giant Jamie's left shoulder, sailing into the adjoining laboratory.

Without so much as a sideways glance, the giant teenager swung his huge left fist in the threat's direction. The blow missed Barton by inches, turning drywall to dust as it rammed the wall next to the gas system control box.

Barton scrambled across the floor, took shaky aim with the gun, and fired once more. This time the dart found its target, sticking Giant Jamie in the neck and delivering a dose of tranquilizer sufficient to knock out an elephant.

But only an elephant.

Giant Jamie ripped out the dart. "Barrrton!" The slurred shout shook the glass overhead like a furious thunderclap.

The tranquilizer circulated in Giant Jamie's system as he made a fist and eyed up Barton. The woozy giant missed his mark again and crushed a new section of wall.

Terrified, Barton dropped the tranquilizer gun and dashed for the exit at the front of the lab.

Giant Jamie Fitzgibbons's huge lips puckered as—*puhtoo*—he launched a one-gallon ball of spit in Barton's direction. It nailed him in the back and knocked the man into the door.

"Haaaw, haaaw, haaaw . . ." Giant Jamie's punch-drunk laughter was eerily distorted by the tranquilizer. He turned to see his father with a gas mask over his face, creeping for the control box. "What the heck are you wearing, Dad? You look stupid." Barton, covered in saliva, used the distraction to slip out of the lab.

"Jamie, you're not yourself," said Fitzgibbons, his voice hollow inside the gas mask. He placed his hand on the security panel. "Lie back down."

"Make me." Giant Jamie's eyes regained some of their focus.

Fitzgibbons's hand wavered on the console.

Giant Jamie boomed down condescension from up high. He leaned toward his father. "What's the matter? Are you scared?"

Fitzgibbons activated the security system.

A powder-blue mist filtered into the room from long steel pipes that ran the length of the greenhouse roof. Fitzgibbons counted in his head—the gas was designed to take effect in as soon as ten seconds.

One stinging snort of the gas in his nostrils was all it took for Giant Jamie to lash out at the pipes, wrenching them away from the ceiling. But his savagery only let more anesthesia into the room. Howling in frustration, he leaped into the air and battered the greenhouse roof. The glass splintered with each blow before finally shattering.

Fitzgibbons covered his head as a shower of glass rained down. The blue mist rose harmlessly into the night air, mixing with the steady rain now pouring down inside the lab.

Giant Jamie raised his arms to the sky. He let the cool rain wash over him and sucked in the fresh air. His huge eyes cleared.

Fitzgibbons sprinted for the tranquilizer gun, which still lay on the floor where Barton had dropped it, but Giant Jamie's huge foot smashed down on the weapon.

Science had caught up to Sean Fitzgibbons, as it had in his youth.

"Sounds like Barton found the stinky idiot who hung me on that sign." The giant boy picked up his dad so they could talk eye to eye. Fitzgibbons trembled in his son's fist. "So where is he?"

"That doesn't matter . . ."

Giant Jamie launched into another tantrum. "It's payback time!" he shouted, stomping the ground and swinging his horrified father through the air. The tablet on the floor chirped and caught the giant's attention. He reached down with his free hand and after a few clumsy attempts, picked the stamp-size device up off the floor. Closing one eye, he held the tablet at arm's length and squinted at the image on the cracked screen. "I know this place," he bellowed. "It's the quarry. Varsity guys go there to party all the time!" Giant Jamie flipped the tablet aside and dropped his father amid the broken glass.

Fitzgibbons struggled to his feet and grabbed onto one of his son's massive toes. "Jamie, you have to listen to me!"

Giant Jamie shook his foot like he was shooing off a pesky puppy. "Not anymore, I don't." With an incredible leap, Giant Jamie bounded out of the greenhouse and into the storm toward the quarry.

Charlie stared out his bedroom window at the warehouse. No activity. Zero evidence of the giant coming or going out the elevator shaft. Not a trace of the old man's truck. In desperation, he'd even tried to raise the giant on the walkie. Charlie had been home from the drive-in for more than an hour, which made him all the more anxious.

Where was Bruce?

There was way more traffic now compared to when he and the giant had snuck out earlier, probably from the fair closing for the night. Maybe Bruce, even with his crazy stealth skills, couldn't get back inside the warehouse unseen with all the headlights. Then again, maybe he had snuck back after all, and now he was just being careful.

Either way, the giant was definitely in big trouble with the old man.

Charlie had to find out where the big guy was. He'd start with the warehouse first to make good and sure Bruce wasn't there. There were other ground-floor windows in the back alley—he'd break one if he had to. Charlie didn't care if he got in trouble. But first, he'd need to get past DJ and his mom, who were watching a movie.

He nudged his bedroom door open and slipped into the living room, which was lit only by the TV. Getting past the couch seemed easy enough, but how would he get the heavy back door open without . . .

"Hey there," said Rita, hearing the boy's footsteps and turning away from the screen. "Someone had a big date tonight. Can a mother ask a few questions?"

"No?" said Charlie hopefully.

"I hope you bought her popcorn!" she teased. "Did you hold hands?"

"Mom!"

"A gentleman never tells," reminded DJ, even as he slipped his arm out from around Rita's shoulder. She playfully punched him in the arm. It was hard for Charlie to tell what was more embarrassing—telling his mom about kissing a girl (wasn't going to happen) or actually imagining DJ and Rita kissing on the couch (maybe even worse).

"I want details," she said, turning off the TV and flipping on a lamp.

Charlie groaned as a loud *boom* sounded from across the horizon. His head jerked in the rumble's direction. At first, he thought it was thunder, but the booms kept coming at regular intervals. Almost like footsteps.

Was Bruce out running around like crazy? If he kept making so much noise, someone would see him for sure. Did Bruce need help? Charlie had to leave and find out.

"Will you listen to that thunder? I thought that storm wasn't due through for another hour!" DJ frowned and slapped his forehead. "And I just bet you my moon roof is still open." He shoved his hand in a pocket for his keys.

"I can go for you," volunteered Charlie.

"You're the man, C-Lion." DJ threw his keys to Charlie, who dashed out the door and down the wet stairs. The rain had already started. Another set of booms sounded as he reached the bottom of the steps.

Charlie felt the weight of the keys in his hand. The chips were down. It was time to play the biggest card he had.

He dashed inside DJ's ride and slammed the door, checking the apartment windows to make sure no one was on to him. Charlie scooted the seat up, then tested his foot on the brake. The accelerator. The clutch. He felt the gear shift, cool and smooth, against the palm of his damp hand. He found the gas gauge, the speedometer, and the tachometer. *It's just like* Total Turbo. *I've raced cars through flaming police barricades and enemy minefields—why couldn't I drive this?*

He depressed the clutch, gave it a little gas, and turned the ignition key. The engine roared to life.

The dashboard lit up and blue LED lights spelled out *Driver 1. Whoa,* thought Charlie, *this is even more like a video game than I thought.* He put the shifter in reverse. Out of the corner of his eye, he saw DJ rumbling down the stairs. He must have heard the Hummer start up.

Rain pelted the man as he reached the H2 and rapped on the driver's-side window. "What are you doing, C-Salt?" he yelled.

Charlie lowered the window an inch. "Sorry, DJ, but I

have to borrow your car. Tell Mom I love her, and I'll be home soon."

"Quit goofin' around!"

Charlie slid the window back up and let the clutch out. With an awkward jerk, the huge vehicle lurched backward and out of the driveway.

"Charlie!" DJ yelled as he ran alongside the car, pounding on its side. "You do not have permission to borrow my car!"

Charlie stepped on the gas and ground his way into first gear. The vehicle careened toward the sound of the booms. The storm seemed to be picking up by the second. He pulled away in search of Bruce as DJ grew smaller in his rearview mirror. Soon, he was out of sight completely.

Charlie jerked hard on the steering wheel to avoid a garbage can lid that clattered across Seminary Street in a squall of leaves and trash. The wind hurled a metal lawn chair in front of the Hummer, and he yanked the wheel again. The H2, not built to take such sharp turns, tipped onto two wheels. Charlie counter steered to avoid rolling over. The truck fishtailed. He pulled back under control but not before ripping a long strip of sod out of the Finks' front yard.

Then Charlie ground into third gear. Frustrated, he stomped on the clutch. The big tank of a vehicle didn't respond anything like his *Total Turbo* Lamborghini, which Charlie could count on to swerve around anything short of a heat-seeking missile. The Hummer lurched forward in angry coughs. "I can't drive this stupid thing!" he yelled, smacking the steering wheel.

Tornado sirens sounded, at first low and ominous, then

building into a full-blown distress call. Charlie winced as the alarm rattled in his ears; he could only guess how the eerie sound would unnerve Bruce.

Charlie followed the sound of the thunderous booms, but as he drove closer to their source, there still was no sign of the giant. The boy panicked as he saw a cop car on an intersecting street—it suddenly occurred to him that he was driving a stolen car with no license. But the officer was too preoccupied with a downed tree to pay him any attention.

A strong crosswind pushed against the Hummer as Charlie turned off Seminary Street and onto County Highway N toward another boom. He tried not downshifting so much. It helped. Richland Center was soon in his rearview mirror. Charlie kept his eyes peeled for signs of his giant friend. The crashing noises got louder as the houses disappeared, and the sides of the road turned to alfalfa and fields of corn.

A big rise loomed in the road ahead. The booms were leading him toward the quarry. Then a huge, blue-clothed figure bounced into Charlie's field of vision. *Bruce!* Charlie floored the accelerator. *What's he wearing?*

As he reached the top of the crest, Charlie got a better view of the giant he was chasing. It wasn't Bruce at all! This colossus had red hair and wore a blue version of Bruce's tent-toga.

Charlie eased back on the accelerator as the monstrosity covered another thirty feet of real estate in a single stride. The giant rounded a bend in the road and dashed up Stone Quarry Hill. Charlie saw the giant's face in profile and gulped. It couldn't be.

Fitz!

His dirty-red pimples were the size of baseballs, and his anger had gathered like the storm that raged all around him. The blue gown made the bully look like an escaped twenty-foot-tall mental patient. He took a swipe at a 100-year-old oak on the side of the road. The blow knocked the top third of the tree's branches into the wind.

Whoa.

Charlie slowed down the Hummer to a crawl as he pulled up to the quarry entrance. His head spun. What on earth had happened? How had Fitz become a giant? Charlie watched the red-headed behemoth rumble through the quarry, backhanding construction barriers that happened to be in his way. He was as loud and brash as Bruce was silent and stealthy. Giant Fitz stopped and snarled at the silo at the edge of the quarry.

I've seen that look on his face before—when he was chasing me on his bike! He's after Bruce!

Giant Fitz bounded to the silo, scaled it, and glared down. It must have been empty, because he gave a frightening howl, leaped off, and punched the side, knocking a dozen concrete blocks out of place. He turned and saw Charlie. "Lawson!" he bellowed and broke into a broad smile, like he was seeing an old friend for the first time in a long time.

Charlie inhaled sharply.

In three leaps, Giant Fitz was halfway to the Hummer. "I got some unsettled business with your big buddy," he growled. "Where is he?"

Charlie depressed the clutch, worked the shifter into reverse, and retreated. Giant Fitz chased after the H2, not seeing what Charlie saw on the horizon: Bruce, high atop a wall of stone, running full speed, not making a sound. The scowl on his friend's face let Charlie know Bruce was not going to be quiet much longer.

Without breaking stride, the giant leaped off the edge of the cliff. He sailed through the air, right leg fully extended, left leg bent at the knee and tucked alongside his body. His arms sliced through the storm with incredible control and balance. The move was pure grace, fueled by fury. Charlie had seen it before on the warehouse wall during *Enter the Dragon*.

Bruce's huge foot slammed into Giant Fitz's lower back just before he reached the Hummer, sending the twenty-foot bully sailing face-first into a mountain of gravel. A fountain of rocks sprayed into the air. Bruce landed and let out a high-pitched "Waaaaaah!" His furious eyes never left Giant Fitz.

The giant bully squeezed gravel out of his eyes and rose to his feet. "I'm the new giant in town, Stinky."

"I'm Bruce." He thumped his chest and squared up again, ready to pound Giant Fitz back down to size. Unlike at the drive-in, it was a fair fight now, and Bruce had friends to protect. Charlie was dying to see Bruce kick Giant Fitz's butt.

The red-haired Godzilla ran full speed at Bruce, who stood his ground with both fists up. Giant Fitz cocked his right hand.

At the bus stop, Charlie had seen Fitz's signature move. He knew what was coming next: *the uppercut!*

But Bruce wasn't taken in. He took a deft step to the side as Giant Fitz's monster fist sailed past his head. The miss threw Giant Fitz badly off balance, exposing his huge, pimpled chin.

Bruce tagged Giant Fitz on the jaw in time with a massive thunderclap. The dazed bully staggered backward. Bruce kept the pressure on with a fierce kick to Giant Fitz's stomach, forcing all the air from his lungs and sending him reeling into the gravel once more.

"Give it to him!" shouted Charlie.

Giant Fitz was off the pile again, holding up his hands in mock surrender. "That's pretty good fighting, Stinky," he yelled, an evil grin spreading across his face. "I got to admit— I'm impressed!"

Bruce crouched at the ready as Giant Fitz took another run. Unlike his first attack, however, he stopped short, wound up, and threw an enormous handful of gravel into Bruce's eyes. Bruce reached up in pain, unable to see, defenseless.

And Fitz knew what to do with a defenseless opponent. Just like he learned in football tackling drills, he wrapped Bruce up and drove him into the ground. Howling like a madman, Giant Fitz kneeled over Bruce, pummeling his head with an insane flurry of wild punches.

Charlie couldn't just sit there. He revved the H2's engine. He wasn't big enough to fight even normal-size Fitz, but with DJ's Hummer, Charlie sure as heck could pack a different kind of punch. He raced the Hummer forward and sped toward Giant Fitz. The spinning tires kicked up gravel as Charlie slammed the Hummer into third gear . . . or at least that's what he tried to do.

The engine hacked, sputtered, and died, killing the vehicle's momentum well before it got to Giant Fitz. Charlie had found fifth gear, not third. It had been a rookie move at exactly the wrong time.

But more help was on the way. Like a mutt missile, Powder flew out of nowhere and latched her sharp teeth into Giant Fitz's ear.

Giant Fitz screamed in agony and slapped at his ear, sending Powder to the ground with a bloody hunk of lobe still between her teeth. It was the opening Bruce needed, and he heaved Giant Fitz away.

Charlie winced at the sight of Bruce's face: It was bruised and bloodied.

The enormous bully touched his hand to his ear, then spied the blood on his fingers. He sprang to his feet and unleashed a deafening roar down at Powder, rippling a puddle of water below. Powder stood her ground, bared her teeth, and barked back. Giant Fitz's fist slammed down and cracked the limestone quarry floor as the dog bounded out of the way.

Then the bucket of an end loader smacked into Giant Fitz's chest and stayed on him. Charlie saw the old man, Hank, in the cab.

"You leave my dog alone, Fitzgibbons!"

Giant Fitz's face flamed as he tried to push the bucket away from his chest. He stumbled backward until Hank's gravel loader pinned him against a rock. Powder dashed up and bit at Giant Fitz's ankles. He screamed in rage and tried to stomp the dog while struggling back against the big machine.

Hank kept on the throttle. "Powder, come!" he yelled out the loader's window. The dog got in one last bite before she ran away from Giant Fitz and skittered into the loader's cab.

Bruce rose from the quarry floor, still picking gravel from

his eyes. He started toward the tussle between Giant Fitz and Hank's end loader.

"Enough! Get back to the warehouse!" Hank hollered as Giant Fitz beat down on the loader bucket with bloody fists. "I switched the pickup. Your ride's almost there! I'll hold him off, then catch you at the rendezvous."

Bruce hesitated. Charlie saw that his friend wanted another piece of Giant Fitz.

"Go! Or all of this is for nothing!" The old man shouted down at Charlie, "You're in this now. If he's not at the warehouse in fifteen minutes, he won't be able to join his family!" He ducked back into the cab, maneuvering the loader bucket to keep Giant Fitz pinned.

Charlie gunned the accelerator, banging his hand on the side of the Hummer. "Come on, man! Let's fly!"

"Hank," Bruce stammered. "Powder!"

"You heard him—they'll meet us there!" Charlie slammed the Hummer into gear and took off for the warehouse.

Bruce took one last reluctant look at the end loader and sprinted after his friend.

22

From the cliff above, slabs of limestone tumbled and pelted the end loader. Silicate dust mixed with the falling rain, making a paste that the wipers smeared across the windshield in streaks. Inside the cab, Hank maneuvered the bucket, keeping Giant Jamie pinned against the rock.

Giant Jamie kicked at the base of the end loader, trying in vain to push it back. The unforgiving metal rammed repeatedly into his midsection, and his screams of frustration changed to howls of pain; his ribs would soon crack. "Back up," the towering youth begged. "You're crushing me!"

Hank scowled through his war-painted windshield and opened the throttle three-quarters of the way to keep the pressure on.

Movement in the distance caught the old man's eye, and he glanced out the cab's side window. A familiar white van sped through the quarry toward the loader. The Accelerton vehicle skidded to a halt. Hank kept on the controls.

Dr. Fitzgibbons leaped out of the van and ran toward the loader, looking up in horror as the heavy machine crushed his son.

"Dad!" Giant Jamie panicked. "He's trying to kill me!"

Fitzgibbons jumped onto the driver's side of the loader and climbed the slick, wet ladder that led to the cab. He pounded on the accordion door. "Hank, you have to stop! I'm begging you."

Hank leaned forward on the throttle, about to open it all the way, when he looked up and hesitated. Looking in the giant's huge eyes, he saw that Jamie was still little more than a frightened kid. The old man growled and cursed himself for going soft.

He set the emergency brake and reached across Powder to open the far door. "Go on, girl!" Powder flew out, bounced off the back tire, and hit the ground running through the pouring rain.

Hank turned back to Fitzgibbons and pulled open the accordion door. "You control that monster of yours, because if you can't, I swear to God I will." Then Hank followed Powder out of the cab. He strained to lower himself to the ground, his bad hip almost giving way as he landed. Duster flapping in the wind, he limped away from the end loader. Powder growled at Giant Jamie's feet, ready to attack again.

"Let's go, girl." Hank slapped his thigh, and the two of them set off through the quarry, back to the old man's truck.

Fitzgibbons took Hank's seat at the end loader controls, trying to determine which lever did what. He found the one that backed the bucket off just enough to allow his son to breathe easier.

"Let me go!" Giant Jamie screamed, even angrier now that his father was at the controls. He strained against the parked end loader.

"I will let you go—if you just calm down and listen to me. We have to get out of here. It's dangerous for you to be out in the open—especially here."

"Dangerous?" Giant Jamie laughed through gritted teeth. "Look at me! I'm freaking huge!"

"I'm sure Barton has gone to Accelerton already," said Fitzgibbons, ignoring the wild look in his son's eyes. "We've already called in one man, a professional soldier. If he finds you, they'll harvest your blood a drop at a time for the rest of your life. You have to believe me."

Hot air seethed from Giant Jamie's nostrils as the violent expression left his eyes. "Okay," he relented. "I did what I came to do. Let's get out of here."

Relieved, Fitzgibbons pulled the bucket back. Giant Jamie extended his leg and found the leverage he needed to shove the machine out of his way. Fitzgibbons bailed out of the cab just before the end loader tipped over and landed with a heavy crash. Giant Jamie stalked the wet, rocky ground through the driving rain, searching the quarry for Hank and Powder.

Fitzgibbons pulled himself out of the mud and blocked his son's path. "We had a deal! You said you'd leave with me!"

"It's like you always said, Dad." Giant Jamie stepped over his father like he wasn't there, trying to spot the old man and his dog. He owed them a serious beatdown. "Refuse to lose!"

Giant Jamie's head snapped around as the warning siren from the office trailer sounded. The high whine hurt his newly sensitive ears. Holding his hands on the sides of his head, he raced toward the sheet-metal office shack. The shabby structure shook in the high winds. "You should have never let me go, old man!" he shouted. "Big mistake!" Raising his muddy foot high in the air, he brought it down on the office trailer. It crumpled like a soda can as the siren bleated out.

From the hillside, Hank dropped his thumb on the detonator and the office trailer exploded.

The blast sent pieces of jagged metal spinning through the air in all directions and knocked Fitzgibbons from his feet. A fireball enveloped Giant Jamie. His wild slaps failed to extinguish the flames, which burned even in the pouring rain.

Fitzgibbons tried to stand, but a shard of metal had lodged in his leg. He grimaced in pain and fell back to the ground.

His enormous son rolled back and forth on the quarry floor to extinguish the flames. When Giant Jamie rose, a long cut stretched under his left eye and his blue hospital gown was littered with burn holes. He loped away, screaming, "You're going to pay, old man!"

Hank was breathing hard, nearly to his truck at the top of the cliff. He cursed his arthritic hip. Powder could have been long gone, but she refused to leave her master's side.

Giant Jamie's forehead peeked up over the rock face, his incredibly large fingers digging into the hillside. "First you stopped me from getting Lawson, then it was Stinky!" He vaulted up to high ground. "But you're never going to get in my way again!"

Powder turned and barked at the giant, but Hank reached down and grabbed her collar. "Powder, go home!" he commanded. He let go and waited for her to run, but Powder wouldn't leave his side. "I said go home!" The dog still wouldn't obey. So he scooped her up and the two of them dove into the truck cab.

Two giant feet appeared in front of the truck. There would be no escape. Powder licked Hank's cheek as a monstrous heel came crashing down on the cab.

23

Bursts of forty-mile-an-hour winds slammed against the Hummer as Charlie did his best to steer through sheets of driving rain. The storm didn't have much of an effect on Bruce, who bolted ahead down the county highway.

Charlie tried to keep up. He slammed the accelerator to the floor, determined to go faster. Hank had made it clear: Bruce had to get to the warehouse right away to catch his next ride. Giant Fitz wasn't going to stop until he kicked Bruce's butt, so this was a good time to get the heck out of town.

C'mon, CUGoneByeBye, *drive this thing!*

Experimenting with a lighter touch on the clutch, Charlie downshifted out of a turn and gained on Bruce. With a straight stretch in front of them, Charlie sped up again. The speedometer needle touched eighty miles an hour. He kept within spitting distance of the giant, who ran with his forearm raised to shield his eyes from the storm.

Charlie chased Bruce for about another mile and

approached the city limits. He wasn't making an effort to stay out of sight, but Charlie wasn't worried. The storm had knocked out power to all the streetlights, making it tough to see much of anything through all the rain. With most people probably holed up in their basements, Richland Center looked like a ghost town.

Up ahead lay the sharp turn onto Haseltine Street. Now that he was getting better at shifting gears, Charlie decided to try the heel-toe maneuver—if he kept the motor's RPM level high, he could take the corner faster. He angled his right foot onto the brake and accelerator, but his clutch work was clumsy. Frustrated, Charlie smacked the dashboard as the Hummer lost speed.

But the failed maneuver turned out to be lucky for Charlie. A huge fallen tree blocked most of Haseltine, its branches wrapped in power lines. Charlie pounded the brakes, spun the wheel to the right, and slid across the wet pavement. Bruce hurdled the obstacle as the Hummer skidded sideways, spraying water into the air before coming to a stop right before the upended trunk's ball of gnarled roots.

Farther up the street, Charlie watched the giant bound up the side of the warehouse and down the elevator shaft. At least Bruce was safe for now. The boy punched the clutch and hit reverse, bumping up over the sidewalk, then moving back the way he'd come. A quick trip around the block would put the Hummer in the back alley.

He sped down a side street. Charlie didn't know what vehicle would come for the giant—an eighteen-wheeler?—but he figured Bruce would know his ride when he saw it.

"Lawson!"

Charlie's heart sank as Giant Fitz's bellow reverberated through the high winds. Even Hank and his end loader hadn't been enough to hold him off. Two giant feet landed ahead of the Hummer and Charlie slammed the brakes.

"Where's your stinky friend?"

Charlie wasn't about to tell him. And he knew just the taunt to lure Fitz away. He rolled down his window and shouted, singsong style, "Try and catch me, *Jamie*!"

Giant Fitz's face creased with anger. "Game over!"

"No, it's not," Charlie returned. "And you know why? Because I'm *CUGoneByeBye*."

"No way!"

"You suck at *Total Turbo*! I'm better than you!" Charlie taunted. "You want to kill me? Let's see you catch me first!" He popped the clutch, and the Hummer's tires chirped as he sped away on the wet pavement, just out of Giant Fitz's lunging reach.

Charlie blew right through a stop sign on his way toward the deserted downtown and away from Bruce. He glanced in the rearview mirror. Giant Fitz wasn't trailing him. *He's at it again,* thought Charlie, remembering the bike chase and how Fitz had outfoxed him by following him along side streets. *I'm ready for you this time, you big ape.* Charlie spun the Hummer onto Mills Street and waited.

Sure enough, Giant Fitz raced around the corner one block up and stopped in the middle of the road. Blood escaped the cut under his eye and darkened the street puddles rusty red. He'd cut Charlie off. There was nowhere to run. The giant bully laughed hard enough to shake the windows of the old Farmers & Merchants Bank on the corner. "Game over!"

Charlie punched the accelerator. He downshifted with confidence now, and the Hummer raced forward on a collision course with Giant Fitz, who raised his foot to crush the ant coming at him. But Charlie didn't swerve. He lined up DJ's naked-lady hood ornament with the foot Giant Fitz still had on the ground.

Giant Fitz wasn't expecting a direct attack. He attempted to stomp the Hummer, but it had gotten too close. He lost his balance, tripping over his own feet and belly-flopping onto the asphalt.

The Hummer's brake lights flickered. Charlie beeped the horn twice, just to rub it in. He glanced up into the rearview mirror. Giant Fitz had regained his balance and was after Charlie again.

He used his superior knowledge of the Richland Center streets to lead the angry giant on a crisscross chase through downtown. As they neared Bailey's Paint and Decorating, a screaming Giant Fitz closed in again. Charlie kept the pedal to the floor.

And at the last possible second, he plowed the H2 right into the paint store.

Giant Fitz skidded on the wet pavement headlong into the building. The truck barreled around the store counter, in and out of the paint mixing area, and right through the big loading door on the rear wall. Charlie cranked the wheel hard to the right. Sparks flew off the Hummer's side panel as it scraped up against another building on the other side of the alley.

When Giant Fitz freed himself from the paint cans and rubble, his face was covered with white primer and green house paint. "When I get my hands on you, Lawson," he bawled through the wind, "you'll wish you never even heard of me!"

Charlie's plan was working so far—they were nowhere near the warehouse now and Bruce should be free and clear—but the boy was starting to wonder how long he could hold off his giant pursuer.

Giant Fitz chased Charlie down a straightaway heading back out of town. The speedometer climbed—seventy, seventy-five, eighty miles an hour—as Charlie barreled the Hummer through the worst storm Richland Center had ever seen. And through it all, Giant Fitz was right on his butt.

Charlie continued to build up speed as he raced toward the river. Eighty-five miles an hour. Ninety. He prayed that no one had moved the banked wall of dirt near the dam, the one that almost got him killed the last time he ran from Fitz. If the pile was still there, it would make a perfect ramp.

He'd have to hit the incline hard out of the corner—and the only way he'd have enough speed was the heel-toe maneuver. If he did everything right, the Hummer would fly across the river. Giant Fitz could follow, but the muck of the river bottom and whipping water would slow him down big-time. A long shot for sure, but as far as Charlie could tell, the only shot he had.

He glanced down at the speedometer. *I need to go faster or I'll never make it across!*

Downshifting a gear made the Hummer's engine scream in protest as the dirt incline loomed only half a block away. The shaking speedometer needle scratched ninety-five miles an hour. *Now.* Charlie held his breath as he went for the heel-toe trick. His toes pressed down hard on the accelerator while he found the brake with his heel. The Hummer screeched around the corner with barely a drop in RPMs.

The Hummer rocketed like it had been shot out of a gun, tires charging straight up the dirt pile. Giant Fitz was right behind the truck. He lunged for it with his mammoth hands.

And then the H2 was airborne. The wheels spun with nothing to hold them back. Charlie took his foot off the gas. He peeked down at the raging water churning frothy white below him, waiting to swallow the truck whole if he didn't make it all the way across.

Giant Fitz stopped at the top of the ramp. He watched as the Hummer hung in the air over the river longer than should have been possible. The truck's back tires caught the river's edge when it landed and crashed into a patch of fire-red sumac trees on the other side. Charlie's head banged off the roof as the Hummer skidded to a hard stop about twenty-five yards from the edge of the river.

Back on the dirt pile, Giant Fitz lurched over and slapped his hands on his knees. He drew back up and laughed like crazy. "Awesome jump, Lawson," he bellowed. "What did that buy you, another ten seconds? I can cross this thing in my sleep!" He hopped off the ramp onto the top of the slippery dam. There was plenty of room for a normal person to walk across, but for someone the size of Giant Fitz, the big cement barrier was more of a balance beam. He shuffled across, battling both the slick concrete surface and the roaring winds.

Charlie struggled to unbuckle from the Hummer as blood rushed to his head. If he could squirm out of the damaged vehicle, maybe he could still escape on foot somehow. But the stupid door was jammed. Giant Fitz was nearly across the dam. Charlie slammed into the door with his elbow, even as his monstrous tormentor's words shook the H2:

"This is what I call my finishing move!"

The boy closed his eyes and prepared to be squashed to death—but the blow never came. Instead, he heard a strange rumble from above. It wasn't thunder.

He swung his head over his shoulder and looked out the rear window. Up in the sky, a man dressed in black somehow balanced on the landing gear of a low-flying helicopter that jittered in the violent storm.

Giant Fitz gawked up at the weird sight, forgetting about Charlie for a moment. The man in black dove off the helicopter, steel cable unspooling behind him. He came out of his dive just as he reached Giant Fitz, contorting his body and swinging around the giant in a blur. Lightweight, superstrong cable wound over Giant Fitz's shoulder and across his chest, pinning his arms like a straitjacket. Charlie had never seen a man move that fast.

"What do you think you're doing?" bellowed Giant Fitz. The whirling of the chopper rotors intensified as he strained against the cables. "When I get this stuff off of me, you're . . ."

Before Giant Fitz could finish his sentence, the man pulled a stick from a harness on his back. He twisted the weapon and jabbed it into Giant Fitz's neck. Electric blue flashed against wet flesh, and then his head convulsed. His eyes went glassy before he slumped, unconscious.

Charlie thought this seemed like an excellent time to get

out of there. With the door still stuck, he got the window down and started to crawl out.

The man tapped an earpiece. "Take him up, Barton." The chopper started upward, the cable hauling Giant Fitz into the air.

The man leaped off the giant's shoulder and hit the ground. Heavy rain beat down without mercy. The stranger strode toward Charlie, tapping the stick in his palm as the helicopter towed the lifeless giant skyward. The man's footsteps sounded heavy and threatening as they approached through the mud. The boy wanted to run, but fear froze him in place. Without a ride, he wasn't *CUGoneByeBye*. He was Charlie Lawson, and he knew he didn't stand a chance.

"So here's the thing, kid. I can't leave any loose ends." The man's face turned cruel. He twisted the end of his stick and pointed it at Charlie's head.

But something out of the corner of his eye made the man leap clear. A giant fist appeared from above, pounding a crater into the muddy ground where the man had stood a half moment before.

Bruce shook water from his soggy mane and growled at Charlie's attacker.

"Looks like it's my lucky day," the stranger said. "Two giants for the price of one."

"Bruce, what are you doing here?" shouted Charlie.

He never got an answer as something like the sound of a locomotive came rushing toward them. All three of them turned and looked up at the angry night sky.

On the other side of the dam, a funnel cloud had reached

down from the heavens and was heading straight for them over the millpond. The angry twister threw mud, debris, and heavy tree branches in all directions.

Bruce grabbed Charlie and ran for it. The driving rain was so fierce that he never saw the hunk of wood that beaned him right in the head.

And that's when everything went black.

24

Even when Charlie regained consciousness, he couldn't seem to open his eyes. He had no way of knowing how long he'd been out of commission or whether it was day or night. He was flat on his back, resting atop a vibrating metal surface. Now and again the shaking intensified, and his head bounced up and down. At least something was cushioning the shock to his cranium. Charlie groaned as he tried to turn his head. His skull ached in a way that he'd never felt before, not even after getting kicked in the face during a fifth-grade soccer tournament.

Reaching up to touch his aching temple, Charlie found a thick, gauzy cloth wrapped several times around his head. He had no memory of anyone fixing him up. The last thing he remembered before blacking out was the awful roar of the wind as Bruce carried him away from the dam.

His eyelids felt bruised. When he was finally able to force them apart, he found himself in the dark. Charlie struggled to pull himself up into a sitting position, giving his eyes time to adjust to the lack of light. Eventually, he could make out the broad strokes of a long, narrow enclosure—one that was moving. He found a wall and scooted his way along until he bumped into something.

"Charlie?"

Charlie laughed, relieved to hear the familiar voice, low and friendly. "Bruce! Where are we?"

"My ride," said Bruce, matter-of-fact.

"Your ride? Wait . . . where are we going?" asked Charlie. Bruce stayed quiet.

The boy realized that they must have been long gone from Richland Center. "Oh man, I'm in serious trouble."

The giant snickered. "Trouble," he agreed.

Charlie punched what he assumed was the big guy's knee. "It's not funny, man. My mom is going to kill me." Shadows slowly took shape, and now he could make out Bruce's general outline in the murk. The giant lay on his side, big chin resting in one hand. Charlie wobbled to his knees, too dizzy yet to stand. He suspected they were riding in some sort of trailer, like the kind DJ's company used to haul big shipments. Something underneath them started to whine.

It sounded pretty terrible, like the whole truck was going to fall apart. Then the vehicle made a sweeping turn, and Charlie landed on his bottom. The sound of furious crunching indicated that they'd moved from smooth pavement to potholed gravel. He leaned back against Bruce to ride it out and spotted the hazy outline of a weird figure painted on the wall across from him. Charlie crawled over to get a closer look. He could make out fiery eyes and a malevolent, razor-toothed grin. It was a huge painting of a spooky skull! The trailer lurched to a stop.

The heavy doors at the far end swung open. Charlie's eyes rebelled as the light delivered a shock through his temples. After an uncomfortable moment, his eyes adjusted.

No way. It couldn't be.

Charlie's brother stood at the end of the trailer, dark hair flopping over the sides of his sunglasses. He hopped up into the trailer to give Charlie a long, sweaty hug. "I just get the mummy all fixed," Tim said with a lopsided grin, "and then I have to unravel him to wrap up your dented melon."

Charlie's brain sputtered and sparked. With the benefit of daylight, he could see the huge devil's pitchfork sticking out of the wall, the campy painting of the evil, grinning fortune teller, and Charlie's favorite zombie, lurching for someone to grab. Even Tim's box of crap was along for the ride. The rest of the spooky stuff appeared to have been dismantled to make room for Bruce. "The Creep Castle is his ride? What are you doing here?"

"I'm a giant smuggler," confided Tim with a wink. "We're all giant smugglers. Come on, Charlie, get in the ball game."

"Come on, Charlie," said Bruce, poking the boy in the ribs with his pinkie finger.

Suddenly, Tim leaving home to join the carnival took on new meaning. Was this what his brother had really been up to? "Why didn't you tell me?"

"Probably the same reason you didn't tell me."

"The kid's awake," came a voice from the end of the trailer. "Now he can go."

Charlie turned to see two more people at the end of the

Creep Castle: Juice Man, the bald carnival worker who worked the blimp, and Wertzie, the guy with four fingers who hated the Gravitron.

"Charlie comes!" The giant bared his teeth and growled to make his point.

"Not if I have anything to say about it! Giants are enough trouble. We can't be babysitting brats, too!" The Juice Man pounded the metal bed of the trailer with a meaty fist. "You're not in charge, giant!"

"His name's Bruce," said Charlie.

"Bruce," the giant grunted in agreement. He pounded the trailer bed much harder than the Juice Man had managed, rocking a pallet of crates near Charlie. The bald man swallowed hard and took a step back.

Charlie held up an arm to steady the wooden boxes, then pulled back as he recognized what the Creep Castle had been carrying. "The dynamite! Holy crap, Tim, you know how much we were bouncing around back here? You could have blown us to bits!"

Tim picked up a bundle from a crate. "You mean this dynamite?" He undid the twine, selected a stick, and tossed it in the air. Charlie ducked and threw his hands over his head to protect himself, but a blast never came as the stick landed with a noisy but harmless clank.

Bruce barked out a horsey laugh. "Boom!"

The cylinder rolled down the metal bed of the Creep Castle. Red-faced, Charlie picked it up. It was as heavy as he'd remembered back in the warehouse.

Tim pulled another stick from the stack. "As long as we're coming clean." He peeled back the warning wrapper and held the rod up. It glinted when it caught a ray of sun from the rear of the trailer.

"Is that . . . ?" Charlie unwrapped his and felt the cool metal against his fingertips. The gold was stunning. A single bar had to be worth millions.

"Solid gold," Tim said. "The giants got bank, Charlie. It's what they're using to pay for their new home."

Juice Man tried to inspect a bar of his own, but Bruce snatched it right out of the carny's hands and put it back in the box. Juice Man looked offended at the implication that he was trying to steal the gold.

"How long until this ride is ready, Juice Man?" asked Wertzie.

"What's the use of even trying? There's too much weight!" the bald man protested. "The giant, the gold, it's too much!"

"Nobody's happy about why we're carrying the gold," said Wertzie. The giant smugglers looked at one another without speaking for a moment.

"What?" asked Charlie. "Who was supposed to bring the gold?"

Bruce was the one who figured it out. "Hank?"

"He didn't make it to the rendezvous," confessed Wertzie. "That's why we have the gold—he's usually in charge of the valuables."

"So Giant Fitz got him?" asked Charlie. Now he felt sort of terrible about just leaving the old man to fight the enormous bully all by himself.

Tim looked at Wertzie. "Who's Giant Fitz?"

"Fitz was the one who was fighting Hank," Charlie explained to his brother. "The bully from the fair? His dad's got a lab out at that Accelerton place—somehow he must have turned Fitz into a giant!"

"An actual giant?" asked Wertzie. "Like your friend here?"

"Why would I make it up?" asked Charlie.

Bruce nodded his head in agreement. "Giant!"

"So where is this other giant? Giant Fitz?" asked Tim.

"He got zapped by the man with the glowing stick."

Tim looked over the top of his sunglasses. "The man with the what?"

"Geez," Charlie said. "Don't you guys know anything?"

The giant smugglers looked at each other in disbelief. This was definitely not business as usual. "We need to sort through this, but the side of the highway probably isn't the place to do it. One thing's for sure: Someone is looking for giants, and we don't want to be here when they show up." Wertzie turned to the Juice Man. "Just grease the daylights out of that bearing. We're an hour out of Peoria. Can you get us that far?"

The Juice Man ran a hand over his bald head. "I doubt it," he spat, but he disappeared to work on the problem anyway.

"Let's move!" shouted Wertzie to the other carnies loitering around their trucks. He left to get the carnival back on the road.

"Before we go," said a woman's voice, "let's get you boys something to eat." Tiger, the one Tim called the roughie, appeared at the end of the trailer with an aluminum cart full of the biggest elephant ears Charlie had ever seen. Bruce's nostrils twitched as he reached for an elephant ear and waved it under his nose. He stuffed a huge handful into his mouth, taking slow, careful chomps to savor every sweet bite. He closed his eyes and moaned with pleasure.

Tim motioned for Charlie to join him and Tiger at the end of the trailer. "We've got to get you home," he said in a low voice, trying not to upset Bruce. He tapped Charlie on his bandaged head. "You've seen for yourself that things can get hairy."

"It might not be safe," Tiger agreed. "Bus ride home is probably your best bet."

Charlie looked back at the big guy, remembering how he'd saved Charlie's butt when the maniac with the stick was about to fry him. Bruce didn't run or leave Charlie behind. Whether it was at the dam or the drive-in, Bruce always had Charlie's back. Charlie thought about what his mom would do in the situation. She helped butterflies on their way—why not giants? If Bruce wanted Charlie to come, then he'd have the giant's back, too. "I'm coming, and there's nothing you can do about it."

Bruce snorted an emphatic grunt, making it clear he wasn't going anywhere without his friend.

Tiger shook her head and took the cart away. Tim wasn't nuts about Charlie's decision, either, but at least he seemed to understand it. "I'll call Mom, let her know you're okay," he said. "Tell her . . . I'll make up something."

"Try it now!" came from outside the Creep Castle. Apparently, the Juice Man had done whatever he needed to do to get the ride moving again.

"Let's get this show on the road!" Tim slammed the heavy metal doors shut and the two friends returned to darkness.

"Looks like we're going to see some more of the world, big guy."

"Big world."

The small, colorful caravan jostled its way back onto the gravel that led to the main road. One by one, the carnival rides, folded up like toys back in their boxes after a day of hard play, rolled onto the highway. It took the trucks a while to accelerate, but soon they were speeding south.

Behind them, hundreds of monarch butterflies rode the air currents in the smugglers' wake, making a migration of their own.

H ank reached for his phone, but found the task impossible with his right arm in a sling. He tried to sit up in the elevated bed and winced. His fingers, purple and bruised, curled into a fist. Even his face hurt.

He was laid up in a patient room at Richland Hospital, the unpleasant smell of rubbing alcohol heavy in the air. Because he kept drifting in and out of consciousness, he had little sense of how long he'd been there. Hours? Days? And he had no idea if the giant smugglers had picked up the last giant in the old warehouse. He had a vague memory of paramedics promising to take care of Powder before he blacked out in the ambulance at the quarry.

A groan to his left made Hank turn his head. That hurt, too—his neck felt like it had been worked over with a meat tenderizer. In the next bed, perhaps unconscious from a recent surgery, was Sean Fitzgibbons. The scientist's face was pale. And his right leg was elevated and heavily bandaged, with a stain the size and color of a bruised orange in the place where shrapnel from the old aluminum shed had ripped through his thigh.

"Guessing things didn't go the way you planned," said Hank, even though he knew the man couldn't hear him.

The old man needed to get out of there. He reached up to figure out the complicated mechanism that held his leg in the air.

He stopped when a businesswoman in a crisply ironed suit appeared in the doorway, her rehearsed smile offset by intense eyes. She held a tablet. The woman sighed as she paused at Fitzgibbons's bed—it was clear she had planned on talking to the scientist. She turned her attention to Hank. "I'm Gretchen Gourmand, with the Accelerton Corporation. Can we talk, Mr. Pulvermacher?"

"How do you know my name?"

Gourmand examined the beeping monitor that was attached to Dr. Fitzgibbons. "You know, I was skeptical. But he did it. Found his fairy tale and better yet, created one of his own."

"What do you want?" asked Hank.

"Right," sniffed Gourmand. "Let's get down to business. Where is it?"

"Where is what? I don't know what you're talking about," Hank lied. He tried to sit up and his body rebelled in painful protest.

"The world gets smaller all the time. It must be terribly difficult for a giant to hide."

Hank saw no use in pretending now. "I thought you already had a giant."

In response, Gourmand selected a thumbnail on the tablet and played shaky helicopter footage of Giant Jamie at the dam. With the tornado bearing down, the chopper had released its giant cargo. The footage showed Jamie being sucked inside the twister, then chaos before the footage went black.

"Even Fitzgibbons's kid didn't deserve that." Hank pinched his eyes shut and shook his head.

"Tragic, yes," said Gourmand, her voice quiet out of respect for Fitzgibbons. "The body will turn up sooner or later, I expect. But our experts have concluded that the boy couldn't have survived. Which brings us to the matter of the other giant at the dam."

Hank gripped the bed rail with a shaky hand. A shock of pain pulsed down his spine. "You'll never find him."

"There are limited ways your giant could have left town in that storm," said Gourmand. "By foot, though that's a very public exit. A few large dairy trucks managed to get on the road. And a certain carnival made the unusual decision to pack up and leave town right as the severe weather hit. Strange, yes? We're tracking all of them."

Hank said nothing.

Gourmand considered his silence, then gave an imperceptible nod. "We will have our giant, Mr. Pulvermacher."

"Why are you doing this?"

"For humanity, of course. We'll develop new drugs. New treatments. The giants' advanced physiology is almost guaranteed to provide the key for a number of discoveries that could improve the lives of millions, Mr. Pulvermacher. Doesn't that sound like a worthwhile achievement? Why don't you pick up your phone and call your friends? You can save everyone from unpleasantness that just doesn't need to happen."

"I'm not calling anyone. I'm sure you've already got my lines bugged."

"We're not the only interested party," said Gourmand, gathering her leather bag. "There's a man from the defense trade, a business far nastier than ours, on their scent right now. A tornado couldn't stop him—it just slowed him down. That's why I was hoping you could help. He won't share my preference for negotiation. He just takes what he wants, and he won't care if your friends get hurt along the way. I'll ask one more time: Tell me where they are, and I'll promise to keep the giant and your people safe."

Hank's silence served as his answer.

"Very well." A gust of cold autumn wind blew in through the open window, but Gourmand did not shiver. "Then be prepared for the consequences when they come."

Carnival trailers circled the Peoria Plaza Tire parking lot like a wagon train, creating an enclosure in which Bruce and Charlie huddled. A swollen moon hung low in the evening sky. For at least the next hour, they couldn't hide in the Creep Castle—the shop's mechanics were hard at work on some road force balancing, or whatever Juice Man had called it. Air wrenches zipped and whirred outside their inner circle.

Charlie and Bruce ate monstrous, greasy cheeseburgers that Wertzie had fetched from a placc across the river called the Burger Barge. Charlie had never got the brat Adele had promised at the drive-in the night before, and he attacked his burger like a competitor in the World Series of Eating. Still, he was only halfway through it before Bruce had worked his way through ten. The giant eyed the rest of Charlie's.

"Don't even think about it."

Bruce found a stray bag of onion rings and emptied it into his maw. He leaned back against the Gravitron trailer and belched. A low rumble came from the other side of the parking lot, and the giant peeked around the edge of a trailer to see what was causing the sound.

"What is it?"

"Wow," Bruce whispered.

There was a "wow" in the parking lot? Curiosity got the better of Charlie as well. He socked Bruce in the thigh and motioned for the giant to lift him up to see what was going on. Bruce picked up the boy in his fist and hoisted him just high enough to peek over the top of the Gravitron.

"Wow."

A fireplug of a man with tattoos that sleeved his forearms worked a crane on his truck, emblazoned with flaming letters that advertised *Stan the Statue Man*. The crane lifted a seventeen-foot-tall ceramic lady into a standing position in the corner of the Peoria Plaza Tire parking lot. She was nearly as big as Bruce. A smile was frozen on her face, and Charlie supposed she was attractive, in a 1960s-president's-wife kind of way. She looked sort of familiar, in her red sweater and navy-blue miniskirt, though he couldn't say exactly who she resembled.

Bruce set the boy back on the ground and scooted around the trailer into the open. "The guy is going to see you!" Charlie said in a whisper-shout, but Bruce didn't respond. Charlie threw up his arms. This was going to be trouble.

Charlie ran out from the circle of trailers to see the giant crawling on his hands and knees toward the queen-size lady. Stan the Statue Man had his back to the ceramic figure for now, checking off something on a clipboard, but if he turned around, there was no way he wouldn't see the giant. His own long-bed truck, the kind that usually carried six or seven cars to auto dealers, was filled with more enormous figures—a replica of the Statue of Liberty, a lumberjack with an ax, a goofy rabbit in red overalls that read *Grady's*. Charlie sprinted over, trying to get to Stan before he could turn around and see Bruce.

"Hey," said Charlie, scrambling for some way to distract the guy. "Um. Hi. Your truck? Wow. What is all this stuff?"

Stan the Statue Man looked up, but he didn't seem surprised. He probably got the question a lot. "The world's finest collection of colossal ceramic mascots," he said with pride. "I design them myself."

"That's amazing," said Charlie, watching Bruce with his peripheral vision while trying to maintain eye contact with Stan. The giant stood next to the lady now, sizing her up. And that's when Charlie figured out who the woman reminded him of—the old-timey girl in Tim's peekaboo pen.

"That gal behind me, she's Vanna Whitewall," said Stan the Statue Man, hooking his thumb over his shoulder. "Proud ambassador of Peoria Plaza Tire for forty years, but she gets dinged up from time to time. Idiots don't check their rearview mirrors before backing up right into her shins. Polished her up and snapped on her new winter outfit."

"Tell me more about the rabbit!" Charlie blurted quickly, successfully diverting Stan the Statue Man's attention just as he was about to turn and point out more of Vanna Whitewall's finer features. "He's got to weigh a ton!"

"Just about," nodded Stan the Statue Man. "He's on his

way to Grady's Family Fun Park in Bloomington, about an hour from here. Kids love him; I think it's the bow tie."

"Uh-huh, bow tie," said Charlie, trying not to panic. Bruce had picked up Vanna Whitewall and was attempting to turn her upside down, just like he did with the girl in Tim's pen! Charlie shook his head frantically whenever Stan the Statue Man's attention was on the giant rabbit, trying to tell Bruce to knock it off. It wasn't working. And then, as if it was happening in slow motion, Vanna's winter sweater and skirt snapped off, revealing a fire-engine-red bikini. Bruce dove for cover as the clothes clanked against the pavement in a noisy clatter.

"What the . . . ?"

Stan the Statue Man spun around. Bruce had ducked behind a carnival trailer and the giant lady was back in her standing position, posing in her summer bikini even as the front half of her ceramic sweater spun slowly on the asphalt. Passing cars honked their horns in appreciation. "That's impossible!" shouted Stan. "There's no way her clothes should just fall off like that! I fastened 'em myself!"

"Weird," agreed Charlie.

Stan cursed and got back in his truck, working the crane to pick up the front half of the scuffed sweater and maneuver it back into place. Charlie whistled and walked backward slowly, disappearing into the shadows of the carnival trailers and then hustling back to the shielded spot where he and Bruce had been eating dinner. The giant was back, and so were Tiger and the Juice Man. They weren't happy.

"Half of downtown heard that skirt fall!" shouted Juice Man, shaking his meaty index finger up at Bruce. The giant gave him a sheepish smirk. "You think this is a joke? We're trying to protect you, moron!"

"And just where exactly were you?" Tiger turned to Charlie. She narrowed her eyes and Charlie felt himself squirm. "Why are you here if you're not going to help us watch him?"

"I was helping!" protested Charlie. "He snuck out to check out Vanna Whitewall . . ."

"Vanna Whitewall?" asked Tiger. "Really?"

"And I distracted the guy in the truck so he wouldn't see Bruce." He looked up at his giant friend. "Tell them!"

"Bikini" was the giant's cheerful response.

"Now we've got to worry about *two* of them screwing this up. I am this close to getting my giant gold," groused Juice Man, holding up his index finger and thumb to indicate just how close he was. He stomped off into the back of his generator truck and slammed the door. "Where's Tim? I want the kid gone! Now!"

"Tim's with the Creep Castle. I'll talk to him," Tiger called after him. She didn't disagree with the Juice Man, Charlie noted. "Meanwhile, you two stay here." She looked up at Bruce, and the barbed tone of her voice made even the giant shrink a little. "You do anything stupid like that again—and you answer to me. Got it?"

Bruce started to smile but thought better of it.

Tiger left to find Tim, leaving Charlie and Bruce to hide once more in the shadows of the trailers. The boy plopped to the ground and leaned against the Gravitron. "I'm mad at you, too, if that means anything. You're going to get me kicked out of here." He picked up a handful of pebbles and threw them across the pavement. "And just so you know, not all girls' clothes fall off when you turn them upside down."

Bruce shrugged. So far, experience had taught him otherwise.

Once the shop's mechanics had finished rejiggering the Creep Castle's suspension to accommodate extra weight, Tiger had sent Bruce and Charlie inside the trailer to wait. There wasn't a lot to do. Aside from the calamity with Vanna Whitewall, giant smuggling had turned out to be a lot of sitting around.

A voice outside the haunted house broke the monotony. When Charlie put an ear to the wall of the trailer, he could pick up bits of Tim's side of a phone conversation with their mom.

". . . know I should have checked with you first but . . ."

". . . sorry, but we hardly get to see . . ."

". . . not going to miss more than a day or two . . ."

". . . really think it's a good idea for someone to come all the way down . . . ?"

Bruce wasn't interested, so he scoured the Castle for something to do. He started playing with Tim's peekaboo pen, but Charlie grabbed it and shoved it in his pocket. "You don't need any more bright ideas." Instead, he poked through Tim's box of crap for some way to pass the time. The only promising item was the musty movie projector, and there was no way to plug it in. Or was there?

"I'll be right back," Charlie said, cracking open the back of the Castle and checking to see if the coast was clear. Tim and Tiger were gone now.

"Go with you!"

"Dude," Charlie sighed, "I mean *right* back. Like ten seconds. Just hang here, okay?"

Charlie slipped out the back, taking care to not make a sound when his tennis shoes hit the asphalt. He wasn't Bruce, but he could be sneaky, too, when he wanted to be. The narrow alleys between the carnival trailers were lit only by the moonlight, and the Juice Man's generator truck was parked just a couple down from the Creep Castle.

Charlie eased the back of the electric truck open and snuck inside. Two gasoline-powered generators hummed, providing the juice for charging power tools needed for assembling carnival rides. Atop the Juice Man's workstation sat a gizmo that Charlie guessed was a GPS device—it looked like the one in DJ's Hummer, except a lot more sophisticated. A digital map placed them squarely in Peoria. A surprising number of gas tanks, labeled *Helium*, were stacked in the back. For the Juice Man's advertising blimp, Charlie guessed. He grabbed a long orange extension cord that was coiled on a hook, plugged one end into a generator, and unspooled the cord back into the Creep Castle.

Bruce laughed when he saw what Charlie was up to. "Trouble!"

"Not me, dude," said the boy. "You're the one who always gets busted." He plugged in the film projector and a brilliant blue square of light hit the back of the trailer.

Bruce Lee whirred to life once more. His alter ego, Bruce the giant, broke into hysterics every time the martial arts master smacked a young student on the head, admonishing him for taking his eyes off his opponent.

The back door groaned, and a sliver of light jumped into the trailer. Charlie looked up, expecting his brother, but it was Wertzie who slipped inside. He eased the door shut so it didn't make a sound. Then he sat next to Charlie and the giant and watched Bruce Lee break a chair over someone's head.

"We're taking off in thirty," he confided. "Juice Man will be back in fifteen—you might want to return his cord before he gets back. He's got a temper, that guy."

"Cool," Charlie said. He kind of liked Wertzie. He always seemed to have his act together, which was probably what bugged Tim. "How long until we get to . . . wherever it is we're going?"

"No one's told you? I guess if you're a smuggler, you should know the details. Grand Isle, Louisiana." Wertzie reached into his back pocket and pulled out a wrinkled road map with a route highlighted in neon yellow. In the light of the movie projector, Charlie could see Wertzie trace a path with what was left of his index finger. "We ought to be down into Tennessee sometime tonight. And then we . . ."

Bruce interrupted. "Finger?"

Charlie gave the giant a "knock it off" look. He was curious about the missing digit, too, but you didn't just come out and ask a guy about something like that. Wertzie didn't seem to mind, though.

"Tim never tell you how he made me lose my finger?"

That one surprised Charlie. Mostly because Tim never shut up with his carnival stories and he wasn't likely to keep one about a guy losing a finger to himself. The boy shook his head, and Wertzie leaned in conspiratorially.

"This is about a year ago, okay? Juice Man and I are setting up the Gravitron and I bet him ten grand I can get the thing up and running in fifteen minutes or less. Usually takes thirty. Going for the new world record."

"Ten thousand *dollars*?"

"When you got giant gold coming, that's chump change." Wertzie grinned. "Call it a bet against future earnings. So I'm slamming the thing together superfast, Juice Man's money is as good as mine, when I get a call from Tim on my cell. I look down at my phone for one second, my fingers got caught trying to line up some bolt holes, and *snap*!"

Charlie cringed. He wouldn't wish a missing finger on anyone. "Dang."

Bruce agreed. "Sucks."

"Sucks is right. Your brother wanted an advance on his draw, which he knew I couldn't give him until the rides were ready to go." Wertzie snorted in the darkness.

Charlie could tell the guy was still bitter. Who could blame him? It wasn't too much of a stretch to imagine Tim

pestering the guy at just the wrong time. In fact, it was exactly the kind of thing Tim would do. "Does it hurt?"

"Only if you touch it," Wertzie said with a wry smile, and
Charlie couldn't tell if he was kidding or not. The carny
pointed his nub at the map. "Anyways, like I was saying. Tennessee tonight, hit the top of Mississippi by morning, then
Louisiana. That should get us into Grand Isle late tomorrow." He cleared his throat. "Well. Most of us."

"What's that supposed to mean?"

Bruce frowned at Wertzie.

"Look, it's out of my hands," he said, holding up nine
fingers as if to prove it wasn't his decision. "I don't think
you two are any trouble back here, and I hate to see you
split up."

Charlie turned off the movie projector. "I'm going with
Bruce," he said. "End of story."

"Yeah," rumbled Bruce.

"Your brother thinks he knows what's best for everyone,
I guess," said Wertzie. "He's got someone coming down to
get you . . ."

Charlie couldn't figure out how his mom could come get
him, not with two jobs. The only person he could even think
of was . . .

"DJ?"

"Yeah, that sounds right," said Wertzie, handing the map
to Charlie and pointing out a town right in the middle of
Illinois. "DJ. Going to meet us at a truck stop in Bloomington or something."

"No!" protested the giant. "Charlie stays!"

The boy's face turned red. "Can't you talk to him, Wertzie?"

"Already tried. But Tim's got his mind made up about what's best for your friend here. And what's best for you. If it was up to me, I'd just put you and the big guy on the Express. It could take you right back to Wisconsin after we dropped off Jumbo."

"Put us on the what?"

"Never mind. Forget I said anything."

"Come on, man."

"The Express. It's how Hank usually gets down south. See?" Wertzie took up the map again and showed Charlie and Bruce a second route, marked in light-blue highlighter. "It's the last railroad car on the line, a big, hollowed-out double-decker. Hank's personal ride, fixed up nicer than you'd guess from the outside. Plan B—if we ever get worried that someone's on to us, we just put the giants on the Express."

Charlie squinted at the map in the pale light, noting the spot where the carnival's route crossed paths with the train's. It was in Bloomington, the same place Wertzie said DJ was coming to take Charlie back home.

Shouting from outside the trailer caused Wertzie to jump up and look out the back of the Creep Castle. It was Tiger and the mechanics, arguing over the final repair bill. "Never let a roughie negotiate money," he sighed. "Better go take care of this before someone gets their wrist broke."

Charlie hustled to the back door after Wertzie. "Come on, man!" he pleaded. "There's got to be something you can do."

"Come on!" shouted the giant.

Wertzie turned back to them. "Family stuff is none of my business," he said. "But the way I figure, Charlie, you got one obligation in this life: Do what's best for *you*."

Wertzie ran off between the trailers, detouring around Stan the Statue Man's truck as it got ready to shove off. "I'll handle this, Tiger!" he shouted. "Don't hit anybody!"

Most of the carnival was well down the road, trailers already packed up for the night, driven by seasonal carnies who knew nothing about giants or gold hiding in the cabs. The Creep Castle, trailing two carnival SUVs, Juice Man's generator truck, and a handful of ride trailers, bounced down a lonely stretch of interstate in an effort to catch up. Only headlights pierced the lonely darkness. Besides the stragglers in the traveling show, the road was deserted of cars.

Inside the cab, Tim yawned and steadied the wheel. Tiger dozed in the seat beside him. The hour was late, even for a carny. He found an alt-rock station on the radio, which didn't seem to disturb Tiger's sleep. He tapped his finger on the steering wheel, then found the straw for the forty-ounce soda that rested in the holder between the seats. He'd need the caffeine to keep on keeping on for a few more hours.

As he tugged at the wrapper, he glanced in the rearview mirror. A lone headlight approached.

Soon a motorcycle had pulled within two car lengths. Tim didn't like having it in his blind spot, so he slowed, but the cycle didn't pass and maintained the same distance. Tim shoved the straw into his right cheek when something else caught his eye. The dim light on the belly of a helicopter glinted as it flew just above the treetops to the east, on a line even with the Creep Castle.

Then the motorcycle roared around the haunted house and pulled in front of it. The rider was dressed in black and had a stick strapped to his back.

Tim jostled Tiger.

"Not now," she mumbled, pushing Tim's hand away.

Tim watched as the man on the motorcycle repositioned himself on the seat. "No, wake up. Something weird is going on."

Tiger lifted her head and rubbed her eyes.

They watched as the man on the motorcycle pulled something from inside his jacket and jabbed it into his thigh. He let go of the device and it flew into the night. The cycle swerved for a moment.

"This," observed Tim, "is not good."

Then the man stood up on the seat of his speeding bike and launched himself high into the air.

They craned their necks as the man turned a backflip. A violent thump behind them indicated the man had landed atop the Creep Castle. His vacant motorcycle skidded off the road and crashed in a ditch. And the straw fell out of Tim's mouth.

"Holy crap and then some," Tiger exclaimed, rolling down the passenger window and hoisting herself halfway out to get a better view.

The helicopter now hovered above the Creep Castle. Tiger squinted through the rushing wind at the man crouched atop the trailer, aiming his stick at the metal surface that protected the top of the haunted house. Blue light exploded from the end of his baton.

"He trying to unhook the trailer?"

"I wish," said Tiger. "He's cutting a hole in the roof."

A tube descended from the helicopter. Powder-blue mist billowed out the end and clouded Tim's view of the road. He caught a whiff, covered his mouth with his sleeve, and coughed. "That's some kind of knockout gas! He's going to put Bruce and Charlie to sleep, then come up here and take the wheel."

"No he won't." Tiger hoisted herself the rest of the way out of the window and sprang up on top of the cab.

Tim kept driving. To stop meant becoming sitting ducks for whatever other surprises might be in store for them.

The man in black was so busy stuffing the tube into the hole and pumping gas into the trailer that he didn't see Tiger until she was nearly upon him. He looked up and laughed. "Let me guess. *You're* the muscle?"

Tiger responded with a leap that planted her foot square in his chest.

The blow sent him sprawling onto his back, which for some reason put a wicked smile on his face. In an instant he kicked back up to his feet, a mean glint in his eye.

Tiger launched herself at the man once more, even as light posts whizzed by ten feet away. She wasn't about to let her larger opponent extend his arms. Tiger got in very close range, sending a furious flurry of Wing Chun–style punches and kicks to his midsection and neck. The attack would have made Bruce Lee proud.

Tim snuck glances through his tilted side-view mirror. The man easily deflected most of Tiger's blows, and the ones that connected seemed to have little effect. She'd beat up plenty of meatheads twice her size, but this guy was different.

She changed up tactics and tried to sweep his leg. Before she could connect, he was airborne. The miss left Tiger exposed, and he took full advantage of the opportunity, spinning deftly to kick her hard in the chin with the steel heel of his boot. She fell to the trailer top, unconscious.

"Not bad, roughie." The man calmly removed a device from his belt and scanned the trailer with its WiVi app, making sure his intended victims were unconscious. He frowned at the readout, then tried again. Finally certain of what he saw, he replaced the device in disgust, pulled the tube from the hole, and shinnied up the conduit toward the helicopter.

Up in the driver's seat, Tim couldn't believe what he was seeing. "Tiger!" There was no sign of her. He watched the man reach the helicopter in uncanny time, and it flew away. Tim hit the turn signal and slowly pulled the Creep Castle off the road.

Tim parked the trailer, bailed out of the cab, and climbed atop the Creep Castle. There was Tiger, barely conscious, crumpled near the ragged hole that the man had cut. Tim rushed to her side and dropped to his knees. "Tiger! You all right?"

She opened her eyes and rubbed her tender jaw. "I don't think so. That guy almost kicked my face off. What happened after that?"

"The guy just split." Tim helped Tiger down to the back of the Creep Castle and threw open the trailer doors. Gas billowed out, and Tim swatted it away from his eyes. "Charlie? You all right?"

There was no response. Tim coughed violently, with no choice but to let the gas clear. When the blue haze finally lifted, they stared into the trailer. Then Tim slammed the doors shut.

Wertzie had doubled back in one of the carnival's SUVs and skidded to a stop on the other side of the highway. He dashed across the four lanes. "What happened?" he asked. "Are Charlie and the giant all right?"

"They're gone," Tim said.

"What? How can they be gone?"

"That dude must have seen the trailer was empty, and that's why he broke off. We got to find Charlie!"

Tiger worked her sore jaw. "At least the gold's still there."

Tim wheeled to her. "Thanks for your concern!"

"You know I'm worried about your brother. I'm worried about the giant, too. But let's not kid ourselves—we're all doing this for the money."

"Some of us more than others, apparently."

"No one is getting any gold," Wertzie reminded them, "if we don't deliver the giant. It's not one or the other."

"That psycho knew the giant was with us. I don't know where Bruce and Charlie are, but that guy's not going to stop until he finds them."

"So we'll find them first," said Wertzie.

"Charlie's my brother," said Tim. "I'll find him."

The lack of streetlights along this particular dark stretch of Interstate 74 made it pretty much impossible for passing cars to get a good look at Bruce. When Stan the Statue Man's trailer of massive fiberglass mascots had pulled out of Peoria Plaza Tire, Charlie and Bruce had snuck out of the Creep Castle and stowed away, with the giant taking Vanna Whitewall's vacated spot.

Tiger's argument with the mechanics had turned out to be great luck—in Wertzie's rush to break up the scuffle, he'd left his map with Charlie. And using it, he made a plan: Piggyback on Stan the Statue Man's trailer to Grady's Family Fun Park in Bloomington, find the train with Hank's double-decker car, and ride the sucker to Grand Isle. He didn't expect the giant smugglers to check the Creep Castle until breakfast. By the time Tim and the rest of them put two and two together, Charlie and Bruce would be well on their way to Louisiana with no one to stop them. Maybe the smugglers would be worried, but it served Tim right for trying to send Charlie home. After all they'd been through, he wasn't about to ditch Bruce just because Tim said so.

Charlie was impressed with the way Bruce stayed stone-still, posing with his hand up like some kind of goofy, waving statue. The boy hid in the crook of the gigantic rabbit's arm, straddling a rusted beam that ran the length of the rumbling trailer. In the spaces between the truck bed's slats, he could see the pitch-black asphalt rushing beneath them, and it freaked him out more than a little. Stan the Statue Man was visible through a small, rectangular window in the back of the semi's cab, but he hadn't looked back once. Charlie wasn't too worried—it wasn't like truck drivers used a rear-view mirror anyway. As long as he and Bruce didn't screw around too much, they were as good as out of sight.

"Hey," Charlie yelled over the roar of the truck barreling down the highway, "how you doing?"

"Good." Bruce grinned and opened his mouth as wide as it would go to catch the wind in his cheeks. He probably swallowed a mouthful of bugs, which Charlie thought was pretty gross. The faster the trailer went, the more the giant seemed to like it, and if he shared any of Charlie's fear that one funky bounce could turn them into roadkill, he wasn't showing it.

A white minivan pulled up alongside the trailer. Charlie ducked as far as he could into the rabbit's armpit to avoid being seen. Inside the van, a little kid in a car seat, maybe four or five years old, pressed his face up against the window. His eyes went wide at the sight of the humongous creatures, and he gave a cheerful wave.

Bruce winked and stuck out his tongue.

The kid went nuts, pointing at the giant and slapping the window. The father at the wheel of the minivan heaved his shoulders in a sigh and threw a granola bar into the backseat, never taking his eyes off the road. The kid shoved the snack into his mouth but kept slapping the window, trying to get another reaction from the funny statue on the big truck. His face fell as the van pulled ahead and away from the semi.

"That kid's going to have crazy dreams tonight," Charlie shouted.

"Crazy," Bruce agreed. He grimaced and shifted his weight, and the trailer let out a low groan.

Charlie froze. "Don't move!" He watched the window at the back of the semi, and sure enough, Stan the Statue Man's grizzled face was checking the passenger-side mirror to see what was causing his trailer to complain.

"Keep low," the boy shouted to Bruce. Stan the Statue Man wasn't visible in the side mirror, and that meant he couldn't see them. Still, Charlie held his breath, half expecting the whole rig to come screeching to a halt.

Instead the driver shifted gears and steered toward an exit ramp. Charlie exhaled—there would be no roadside inspection. But Stan the Statue Man would soon be at his destination and they would have to find a way to get off the trailer without being seen. The giant's ninja skills would be put to the test once more.

The trailer worked its way through sleepy neighborhoods before hitting a stretch of industrial road. Finally, it turned past a sign that read GRADY'S FAMILY FUN PARK—END OF THE SEASON BLOWOUT in vibrant blues and reds. Little kids straddled pint-size railroad cars that chugged around the exterior of the park, a miniature locomotive puffing indigo smoke into the night.

"Fun," Bruce said.

Stan the Statue Man worked the truck around the edges of the crowded parking lot, looking for a sane place to unload the outsize rabbit. The aroma of freshly baked pizza hung in the autumn night air, and Bruce's nostrils started to twitch.

"Hungry!"

"You just ate like a hundred burgers," Charlie complained, though by now he knew giant teenagers ate a ton, literally. "You can eat later. We've got bigger problems."

Problems like lots of people, all possible eyewitnesses to the giant hiding on the mascot trailer. Lucky for Charlie and Bruce, most of them were near a temporary stage at the front of the park, where a man in an old-fashioned straw hat shouted into a microphone, "And the best way to thank you for our biggest season ever is with the biggest pizza in Illinois!" The man pointed to a massive makeshift pizza oven to his left, where a crew of chefs worked a ten-foot pie into position. The crowd erupted in cheers.

"Don't even think about it," warned Charlie.

The giant grinned and licked his lips.

The truck continued past all the cars, past the shadowy miniature golf course and deserted bounce house, and groaned to a stop at the end of the lot where the pavement turned to dirt. One by one, lights were turning off throughout the park, leaving the bumper boats and batting cages shuttered until next year. The mini train chugged to a stop, despite the kids' disappointed groans. "You guys really expect me to deliver this thing in the dark?" shouted Stan the Statue Man out the driver's-side window to no one in particular.

The lights had been turned off for a reason. Something was about to go down. "Everybody, get ready," barked the man in the straw hat.

Stan the Statue Man jumped out of the rig and slammed the driver's-side door. "A little help!" he shouted. When everyone ignored him, he kicked at the dirt and turned for the trailer, heading right for the bow-tied rabbit where Charlie was hiding.

The boy slipped down from the rabbit's armpit, sliding as quietly as he could behind an enormous ceramic fish, its cartoony lips pursed as if it was blowing bubbles. "Stay still," he whispered to Bruce. The giant didn't respond, frozen in place.

Stan the Statue Man shuffled down the opposite side of the trailer, muttering to himself the whole way. He was lost in his own frustration as he undid one of the straps that secured the huge Grady's rabbit, paying no attention to the flesh-and-blood behemoth that lay motionless on the other side.

Charlie bit his lip. Once the man moved the rabbit, there was no way he wouldn't see Bruce. They had to think of something—fast.

"Thanks for a great season, Central Illinois!" boomed the voice over the loudspeaker. The last floodlights in the park went black. "See you next year!"

A huge burst of fireworks detonated over the park with a bright scarlet flash and thundering boom. Stan the Statue Man craned his neck to the sky, watching the lights create a colorful weeping willow that melted into the night.

Charlie felt Bruce's enormous hand close around him. Then the two of them slid to the ground on the side of the trailer away from where Stan the Statue Man stood. Bruce watched the fireworks' light fade, and just before the next one exploded into the darkness, he leaped onto the mini golf course, landing near the Statue of Liberty hole. Bruce stashed Charlie on the ground behind Lady Liberty's skirt.

"Are you nuts?" whispered Charlie as the sky exploded green and blue. "Somebody will see us now for sure!"

Stan the Statue Man came around the trailer and stopped, perplexed. He squinted at Bruce on the golf course, lit only by the muted colors in the sky.

Bruce stood perfectly still, posing like a fierce caveman right above the waterfall on the seventeenth hole.

"Those sons of guns have been buying their giant figures someplace else," muttered Stan as more fireworks boomed overhead. "Pretty lifelike though, I got to say." He gave up on unloading the rabbit for the time being and made off in the direction of the largest pizza in Illinois.

Charlie peeked around the statue. "Dude."

Bruce lowered his fist for a bump. For someone without a lot of real-world experience, Charlie thought, the big guy was pretty quick on his feet. But there was no time for celebrating this small triumph.

They were going to be in real trouble if they missed the train. Charlie wished his phone hadn't been crushed at the drive-in. If they got stuck out in the middle of nowhere, he had no way to contact the giant smugglers or anyone else to bail them out. Charlie pulled Wertzie's map from his back pocket, then surveyed the line of dark trees that ringed the amusement park. According to the smugglers' map, they needed to go west of the amusement park to catch the train. But Charlie had no sense of which way was which. Neither his surroundings nor the map offered potential landmarks to help point the way.

"Bruce?" Charlie looked up from the map and the giant was gone. "Quit screwing around, man! We've got a train to catch! Like now!"

The giant's head poked around from behind a fiberglass giraffe that towered over the twelfth hole. "T-t-train?"

It was another word that the giant didn't understand. "Train," repeated Charlie. He pointed out the miniature version over in the kiddie area of the park they'd seen coming in. "Like that but bigger. The trees are the problem. They totally block the view. And the train could be coming from any direction."

The giant stared at the trees, then took a look around the darkened park. He closed his eyes in thought, then opened them. "Got it."

"Got what?"

Bruce once again picked up Charlie in his right fist. He crouched low as another set of fireworks boomed overhead. Then in the brief moment when things went dark, he sprinted out of the miniature golf course and leaped atop the deserted bounce house. The inflated structure sagged, then threw them high in the air.

Charlie had the presence of mind to get a good look at the Bloomington skyline even though he'd just been jerked into the night sky. The city, way bigger than Richland Center, blinked its downtown lights just past the trees. No train in that direction.

"Turn another way," Charlie urged as they fell. Bruce torqued his body as he landed on the inflatable house. When they returned into the air, they faced ninety degrees to the right. In the distance, Charlie glimpsed the remote lights of the train as it made its way around the perimeter of the town.

"There! You see it?"

"Yep!"

Bruce and the boy landed once again on the bounce house, this time puncturing the structure with a rowdy *pop* that coincided perfectly with a booming explosion in the night sky. The two tumbled into the grass.

"Think we can make it?"

Bruce grabbed Charlie and tore off into the darkness. Staying hidden took a backseat to catching up with the train. Charlie held his arms in front of his face as Bruce ran straight through the line of trees, noisily busting off branches and sending fall leaves swirling in a million directions. They tore through an apartment complex parking lot in a blur, then along a lonely road in the direction of the rail cars.

A whistle blew up ahead, long and low. Charlie and Bruce saw the train chugging under an overpass. They were going to miss the ride for sure. "Come on, Bruce! It's getting away!"

Bruce responded by kicking it into a new gear, sprinting down a grassy slope toward the train like a rocket. They reached the tracks, but the train had put some distance between them. Charlie identified the final car in the line, its tall profile perfectly fitting Wertzie's description of Hank's double-decker, the Express. "We can still make it!" he shouted.

Bruce sprinted along a path parallel to the tracks. The train had slowed as it passed through town, but it was picking up steam now. Bruce took big gulps of air, and Charlie felt the giant's palm get sweaty as he galloped after the final car. They closed the distance, and Charlie tried to figure out how they would get inside. If Hank had transported other giants in the past, there must be an entrance big enough for Bruce. How could he open it?

Bruce jumped onto the back of the Express, straddling the double-decker car like the kids he'd seen riding the miniature train. "Wooooohooooooo!"

"No, not like this, we're supposed to ride *inside*," yelled Charlie from the giant's fist. The boy surveyed the roof of the double-decker and spotted a release lever at its far end. "Let me down and I'll see if I can get us in."

Moving down the top of a rumbling train was tricky. The car shook so hard that Charlie could barely keep his balance. He got down on his hands and knees and worked his way to the latch, and with some effort, he pulled it up.

With a hydraulic hiss, the door on the back of the double-decker swung down like a pickup truck tailgate. The hatch door was now parallel to the tracks, creating a platform that Bruce could easily step down on to enter the car. He reached up and grabbed Charlie, bringing him inside. Then Charlie found a button on an interior control that raised the door back into its closed position, just as the train whistle gave off another long blast.

Charlie looked around the car, modestly furnished with plenty of room for a giant. "We did it!"

Bruce flopped onto his back and caught his breath. "Fun," he agreed. He reached inside his tunic and from somewhere pulled out a massive piece of pizza that he'd stolen from Grady's. He shoved the entire greasy thing into his mouth.

"You're disgusting," laughed Charlie.

30

The sound of rain slapping against metal nudged Charlie awake. He looked up. Silver clouds streaked past high windows twenty feet above him. It took a few seconds to shake the cobwebs free and remember just where he was—in Hank's train car, the Express, rumbling south toward Louisiana. Once he and Bruce had gotten safely inside, the rush of their mad dash to board the train had given way to exhaustion. Charlie had been knocked unconscious back in Richland Center, but that wasn't the same as sleeping. Both of them had been up so long they pretty much collapsed and passed out.

Even though Charlie's head still ached, he realized that right about now he should have been racing to beat the first bell at school. Instead, here he was, long gone from boring Richland Center and riding in a tricked-out train car with the best dude ever (who just happened to be a giant).

He looked over at the big guy taking up nearly the whole

length of the car, snoring like crazy despite the hard wooden floor. Giants were used to sleeping on the ground, Charlie guessed.

He rolled off the fold-down cot he'd slept on and quietly refastened it to the wall. The interior of the car was nice enough, though nobody would call it elegant. The walls were paneled with dark cherrywood, and a lower bank of tinted windows were protected by thick red drapes that kept out the sun and prying eyes. The car had two doors—the fold-down hatch in the back that they'd used to get in and a regular-size entryway at the front of the car.

Furnishings were sparse. A lone leather chair and empty coffee table stood across from a wall adorned with framed pictures. Charlie tiptoed around the sleeping giant and took in the shots: a forest of incredibly tall trees blanketed in snow; a dented coffeepot atop a campfire; several shots of Powder running through the wintry wild. The display was a reminder that had there been a different turn of events, it would have been Hank riding in the car. Charlie turned away.

Positioned near a far window, several potted plants rested atop a large box with a slatted wood-panel surface. Next to the box, Charlie opened the door on a small enclosure to find a tiny bathroom. Perfect—he was worried that he'd have to leave the car to find a place to relieve himself.

"Me too."

Charlie wheeled around. The ceiling was just high enough for Bruce, and there he stood. Of course he hadn't made a sound. "You got to go?"

"Yep."

"Number one or number two?"

Bruce held up three fingers.

"There is no number three, man."

Bruce crossed one leg in front of the other, a distressed look on his face. He was serious about having to go. "Bad."

Charlie looked around—there wasn't a giant enclosure for . . . wait. He looked more closely at the box. The slats on the surface were spaced close together, but Charlie could see through them—the boards concealed a monstrous toilet! "Looks like Hank thought of everything," he said, holding up a "just a second" finger. He began pulling the potted plants from the giant toilet lid, looking for a place to put them so Bruce could flip up the top.

"Now!"

"I'm going as fast as I can," Charlie protested.

But it wasn't fast enough for the giant. He pushed the button at the back of the car, and the hinged panel folded down to expose the outside world. In contrast to the colorless clouds overhead, autumnal America streaked by in vibrant golds and greens. They were long gone from Illinois, rolling along a horizon that stretched into forever. This was what the middle of nowhere looked like, and it was beautiful. Bruce stepped out onto the platform, hiked up his tunic, and relieved himself off the back of the train.

Bruce had it right. To heck with toilets. If it was good enough for the giant, it was good enough for Charlie, who joined his friend on the back of the train. The two christened the tracks, expressing their newfound freedom to the fullest. When they'd finished their business, they shouted out to the plains—no actual words, just whoops that traveled into nowhere with no chance of being heard over the roar of the train.

Finally, they returned to the car, and Charlie raised the wall. As it shut tight, a clicking sound at the front of the car startled them. Had somebody heard them? Charlie looked around frantically for a place for Bruce to hide, but the car offered no such cover.

Then the door at the front opened. A white cane with a red tip poked through. Bruce balled his fists, ready to take on a dangerous intruder, but Charlie held up his hand. He'd seen that type of cane before. It was the kind blind people used.

A large man dressed all in black followed the staff into the car and shut the door behind him. He wore dark sunglasses and a long tangle of white billy-goat whiskers hung from his chin. His cane explored the floor with a wooden *tap-tap-tap*. Charlie had been right—the man couldn't see a thing. As long as Bruce kept his mouth shut, he wasn't in immediate danger of being discovered.

The man stopped tapping and held very still. "Who's there?" he croaked in a raspy voice that sounded like Charlie's Uncle Harvey, a man who smoked too many cigarettes.

Charlie tried not to breathe.

"Come on, I know you're there." The man rapped the floor with his stick.

"Who are you?" The words rocketed from Charlie's mouth. "What are you doing in my car?"

"Name's Parran. I'm aiming to take a rest," he said, revealing a wide smile full of tobacco-stained teeth. He poked his cane in Charlie's general direction. "This is the sleeper car, ain't it?"

Charlie winced. He hadn't checked the front entrance to ensure it was locked. They were lucky that it had been a blind man who had wandered in. "No, this is a private car," the boy said, trying to make his voice sound deep and grown-up. Bruce gave him a funny look.

"That so?" Parran reached into his front pocket and pulled out a toothpick. He rolled it between yellowed fingertips before stashing it in his cheek. "The door was open."

"You're going to have to leave," warned Charlie, clearing his throat. The deep voice wasn't working so well. "Sorry."

Parran paused as if he was going to argue with Charlie, or perhaps call a porter to sort it out. But instead, he turned and shuffled back the way he came. "Sorry to trouble you, good sir. I'll show myself out." He tapped his way through the door, and Charlie locked it tight behind him.

"Trouble?" Bruce asked.

"I don't think so." Still, it was a close call. Charlie plopped down in the easy chair by the coffee table and pulled out the smugglers' map, trying to figure out how much longer they'd need to hide on the train. He remembered Wertzie's time estimates from the night before. "My guess is we're somewhere in Tennessee, not far from Louisiana. Almost there, big guy."

Bruce didn't respond. He was staring at the pictures on the wall, inching closer for a better look. He reached out, touched an imperceptible seam, and pulled to the side. The wall parted, revealing a hidden compartment. A light snapped on inside. Bruce leaned in, and Charlie got out of the chair. Hanging inside the partition was a second series of framed, faded pictures, ones that were not meant to be seen by just anyone.

"Whoa," said Charlie. He gawked at a picture of an unfamiliar giant, bearded and noble, staring up at a towering tree twice his size. The shot captured an eagle leaving its nest, soaring high above the giant. "Where is this?"

"Home," Bruce said.

Other shots included a giant wrapped in some kind of animal skin throwing a spear the size of a small tree, a catch of silvery fish large enough to fill a dump truck, and a close-up shot of a giant woman's face, smiling and peaceful. A mountain stood in the distance behind her.

Bruce pointed to the snowy mountainside and let his fingertip linger on the glass. "House."

"You lived on that mountain?"

"Caves," Bruce responded. He pulled the picture from the wall and carefully pointed out several openings in the mountain, joining them with his finger.

"A bunch of them, all connected together?"

"Yep."

"Jeez, dude, weren't you freezing?"

Bruce smiled and shook his head.

Charlie imagined the world's most amazing collection of underground forts, all connected by enormous tunnels. "I'd love to see your caves sometime."

Bruce's brow furrowed. "Gone."

"What? How could they just be . . . gone?"

"Hank," the giant explained. "Boom."

The old man had talked about blowing up the dam back in Richland Center, so he knew his way around dynamite.

And the smugglers were pretty serious about keeping the giants a secret. Charlie guessed that meant making sure nobody could visit their former address. That didn't mean Bruce had to like it. Charlie hated moving all the time. No place ever felt like home. "Sorry, man. You excited about going to your new place?"

Bruce thought about that one. His lips tightened, and finally he shrugged. "Big world."

Charlie thought about Bruce's future, secluded and safe with the other giants in a new home but cut off from everything the world had to offer. He had never known about hamburgers or trains or carnival rides before, but he sure seemed to like them. And there was so much more that he had yet to see. "What would you do if you didn't join up with the other giants? Just . . . hang out? Watch movies?"

Bruce's face brightened. "Sure," came the matter-of-fact reply.

Charlie chuckled. "It's not that easy, man. You can't just hang all the time. People in my world have to do something, like work or go to school before they get to watch movies . . ."

Movies. Of course! It was a crazy idea, but why not? With Bruce, movies wouldn't need special effects. He *was* a special effect! A giant who could do martial arts moves? Charlie couldn't think of anyone who wouldn't pay money to see that. They were on to something.

"What?"

"It probably wouldn't work." One of the giant smugglers had to have thought of this idea before and dismissed it for some good reason he hadn't thought of yet. But why couldn't Bruce be a movie star? Charlie began to reconsider. The giant was a couple of years older than Charlie, close to the age when Tim started making his own decisions and ran off on his own. "But maybe you could be in the movies!"

Bruce's mouth curled up at the corners. "Me?"

"It wouldn't be a sure thing," Charlie said, realizing he really had no idea how someone got into the movie business. "We'd have to go to California, probably, and we'd need some money to get started."

"Gold," offered Bruce. He broke into his fist-pumping dance move, excited that his friend was even considering the idea.

Charlie had forgotten all about the gold. A stick or two could probably buy a mansion, and Bruce was entitled to his fair share. "What about your parents? Won't they be worried?"

"Visit," Bruce offered as a compromise.

The boy's head spun. His own mom would put up a fuss, that was for sure, but with that kind of money, maybe he just could talk her into moving out west. She could leave both her crummy jobs and finally get the big house she deserved.

"Movies!" the giant insisted. Now that Charlie had planted the idea, Bruce wasn't going to let it go easily.

"Movies?" Charlie said again, testing the idea out loud to see if it sounded as crazy as he feared.

"Movies!"

"Okay," the boy said, becoming convinced himself. The giant's enthusiasm was contagious. "Okay! Let's do it, man. Let's get your share of the gold and go to California!"

31

The afternoon hours flew by as the train sped to their Louisiana destination. Charlie and Bruce spent the rest of the ride planning the giant's movie career. And what better place to start than their current adventure? It was a natural. Who wouldn't want to see a movie about a bunch of giant smugglers when the main part was played by an actual giant? The story wrote itself: Bruce coming to town, Charlie finding him in the warehouse, sneaking out to the drive-in, fighting Giant Fitz in the quarry. Bruce wanted that part changed a little bit—less Giant Fitz hitting him and more him hitting Giant Fitz. Charlie had an idea about spinning Bruce off into a video game: *Total Turbo: Giant Trouble*. Even if Bruce's career as an actor didn't take off, his future as a celebrity was all but assured.

Finally the train pulled to a stop. Charlie wanted to take a victory lap—it wouldn't be long now until they collected Bruce's gold and set off on another adventure, leaving his boring old life behind forever. But when he parted the curtains and looked out the tinted windows, the feeling of triumph deflated to confusion.

He'd expected to see the Gulf of Mexico or at least a sleepy town deserving of the name "Grand Isle, Louisiana." Their destination was just a speck on Wertzie's map, even smaller than Richland Center. But outside, even though it was nighttime, the train yard was bustling with activity. Towering above the dozens of tracks full of freight and passenger cars, Charlie saw brightly lit buildings reaching into the sky. This couldn't be the end of the line.

The giant was antsy. "Out?"

"Not yet."

Charlie made a peephole in the space between the thick red curtains, trying to get a sense of what was going on. A tram rumbled past, the back end full of passenger luggage. Stenciled on the vehicle's side were the words *New Orleans Union Passenger Terminal*.

New Orleans?

Charlie fumbled the map open again. New Orleans was close to Grand Isle—close in the sense that both cities were in the state of Louisiana—but they had to be a hundred miles from their final destination. Wertzie never mentioned anything about the train not going all the way! How were they supposed to cover a hundred miles? That was one heck of a walk, even for Bruce.

In the space between the curtains, Charlie saw motion near the front of the double-decker car. Someone was snooping around. He closed the drapes just as the lock in the forward door clicked and turned.

Tim quickly slipped inside and shut the door, locking it behind him. Bruce stuck out a fist for Charlie's brother to bump, but Tim's usual crooked grin was nowhere to be found. "What were you guys thinking, running off like that?"

Charlie was in no mood for lectures, especially after Tim had betrayed him back in Peoria. "What did you think we'd do? Wertzie told us everything! You were going to send me home!"

Tim shook his head. "Wertzie told you . . . Wait, what did Wertzie tell you?"

"That DJ was coming. Don't act like you didn't tell him to." It felt good to call out his brother on his bullcrap for once. It was about time someone did.

"I can't believe he told you that."

"Wertzie," agreed Bruce, endorsing the smuggler who'd confided in them.

"Forget Wertzie," Tim said, opening a streaming-video app on his phone. "Let's talk about this."

"Movie!"

"Yep, it's a movie," said Tim. "Starring you two dopes. Somebody named Adele found my e-mail and sent me the link. She's worried sick about you, Charlie."

Bruce made kissing noises, and Charlie slugged the giant in the shin as hard as he could. "The link for what?" he asked. He wasn't surprised that Adele had tracked them down online; it was her specialty.

In response, Tim pushed "Play." Charlie and Bruce watched the video, a blurry handheld clip titled *Bloomington Bigfoot???* Even though the video was dark and fuzzy, Charlie easily recognized Bruce racing through the apartment parking lot back in Illinois to catch the train. Some guy narrated about how he'd been barbecuing on his balcony when he heard a monster running through the trees and caught it on his phone. It was impossible to tell exactly what it was, but there was definitely something big rumbling past the pickup trucks and mopeds.

"Me!" said Bruce, excited to see himself on-screen.

"You can barely see anything," Charlie countered, his voice defensive. There were only 325 views on the video, anyway. Practically no one had seen it.

Tim stashed his phone. "Once I saw how close you were to the train, it wasn't hard to put two and two together. The train, Charlie! There's a reason Hank only uses it for emergencies. Too many people all along the way. How do you know someone hasn't seen you back here?"

"Nobody," protested Bruce. "Careful!"

"Well," said Charlie. At this point, there wasn't much to lose by coming clean. "I did meet a blind guy, some kind of drifter. But he had no idea Bruce was here. Like he said. We've been careful."

"Careful doesn't always keep trouble away, Charlie. Remember your friend with the stick?"

"Dead!" argued the giant.

"Bruce is right. We saw a tornado coming right at him!"

"That twister must have chickened out, because Stick-O is very much alive," said Tim. "Last night he backflipped off a motorcycle going seventy and attacked the Creep Castle!"

Charlie couldn't believe the guy had survived the tornado. And he remembered the merciless look in his eye as he was about to zap Charlie in the head. To counter his fear, he puffed out his chest. "Sounds like we made the right decision to get out of there."

"Way to go. You snuck off like a real hero," said Tim, his voice sticky with sarcasm. "But we know someone's after Bruce. We got to keep him safe until he gets to his new home."

"No."

Tim looked up at the giant and snorted. "What do you mean, *no*?"

"He means he's not going," said Charlie. "Not to the place with the rest of the giants."

"Where does he think he's going instead?"

Charlie swallowed hard. "To California. He's coming with me. He's going to be in the movies."

"Movies," Bruce agreed, pointing to Tim's phone as if the online video was his big debut.

Tim exhaled and ran his hand over his face. "Charlie. You guys get major props for what you've pulled off so far. But you're in *middle school*. How exactly do you think this is going to work?"

"We're still hammering out the details," Charlie admitted, the words *middle school* stinging like a slap across the face. "But we decided. He wants to hang with me in our world. He's about the same age you were when you left home. So he's getting his share of the gold in Grand Isle. And he's not going where you tell him to go."

"So you and Bruce are just going to waltz down the streets of Richland Center? Or Hollywood? What do you think people will do when they see him for the first time? Applaud? Or maybe they'll get big-time scared. What are the odds someone panics and whips out a gun? This isn't hypothetical, Charlie—you know people are after him, bad people. What happens when your friend with the stick knows just where to find Bruce?"

The giant made two fists to show that he wasn't afraid of any man, stick or no stick. Tim rolled his eyes and kept right on talking.

"There's one other thing Adele told me—she's seen Accelerton vans crawling all over Richland Center looking for something. That's the place where the other giant's dad worked, right? I've seen the vans myself, right here in this rail yard." Tim pulled one of the red drapes back an inch. On the other side of the yard, a security vehicle was stationed near a gate where big freight trucks came and went. The green Accelerton logo was stenciled on its side. "Quite a coincidence, huh? Can you guess who they're looking for?"

Charlie swallowed hard. Maybe there were a few things he and Bruce hadn't thought through. But winging it had worked great so far. "We got each other's backs."

"Having fun, hanging out—that's only one part of being a friend, Charlie," said Tim. "It's not just about what's best for you. What about what's best for Bruce?"

"Friend!" The giant crossed his arms. The two of them were in this together, no matter what.

Tim gave a frustrated laugh and threw up his hands, the sign of a man who could tell he was getting nowhere fast. "Tell you what. You're going to Grand Isle anyway, right? For the gold, if nothing else?"

"Yeah, we're going to Grand Isle," said Charlie, though he had no idea how they were getting there.

"Gold." Bruce was emphatic. He was getting his share.

"Then let me help you get there. And give all of us some time to think along the way."

Charlie looked at Bruce. They had agreed to do this on their own, but grabbing a ride didn't seem like such a bad idea. Bruce gave the boy a small nod, and Charlie turned back to his brother.

"Okay, fine. We'll go with you."

"Not with me. Hank has a guy who can help you get out of town. He's the man down here." Tim reached into his pocket and pulled out a cheap plastic cell phone, the kind convenience stores sold for twenty bucks. He handed it to Charlie. "My number's in there in case there's trouble. Meantime, I've got a few things to take care of."

That sounded familiar, like the note Tim had left their mother a few years back. "How will Hank's guy find us?"

"Oh, he already knows you're here. He'll get you out, as long as you don't go AWOL again." Tim opened the back door of the car and slipped halfway out. "And Charlie? Think about what I said, okay?"

Tim disappeared into the night.

"What now?" asked Bruce.

"Wait, I guess." Charlie looked up at his giant friend, and considered Tim's warning. His brother was probably right: The world might not understand Bruce without the proper introduction, but Charlie figured there were people in Hollywood who could help them with that. They'd schedule a press conference. Adele could help them make a website: brucethegiant.com or meetthebigguy.org, something like that. People would love Bruce, as long as it was all handled in just the right way. The whole thing was so real in Charlie's mind that he couldn't imagine a way that it wouldn't . . .

Tink tink tink.

The car was moving again.

Tink tink tink.

Where were they going? Charlie split the drapes on a window and peered out. They were heading in the opposite direction from the Accelerton van, where a man in a security uniform waved some kind of device over the trucks hauling freight in and out of the yard. He was definitely looking for something big, but as far as Charlie could tell, he wasn't paying any attention to the double-decker passenger car slowly rolling away.

Charlie and Bruce peeked out through the curtains on the other side of the car. The Express had been unhitched from the long line of cars and a locomotive was towing it down a side track into a building that looked like an aircraft hangar. Once the car was safely inside, the locomotive disengaged, and the hangar's huge doors slid shut.

The car's forward door opened again with a loud click. And for the second time, in walked the blind man, Parran. He pointed his cane at Charlie.

"Gotcha," Parran croaked in his Cajun accent. He swiveled his cane to Bruce. "And your giant buddy here, too."

"You're . . . you're Hank's friend?"

"I'm the old man's eyes in this here part of the country. Ironic, ain't it?" Parran slapped his knee at his own joke, hacking out a laugh that quickly turned into a cough. "Make good and sure nobody is sniffin' around this car, and I'm good at dat. No one ever thinks a blind man is watching. Then, of course, when Hank needs a fixer, I'm his man."

"F-f-fixer?" asked Bruce, trying to get his teeth and tongue around the new word.

"I arrange things, so the story goes on," said Parran. "Dat brother of yours tells me you desperately need some fixin' right about now."

"Great," Charlie said. "You'll give us a ride then?"

"Well," Parran huffed, "it ain't as easy as all dat. You can't be seen, and we can't be using no truck. People are on to you."

"Then how are we going to get out of here?" asked Charlie.

"We put you where they ain't lookin'," laughed Parran. "And then we roll you right outta the Big Easy."

"You didn't find them?"

Even in the dim midnight moonlight, Tim saw the frustration and fatigue filling the Juice Man's face. The guy looked like he could use some sleep. He'd been on guard duty at the back of the Creep Castle for nearly four hours now, fiddling with his GPS device to pass the time. His jaw had to be sore from holding that penlight in his mouth.

"Oh, I found them all right," explained Tim, just as Tiger and Wertzie arrived at the back of the haunted house to get the update. The carnival had arrived earlier in the evening, and Wertzie had paid the local crew early, ensuring they'd head into town to blow their earnings. The Creep Castle was parked at the very back of the caravan, away from prying eyes. Even so, the giant smugglers kept their voices low. They were barely audible over the rush of the gulf tide on the beach adjoining the park.

"So where are they?" asked Wertzie, rubbing sleep from bleary eyes with his four-fingered fist. "That giant needs to get gone tomorrow."

"New Orleans," said Tim. "Parran's got 'em. They'll be here tomorrow, right on schedule."

"New Orleans?" asked Tiger. "How in the world did they . . . ?"

"Doesn't matter," said Tim, waving off her questions. "They'll be here." He didn't mention Charlie and Bruce's plan to grab the gold and go. He still had time to talk some sense into them, and spooking the rest of the smugglers wasn't going to help.

"New Orleans," muttered Juice Man. "Your brother's bright idea to go to Mardi Gras, Lawson? I knew we should have left him back in Wisconsin!"

"Tell it to the giant."

Juice Man spat in the dirt.

"Parran gives me the creeps," complained Wertzie. "That whole blind act seems fishy to me. I don't trust him."

"Hank trusts him," said Tim. "Good enough for me."

"Since you didn't bring the giant back with you, we don't have a whole lot of options, do we?" Tiger said, glaring at Tim.

"Everything's cool. You guys get some sleep," he replied. "I'm so wired, I couldn't sleep if I tried. I've been chugging energy drinks all the way back from N'Awlins. I'll take Castle watch. Tomorrow, we'll hook up with Parran and get the giant on his way."

"And then we get paid," snapped Juice Man.

"And then we get paid," Tim agreed.

"Fine," Wertzie said, giving the Creep Castle a final once-over. "I'll relieve you at four."

The giant smugglers, save for Tim, returned to their trailers. He hopped up on the back of the Creep Castle and checked his phone for messages. Nothing new, just a few more worried texts from his mom asking about Charlie. He reassured her for the hundredth time, sighed, and opened the doors at the back of the trailer.

Four hours later, Wertzie stumbled back through the dark, ready to take his appointed turn at the back of the Creep Castle. He reached the end of the trailer convoy and stopped in his tracks. He looked over his shoulder. Then he spun entirely around.

"It's gone!" he hissed into a walkie-talkie that he pulled off his belt. "The Creep Castle is gone!"

Wertzie ran up and down between the other trailers, looking frantically, as if something the size of the Creep Castle could have just been misplaced. "I knew we couldn't trust Tim! I knew it!"

Tiger came sprinting to the empty spot where the Creep Castle had stood just hours before. "Tim!" she screamed into the dark. Her hands were balled into angry fists. "I can't believe he did this to us!"

Wertzie kicked at the sandy dirt in frustration. "This whole business with his brother was just a diversion so he could take off with the gold! Our gold!"

"I did my part! Everything I was asked to do!" The Juice Man staggered into the void created by the missing Creep Castle. "I want my money!"

Wertzie took a few deep breaths, cooking up a plan.

"Okay. Okay. It's not like he's going to get far in that thing. Weighted down with all that gold, it can barely go forty-five miles an hour. Tiger, you got this?"

"Damn right I do," she growled, launching herself into one of the carnival's beat-up SUVs, a far more agile mode of transportation than the lumbering amusement ride. "I'll take the interstate—it's the only road out of here. Juice Man, you take . . ."

"The town. I'm way ahead of you." Juice Man hopped into a second SUV, but not before pounding the hood a few times in frustration. "I'm going to kill him! I want my money, Wertzie!" The veins in his thick neck bulged as if to reinforce the message.

Wertzie approached the second SUV, calm and slow. "Oh, I see. You want to get paid." Then he exploded in frustration at the Juice Man. "We all want to get paid! Get moving!"

The Juice Man peeled off in his ride, with Tiger right behind him. Wertzie did a quick check of the dark grounds to make sure none of the other carnies had heard the heated discussion. But they were still in their trailers, sleeping off the fun from the night before.

"Excuse me?"

Wertzie turned to see a man striding in his direction through the shadows. "It's a little early, pal," said the carny, in no mood for conversations with strangers. "We're obviously not set up yet. Why don't you come back later, buy yourself a ticket? Bring a girl or something, have yourself some fun."

"I'm not looking for fun," said the man. "I'm looking for someone. And I suspect you might be able to help me find him." He held out a business card featuring a green double helix in the shape of a leaf.

Accelerton.

"A little more to the right," Charlie coached.

Bruce adjusted the position of twin court jesters, masked and wearing jingling fool's hats. He was trying to fasten them dead center on the front of a massive parade float.

"Yep, right there!"

Bruce lowered the two grinning clowns, and hooks caught the hard edge that rimmed the float, glittering in a garish array of gold and purple. The giant stood back to make sure the jokers hung straight. Then he turned back to Charlie, who had discovered Tim's cheap phone could take photos and even video. The boy was documenting the whole escape for history.

"Bruce, what you got there?"

"Ride," the giant proclaimed, smiling broadly for the camera.

After allowing the guys to grab a few hours of sleep,

Parran had roused them at an absurdly early hour to decorate the rolling spectacle. It was practically complete now, with room for an entire marching band to perform on its wide platforms. The words *King's Court* were emblazoned in dazzling gold on both sides of the float. Charlie still hadn't figured out where Bruce was going to ride without being seen.

Parran emerged from a room at the back of the hangar pulling a wagon full of green five-gallon buckets. "Looks good," he called, though Charlie couldn't figure out how he knew that. "I took the liberty of getting lunch for us. Can't visit New Orleans without having red beans and rice. Personally I'm partial to a shrimp po-boy, but dat's impractical in this case." He swung the wagon around, and Bruce rubbed his hands together in anticipation.

Without waiting for an invitation, he threw a bucketful of food into his mouth. The unfamiliar sting of Cajun spices lit up his face, and he squeezed his eyes shut. After an excruciating swallow, Bruce searched frantically for some water. Parran was in no hurry to help the giant. He had a pretty good idea about how the big guy's first taste of Cajun cooking was going to go.

"Thought you might need some water," Parran chuckled.

Finally, Bruce, his big face red and sweaty, found an industrial spigot and swallowed a gallon of water. Then he rushed back for more food.

Parran helped himself to a slice of cornbread. "Bet you're busting at the seams to know how all dat going to work?"

Charlie tried a cautious spoonful of the sausage-filled rice. "Actually, I am. Where's Bruce going to sit?"

"Who said anything about sittin'?" Parran brushed cornbread crumbs from his hands and *tap-tap*ped his cane around to the front of the float. Reaching underneath a lip, he felt around until there was a loud *pop*.

A hidden panel, disguised by white crepe paper, swung open, and a long, rectangular box emerged. Bruce stopped eating and joined Charlie to examine it. Parran flipped open the lid, revealing an interior lined with cushy blue foam. It gave Charlie a queasy feeling.

"Is that a coffin?"

Parran pulled his sunglasses down to the end of his nose, exposing his milky blue eyes. "Don't be morbid, boy."

Charlie winced. The blind man's eyes looked like they hurt.

"Here's what's going down. Big fella, you'll take a load off right in there. Charlie, you'll be beside him the whole time."

"We're both going to be inside the box?"

"See those two clowns?" deadpanned Parran, nodding to the jesters hanging above them. "Dat's you two. After we're finished eating, in you go."

At the rate Bruce devoured the food, it didn't take long. Charlie finished off his meal in short order as well. Someone knocked on the big door at the front of the building.

"Just a minute," Parran yelled. Then he got quiet and held the box lid open for Charlie and Bruce. "It's showtime. Get in there, get comfortable. I'll handle the rest."

Bruce climbed into the box and stretched out. Charlie hopped in after him; there was just enough room along the giant's side to squeeze in. Parran closed the lid of the box, and the two friends were enveloped in darkness. Charlie thought about all the spicy food Bruce had just eaten and hoped the box was well ventilated.

"Too small," the giant complained.

"Relax! Sorry the accommodations ain't first class!" Parran reached under the lip again, and the box sucked back into the float, which sealed up tight. "It ain't dat bad. See them air holes along the sides? You might even watch the city go by. Lots to see!"

Even though it was plenty dark, Charlie saw what Parran meant. The walls of the box had perforations at regular intervals that coincided with lookout points on the float. Charlie and Bruce found the ones closest to their heads and peeked out at the hangar. Charlie found his phone and pointed it at Bruce. The picture was dark and fuzzy, but that made it look cool.

"This is the part," he whispered, "where the heroes escape!"

"Yep!"

"Let us venture forth," Parran cried. The boys heard the sliding front doors to the building open.

Charlie couldn't believe what he was seeing through the peephole: at least thirty people, dressed in eggplant-colored coats with gold trim. Matching hats sat atop their heads. They all carried instruments—tubas and trombones, snare drums and saxophones. A few others twirled ornate umbrellas. A big truck crept along behind them.

"Good afternoon, everyone," bellowed Parran. He

pushed his hat back higher on his head. "And thank you for coming."

One man at the front of the line twirled his parasol and frowned. His salt-and-pepper goatee scrunched up at the corners as he looked dubiously at the massive float. "What kind of job is this, Parran?"

"We having a short parade up to Woldenberg Park," replied Parran. "Climb aboard."

Several of the musicians stormed their way up onto the float. Inside the box, it sounded like a particularly nasty hailstorm. Charlie and Bruce rocked back and forth.

"Crazy," whispered the giant.

"My man, Parran," came the voice of the fellow with the parasol. "What are we doing here? Some kind of new holiday or something?"

Parran motioned for the truck to back up and hitch to the float. "As if the Big Easy needs a reason to have a parade! But if you must have one, think of it as a celebration of our rich heritage. And in case anyone is wondering, your friend Parran does have a permit. Dis is a legal parade sanctioned by the proper authorities."

The man with the parasol laughed. "That must have been one serious bribe."

"Well, we are in New Orleans. Now, if the truck is in place? Music, please!"

The musicians raised their instruments and played a soulful tune. Some marched alongside the float, while another bunch played up on the platform. Parran pulled on a colorful hat and twirled his walking cane like a baton. The truck pulled the Trojan horse of a float slowly out of the building and through an exit reserved for rail yard workers.

Across the yard, the Accelerton man turned his head in the direction of the brassy music. He squinted at the strange spectacle, then switched to another app on his phone. A bizarre float wasn't an unusual sight in New Orleans, but he snapped pictures just in case and sent them along to his superiors.

The float moved down the streets of the city. Inside the box, Bruce mugged for Charlie's camera, bopping his head side to side in time to the Dixieland beat.

Even with their limited view, there was so much to see: The buildings of New Orleans were as colorful and unique as the float itself. Colorfully dressed onlookers waved white handkerchiefs and danced alongside the float. A red streetcar rolled past, clanging its bell in time to the music. The tombs in a neighborhood graveyard jutted above the ground as if the dead were buried that way in case they wanted to rise up and join the party. Charlie couldn't think of a city less like Richland Center.

"Crazy," whispered Bruce.

"I'll say."

Finally they reached Woldenberg Park, full of joggers, rollerbladers, and people posing as living statues, trying to coax coins from tourists. The muddy Mississippi River ran alongside the procession. Parran sniffed the air.

"You see a hovercraft nearby?" he asked a trombone player.

"Yes, sir, there's one tethered to the pier up ahead."

"Outstanding! Dat's our destination."

The float turned in the direction of the pier to the strains of "When the Saints Go Marching In." Soon the brassy procession was at the pier, with a beat-up hovercraft moored at its end.

Charlie peeked out the viewing hole. Onboard the hovercraft, he saw four unsavory-looking characters, two older and two younger. *Fathers and sons?* wondered Charlie. All of them had goatees and wore sleeveless shirts over their ample bellies. Gnarly alligators were tattooed on the younger men's sunburned biceps.

One of the fathers, squinting beneath a camouflage baseball hat, raised his arm and shouted over the music. "Heyo, Parran!"

"Benoit," Parran hollered back. "Good to hear your voice!"

"Charlie?" The giant kept a wary eye on a peephole.

"Keep it down," Charlie whispered back. "We're almost there."

"Charlie!"

The giant pointed out the viewing space at the end of the float. Weaving in and out of traffic, and moving dangerously close, was an Accelerton security van.

"Oh man." Charlie tried not to panic, but fear and the stuffy air inside the box made him feel claustrophobic. "How are we going to tell Parran?"

Charlie watched the van pull over to the side of the road, and two guys with dark glasses and green Accelerton jackets hopped out. One produced a phone, letting someone know that they were getting close. A phone! Was Tim smart enough to . . . ? Charlie checked the contacts in the one that his brother had left him. *Parran!* He punched the name and waited impatiently for the blind man to answer.

"Who dat?"

"Charlie! There's bad guys right on our tail!"

"Band!" Parran pocketed his cell, spun on his heel, and addressed the musicians with a toothy smile. "Please retire to the rear of the float and play 'Bon Ton Roulet'! With feeling, boys!"

A slew of bodies marched into place, blocking the peepholes at the end of the float. Many were band members, but overweight tourists in shorts and sandals also joined them, attracted to the jazzy music. The Accelerton men tried to push their way through the party, but no matter which way they turned, swaying sousaphones pushed them backward.

"Yeah!" shouted Bruce, laughing as a trombone slide poked one of the Accelerton guys in the side of the head.

At the front of the *King's Court* float, Parran popped the panel and the box rolled forward. Wheels folded out from beneath the crate, and the container rolled out onto the pier and aboard the hovercraft. Now that they were outside the float, Charlie got a real sense of how loud the music was. The band was blasting its Dixieland sound right at the Accelerton security guys, who couldn't make their way through the throng of dancing sightseers and high-stepping musicians. As far as Charlie could tell, they couldn't even see the Cajuns sliding the box onto the hovercraft.

"Parran is the man!" he said to Bruce and started filming the next leg of their journey.

"Yep!"

When the case was secured onboard, Parran waved a

handful of crisp twenty-dollar bills to the band members. The man with the parasol ran to the end of the pier, retrieved the cash, and raised it triumphantly to the musicians. A joyous cheer erupted, and the band rocked even harder. When the Accelerton security men finally broke through the multitude and sprinted down the pier, the hovercraft had already slipped away down the Mississippi.

The hovercraft hummed through the water at a good clip, but Charlie and Bruce were getting pretty sick of lying inside the box. In the giant's case, that sickness was literal. The cramped space, the lack of fresh air, and the stale smell of swamp water combined to make his face turn green. He wasn't used to traveling by boat, and the rocking waves were playing havoc with his stomach, full of red beans and rice.

"We deserve all the gold after this," Charlie griped.

Bruce just moaned.

Parran was at the front of the hovercraft with the two older guys, sharing a bottle of something that sounded, from all the hooting and back slapping, like it was full of good mood. The men leaned back in canvas lawn chairs, watching the sun turn orange as it touched the horizon.

"Mighty appreciative dat you boys could help me out on short notice," Parran said.

"Yep yep!" said the second man, Lambert, cracking back the pop-top on an aluminum can.

"We can put down the gaff hook anytime for the kind of money you talkin'," laughed Benoit. "Plus we're outta gator tags as it is. And nothing worse than goin' back to fishin'."

"True dat. Alligator season should be longer," agreed Parran. "A man can always use a new pair of boots."

"Yep yep!"

"Those dummies that run the show are blinder than you, Parran. Gators everywhere in Louisiana!" Benoit raised his bottle. "Here's to new boots!"

From the holes in their box, Charlie and Bruce watched the two younger guys futz with fishing equipment—beat-up poles of all sizes, ratty-looking nets, and dangerous hooked sticks that Charlie surmised were used to land fish that were too big to get aboard any other way. The two had plenty of arguments about what line should go where, and they weren't afraid of yelling and shoving to make their points.

That's why they didn't notice the first time Bruce pushed up on the top of the box, anxious for a gulp or two of fresh air. Charlie punched him in the arm.

"You want these guys to see you? We're almost there!"

"Don't care," he burped, raising the lid a couple of inches and sucking in as much fresh air as he could handle.

The box rustling finally caught the attention of one of the young fishermen. "Hey, Dag," said the one called Junior, eyeing the box with suspicion. "That box just moved."

"Yeah," drawled Dag. "It's called the boat rocking."

"I know what I saw. I'm having a look."

"Don't need me to tell you," said Dag. "That's a dangerous game you playin'. If your pa catches you . . ."

Junior approached the box with one of the hooks. "If
there's trouble in there, he'll thank me. Just a peek."

"What do we do?" Charlie whispered. "Call Parran
again?"

The lid of the box flipped up. Junior got a good look at
what was inside and screamed at the top of his lungs, flailing
backward to where Dag stood. It was only a second before
he joined in the frightened yelling.

"What the . . . ?" Benoit and the other men rushed to
the back of the hovercraft, just as Bruce stood and stretched
his limbs into the sky, breathing in the fresh air. He craned
his neck from side to side and it cracked loudly.

"Let me guess," Parran said, tapping his cane around the
deck. "Somebody opened dat box."

"What in blazes is that thing?" screeched Benoit. "Skunk
ape? You gone and caught yourself a skunk ape?"

"Yep yep!"

Charlie crawled out of the box just as Junior and Dag
found some courage and cautiously approached Bruce with
gaff hooks.

"Get back in that box, skunk ape!" yelled Dag.

"He ain't no skunk ape," said Parran. "And you boys
need to settle down. I'm paying you good money."

"Hi," said Bruce, flashing the Cajuns a smile that showed
off his yellowed, crooked teeth.

"The skunk ape can talk!" shouted Dag.

"A deal's a deal, Parran," said Benoit, tentatively motioning for his boys to stand down. "But this here's another thing altogether. You never said nothin' about no monster."

"He's not a skunk ape and he's not a monster," said Charlie.

"Relax," said Bruce, but it sounded vaguely like a threat as he motioned for the boys to drop their hooks. Dag and Junior let them fall to the deck and held up their hands in surrender.

"This here's what you call a friend," Parran said calmly. "Dat's all you need to know, and you don't need to tell anyone what you seen."

"Forget that," said Dag. He reached into his shorts and pulled out his phone. He held it up and started taking a video of Bruce. "No matter how much you payin' us, I can get more sellin' this on the Internets!"

Someone fired a shot into the air and everyone, including Bruce, jumped and turned to the explosive sound. Parran stood still with a pearl-handled pistol pointed straight up into the air. "Here's the thing. I'm a crack shot, but not like you think. I keep shooting this thing until it cracks somebody." The blind man swung the gun around, and everyone on board the hovercraft ducked and weaved when it pointed their way. "Now, Benoit, I suggest your man here toss his phone over to my big friend."

"Do like the man says, Dag," grumbled Benoit.

Dag threw up his hands. "But Pa . . ."

"Do it!"

Dag reluctantly tossed the phone up in the air. "There you go, skunk ape." The giant snatched it midflight.

"Got it, big boy?" asked Parran.

Bruce held the phone between his thumb and forefinger. "Yep."

"Then smash it up good." Dag groaned a little at the sound of cracking metal and plastic, and the blind man cackled. "I'll buy you a shiny new phone, don't you worry. This ain't no big thing. You boys know how important it is to keep secrets. Y'all got a few right here on this boat, am I right? I know your business is built on transportin' contraband from time to time. Probably some on here right now—stuff you don't need anybody knowin' about?"

Benoit and Dag exchanged awkward side glances.

"You needn't worry about me tellin', and I'll double your fee. We all in the smuggling business. You feelin' me?"

Lambert cleared his throat. "Yep yep."

"We ain't seen nothin'," mumbled Junior even as he stared up at the grinning giant. "Ain't that right, Dag?"

Junior elbowed Dag in the arm. "Right," he said, shuffling his bare feet on the slick deck. Losing a phone was worth a guaranteed double payday. "Just takin' a ride down the river, tryin' to catch a few fish."

"Like you was sayin', Parran—we carry the rare, valuable, and illegal," said Benoit, who looked like he'd seen a ghost. "But this here creature's something else entirely. I don't want it on my boat. I'll take your double fee, but ride's over. Grand Isle's just up ahead."

Benoit pointed to the shoreline, where Charlie could see the hint of the Century Wheel peeking above the piers along the beach front.

Parran sighed. Waving his gun around wasn't going to change Benoit's mind. "What about my friends?"

"I suggest they start swimmin'."

Parran tapped his way to the crate. "End of the line, boys," he said. "You know how to swim, Bruce?"

"Yep," said Bruce, insulted. Of course he knew how to swim.

"Then I suggest you be on your way, quick as you can now."

Bruce launched the crate into the water and, seeing it was sea-worthy, tossed Charlie inside.

"Hey!" shouted the boy as he bounced down in the box. "Take it easy! I can swim, too, you know."

The giant took one last look at Benoit and did a massive cannonball off the side of the craft, soaking the crew that had just kicked him off their boat. Then, using the wooden box as a kickboard, he began flipping his feet toward shore.

The hovercraft rose, and in an instant it zipped away in the opposite direction.

"I gotcha this far, boys," hollered Parran. "Good luck the rest of the way!"

Charlie held on tight as the box skittered across the water. Bruce's powerful kicking was better than an outboard motor—they neared the shore of Grand Isle in no time. Despite the spray of water in his face, the boy could make out the outline of the darkened carnival that had been set up on the sandy shore. The gold was within their reach at last.

When their makeshift boat bottomed out, Bruce plucked Charlie out of the box, which they abandoned in the muck. They walked the hundred yards through the shallow gulf water between them and the lonely beach.

"I think we made it, dude."

"Made it," the giant replied, a look of triumph on his face.

They didn't see a soul as they walked the sand toward the carnival rides that were silhouetted in what remained of a scarlet sunset. Charlie wasn't exactly sure where to find the giant smugglers and the gold, but the Creep Castle seemed a good place to start, even though the carnival looked deserted. Charlie scanned the beach for signs of life. On the waterfront, just across the beach from the rides, a huge crane towered over a long pier, probably to load the huge ship moored there. Farther down the beach, a run-down snack shop sat at the end of a rickety, shorter dock. Where was everybody?

"Wertzie?"

Bruce pointed to the carny, who was standing in the shadows at the front of the nearest pier.

"Yeah!" shouted Charlie, happy to see the guy again. They really had made it. "Wertzie! We're here!"

He and Bruce ran the rest of the way, and Wertzie's face lit up at the sight of them. "Charlie! I knew you guys could do it!" He looked past them down the beach. "Wait a minute. Where's your brother?"

"What do you mean?"

Wertzie's face fell. "We hoped he was with you." He hesitated. "I hate to say this, Charlie, but he stole the gold."

The revelation was like a punch in the giant's gut. "Gold!"

"What are you talking about?"

"Gone without a trace. It's supposed to be up there." Wertzie nodded over his shoulder at the crane and huge ship. "Bruce was supposed to leave on that ship with the giants' gold," he explained. "But Tim has taken his ticket, so to speak."

The boy was stunned: Tim was a lot of things, but Charlie never thought he could be a thief. "I don't believe it."

"Oh, you can believe it," called a chubby man who

emerged from the ship. He hurried down the pier to meet them, looking up at Bruce. He stopped halfway to take in the giant, hands trembling with excitement. "Remarkable! Simply remarkable!"

"Who?" asked Bruce.

"That's Mr. Barton," said Wertzie. The carny pulled a gun from the back of his pants and grabbed Charlie around the neck. He pressed the pistol against the boy's temple. Bruce roared at Wertzie, but that just made him push the gun harder into Charlie's hair. "Back off, Stretch," he warned.

"Don't listen to him," shouted Charlie. "Smash him, Bruce!"

But the giant had just seen how dangerous guns were back on the boat. He glowered at Wertzie, then at Barton, but didn't attack.

"Your brother won't answer my phone calls," said Wertzie. "Would you mind giving him a buzz and letting him know you're here?"

"Forget it," snapped Charlie.

"Fine," said Wertzie, releasing the tension on Charlie's neck just enough to grab the phone from his pocket. "I'll do it." Wertzie found Tim's number and pressed the screen. It only rang once.

"Charlie?" came Tim's voice over the tinny speaker.

"I got your brother at the carnival," shouted Wertzie. "And if you don't show up with the gold in fifteen minutes, he starts losing fingers!"

"Don't give it to him!" shouted Charlie, but Wertzie had already hung up.

Barton took a tentative step toward Bruce. "Hey there, fella," he coaxed. "How about you come with me? This doesn't have to be difficult."

Bruce lowered his face to Barton's and grunted through bared teeth. The bespectacled scientist rocked backward on the splintery dock.

Wertzie dragged a flailing Charlie across the sand toward the carnival, gun still to his head. "Let's go, Lawson."

Bruce clenched his fists and raised his arms in the air. "No!"

"Hey," someone yelled from high above the giant. "I'm ready for you this time."

Bruce looked up to see the Stick balancing on top of the crane, at least half a dozen weapons strapped to his back. He thrust hypodermic needles into both thighs and dropped the plungers. His eyes bulged and the muscles flexed under his skintight black suit. Then, with a twirl of his namesake, the Stick leaped off the crane.

36

Bruce swung a furious fist through the dark, but the Stick contorted his body as he fell, dodging the blow. He landed on the giant's left thigh, using it as a springboard to launch himself onto Bruce's shoulder in the blink of an eye. The end of the man's stick glowed blue with an ominous, electric hum.

"Bruce!"

Charlie's shouts faded into the distance as Wertzie dragged him behind the carnival trailers, but not before he saw the Stick jab his pulsing weapon into the side of the giant's neck. Bruce howled in pain as a jolt of electricity sent him reeling. But unlike Giant Fitz, the shock did not knock him unconscious. Like a man stung by a bee, the giant slapped at his attacker. The Stick used a lock of Bruce's long hair like a vine to swing clear, but the giant's flailing fist found him. The glancing blow sent the man spinning to the ground.

"Remarkable!" shouted Barton, who pulled out a phone

to document the fight for posterity. He established a satellite connection with Gretchen Gourmand so she could witness their triumph. "What you're seeing cannot begin to convey how incredible a giant is in person!"

The sting in his neck enraged Bruce. He charged down the dusky beach toward the Stick, who simply stood and waited, letting the giant get close. Then a tremendous flash of blue light from the end of his weapon blinded Bruce. The giant stumbled, hands over his eyes, and fell face-forward into the sand. The Stick reached over his shoulder and retrieved a new weapon from his arsenal.

"Brilliant," exclaimed Barton, chasing the action to make sure he caught every moment of the encounter. "We were right to hire the Stick—the giant is five times his size and he hasn't backed off an inch!"

A small box in the top of Barton's screen showed Gourmand conceding the point but not satisfied. "Enough playing with it," she warned through Barton's phone. "Finish the job and get him aboard the ship! I want that creature in international waters as quickly as possible!"

Bruce tried to clear his vision as the Stick gave his new weapon a hard shake. It extended into a much longer staff. He heaved the javelin at Bruce and halfway there, a burst from its back end propelled the weapon like a rocket. The lead tip crackled with an electrifying cobalt glow.

The angry giant's reflexes were too quick for the intended finishing blow. He backhanded the missile right out of the air, sending it to explode over the ship in a blue blaze.

"That's not good," wheezed Barton.

Gourmand slapped the camera lens. "Finish him!"

The shout caught Bruce's attention, who wheeled to snatch up the scientist. The giant lifted the thrashing man to eye level and roared in his face.

"Put me down!"

Bruce turned toward the gulf and wound up like a baseball pitcher ready to bring the heat.

"Not like that!"

With a whirling heave, the giant flung Barton far out over the boat and into dark, deep waters.

Barton's voice trailed off in the distance as he flew through the night. "I can't swiiiiiiiiiiiiim . . . !"

Bruce spun back around. It was time to focus his fury on the Stick.

37

Wertzie peeked around the corner of the Pick-a-Duck game, trying to stay out of sight while watching for Tim's return with the missing gold. He checked the time on his phone and ground his teeth. "I gave your idiot brother fifteen minutes, and he's used about fourteen already. He better show!"

"Why are you doing this?" asked Charlie. "That guy's going to hurt Bruce!"

"I don't care about stupid giants—I want the gold. All of the gold! Why do you think I tricked the two of you into leaving it unguarded in the first place? Your brother beat me to it. Now I'm going to get it back."

A scream from the beach caused both Wertzie and Charlie to jerk their heads. It sounded like the wormy scientist, and his shrill shriek was one of pure terror. Both of them looked up in the sky to watch a flailing figure soar out over the gulf. "What's going on?" shouted Wertzie.

Charlie saw his opening. He searched the sandy ground in vain for a rock or stick he could use as a weapon. In desperation, Charlie reached into his pockets and found something that would have to do.

Charlie lunged forward and stabbed Wertzie right in his sensitive stub with the peekaboo pen, the girl's clothes disappearing as the carny let loose with a horrendous squawk. His pistol flew from his hand and landed with a splash among the rubber ducks. He dropped to his knees in pain, clutching at the pen that was still stuck in his flesh. Wertzie hadn't been kidding—the nub did hurt when you touched it. When you stabbed it, the pain got downright excruciating.

"I'll kill you!" he shouted, pulling the peekaboo pen from his hand. Blood the color of brick oozed from the wound. Wertzie lunged to his feet.

Charlie took off running for his life. He looked for someone, anyone, who might help him, but the carnival grounds were hopelessly empty.

Wertzie grabbed a crowbar near a pile of crates left over from the day's carnival setup. He held it in his good hand while clutching his injured mitt to his T-shirt, trying to stop the bleeding. "I'm going to beat you like I should have done to your brother a long time ago!"

Charlie thought about making a break for the beach, but Wertzie was definitely faster than he was, a sure bet to catch him in a flat-out race for Bruce. Charlie would have to lose him.

He shot across the midway and darted around the lemon shake-up stands and down the row of carnival games that backed up to the beach. He turned a corner and hurdled the counter at Tim's "Guess Your Weight" booth, ducking beneath the prize table and hiding there in the shadows. He didn't move a muscle. Determined not to let his breathing betray him, he listened for the telltale sound of Wertzie's footsteps. His own pulse pounded in his throat. He could hear Bruce and the Stick continuing to battle down by the water—Charlie even thought that the giant was winning—but there wasn't a sound along the midway. He was just about to attempt to sneak back to the beach when the crowbar smashed a novelty mirror that hung among the stuffed animals. Shattered shards of silver rained down around the prize table.

The carny was dead serious about wanting to break a few bones as payback for the peekaboo-pen puncture. The boy pulled the booth awning down on Wertzie and scrambled out while the man untangled himself. Then Charlie tore across the carnival grounds looking for any place he could hide, the furious sounds of a stumbling Wertzie not far behind him.

Most of the rides were closed up, offering no escape. Finally Charlie found one into which he could at least duck—the Gravitron. He tumbled in, looking for refuge.

Wertzie burst inside just behind him, waving the crowbar like a flyswatter.

"No place to run, Lawson!"

The crowbar crashed into the Gravitron control panel at the center of the ride, just inches from Charlie's head. The boy dove for the controls, remembering his brother's claim— "Any idiot can run the Gravitron"—and pushed the big red button in the middle of the control panel. The door to the outside slammed down.

"Oh no, you don't!"

Wertzie lunged after Charlie with his free, bleeding hand, missing the boy by the length of a missing finger just as the ride roared to life.

The crowbar flew backward. Wertzie tried with all his might to reach inside the control booth and strangle Charlie even as the laws of physics denied his progress. Then centrifugal force slammed him back into the padded Gravitron wall. The ride spun faster and faster, sucking Wertzie to its surface like a magnet snatching iron filings. His complexion got pasty and pale, while motion-sick tears filled his eyes.

"Slow it down," he pleaded. "I'm going to hurl!"

"It's just going to come flying back at you," warned Charlie from the ride's motionless center. He wasn't ever going to let the Gravitron stop, even as Wertzie began making awful retching sounds.

Charlie felt something uneven beneath his feet. He looked down to find a maintenance panel on the floor. He got on his hands and knees, twisting a silver handle that caused a door to flip open with a sudden click and reveal the sandy dirt beneath the ride. He took one last look back at Wertzie— someone was going to have a smelly mess to clean up. Then the boy slipped down through the passage and ran like crazy for the beach.

38

Arriving at the ocean, Charlie watched the Stick tumble out of the way as an enraged Bruce pounded crater after crater into the wet sand. With amazing speed, the mercenary bundled four rods that were strapped to his back. The metallic shafts locked together with a menacing clank, and the Stick slung the four-barreled weapon over his shoulder.

"For you," he said, "I brought the biggest stick."

A warning was useless, so Charlie did the only other thing he could: throw himself at the Stick just as the terrible weapon fired dozens of Taser wires in the giant's direction. Despite the boy's small stature, the collision was violent enough to knock most of the projectiles off course. Only four of the cruelly barbed tendrils hooked in Bruce's side, but their violent electrical discharge was still enough to shock the giant to his knees.

Now the Stick was angry. He tossed the Taser weapon aside then punched Charlie in the midsection. The blow cracked two of Charlie's ribs and forced him to the ground. The Stick put his boot on Charlie's throat.

He looked up just in time to see someone kick the Stick in the forehead. The boy brought himself up on his elbows and watched Tiger launch another fierce series of kicks at the Stick's skull.

"Tiger's got this. Let's move!"

Juice Man pulled Charlie away from the fray and to their fallen giant friend, who was still writhing in the cold damp of the beach. "Don't touch those!" warned the Juice Man as Charlie reached for the wires. The man pulled insulated gloves from his work pants, then carefully removed the pulsating Taser cables from Bruce's rib cage. The giant moaned and rolled over onto his side. He had a dazed, expressionless look in his eyes.

Charlie's ribs hurt so bad he couldn't talk. Juice Man grabbed him hard by the shoulders. "See that concession shack over there?"

Charlie turned, and the movement made him wince in pain. He'd seen the shack when they'd arrived, halfway down the closed-off, rickety pier that barely stood on its tall stilts. "Sure, but what does that . . . ?"

"I know it doesn't look like much, but that's the giant's ride out of here. You got to get him inside, but whatever you do don't set foot on the pier! Wood's all rotten and it probably won't hold two ordinary people's weight, much less yours and his. There's a door on the underside of the dock, you get in that way and everything should fire up."

Bruce was going to escape in a refreshment stand? "Okay, I'll get him there. But then what?"

"Just go!"

"Heeyahhh!"

Twenty feet down the beach, Tiger ducked the Stick's hard right cross. She delivered a powerful knee to his midsection and pulled the last remaining weapon from his back. She used it to bash his face, which knocked him backward into a flip. With an angry sneer, he landed on his feet, reached into his boot, and withdrew a small baton.

Tiger scoffed at the unimpressive cudgel.

The Stick snapped the weapon with a violent flick of his wrist, and the rod telescoped, doubling in size. Once more, the end crackled with electricity. "You're good, but good isn't going to be enough."

"No!" Even in his disoriented state, Bruce wasn't about to let the Stick take out Tiger. The wobbly giant rose to his feet, but the Juice Man jumped in his way.

"Leave that guy to us! Charlie, get him out of here, now! Come on, kid, what are you waiting for?"

Tiger screamed in pain. A brutal blast from the weapon sent her reeling into the sand, followed by the Stick brutally bending her arm the wrong way at the elbow. She slumped to the ground, and Juice Man ran to cut off the Stick's next attack.

"Bruce, let's go!" Charlie grabbed the giant by the tunic and started toward the pier. Bruce took one last look back at Tiger, then staggered after his friend with unsteady footsteps. "Under there!" Charlie pointed to the dark underside of the stilted pier below the snack shack. Bruce scooped him up and waded into the gulf. The water didn't help Bruce shake off the Taser's effects. In fact, the cold seemed to stagger him even more. They made their way under the shadowy pier, searching for what the Juice Man promised Charlie he would find. Finally, he saw a hatch near the end of the dock.

"Up there, Bruce. That's got to be it!"

The unsteady giant set Charlie down on the wooden support webbing on the underside of the pier, then labored to shinny up. He struggled to the top, pushed the door open, crawled inside, and pulled Charlie behind him.

With a long, low creak, the door slammed shut, which triggered some kind of mechanism inside the shack. Digital equipment began to glow and hum. Bruce slumped in the corner and held his head in his hands, trying to reorient himself. Charlie's eyes adjusted to the dim light, revealing the indistinct outline of dozens of helium tanks that he'd first seen in the back of the Juice Man's generator truck. They were hooked up to red hoses that ran to the roof. The GPS system that the Juice Man had been working on back in Peoria sat atop a central computer system. It beeped twice, and the tanks began releasing helium into the hoses, which in turn inflated a large canvas balloon that slowly filled the roof.

Holy cow, thought Charlie. *This thing is a blimp.*

At the far end of the shack, two huge exhaust fans began to spin. *Are those propellers?* he wondered. *Got to be. Maybe they even steer this thing!*

To the left of the tanks, Charlie saw another familiar sight: the pallet of gold. Tim hadn't stolen it after all! The ceiling began to waver and crack.

"Ride?" asked Bruce.

"Yes, sir. And there's your gold!" The floor rumbled and

the whole shack began to detach from its anchoring. It wouldn't be long before the blimp took flight—with Charlie on it. Nothing was going according to plan, but at least for now, it looked like he and the giant would be together.

Without warning, five glowing wires sailed through the window. They struck Bruce dead in the chest. The giant shook uncontrollably.

"Bruce! No!"

Charlie spun. Out a crooked window, he saw the Stick at the end of the rickety pier, his glowing, four-barreled bazooka-stick once again on his shoulder. Charlie looked down the beach. Tiger and Juice Man lay unconscious on the sand. Even as fast as the balloon was filling, the Stick would reach Charlie and Bruce long before the blimp took off. Apparently satisfied that the giant was unconscious, the Stick turned off the flow of electricity. The giant stopped shaking, but he was barely coherent.

Charlie knew then what he had to do. There was no way Bruce could stay. Tim had been right: Charlie had to do what was best for the giant.

"I'm your friend, right?"

Bruce looked up at Charlie as if to say "Are you kidding me?" Even in his weakened state, he held out his fist.

Charlie bumped it, holding it against the giant's for a long moment before finally taking a step back. His throat felt thick and he couldn't swallow. Remembering the phone in his pocket, he withdrew it and left it by the window for the giant to find when he got home. Movies for later, something to re-member him by. Charlie dashed out the front door, leaving

Bruce alone in the snack shack. The giant wouldn't have his back this time. This one was on Charlie.

The Stick was almost halfway down the pier, the end of his weapon blazing the way. "You again?" he said. "For being such a pain in the ass, your buddy gets another one." The treacherous wires crackled with energy. The dock shook as Bruce writhed inside the shack.

Charlie needed to stop him right then and there. The boards creaked and groaned beneath his feet. The Stick looked to be more than two hundred pounds. All the rotting wood needed to give way was some extra weight.

The Stick laughed, amused at the boy's pursuit down the dock. "What do you think you're going to do when you get here, kid?"

Charlie leaped in the air and hollered. "Fight without fighting!"

He landed on the rickety boards right in front of the Stick and the entire section of dock gave way. All the wires from the Stick's weapon pulled free from Bruce inside the shack. The boy somehow managed to reach up and grab hold of a fractured beam dangling from what remained of the pier. His fingers gripped hard as he watched the Stick plunge into the gulf. An eerie electric zap erupted when his shimmering weapon hit the surface. A wide circle of water lit up blue for a brief second, then darkened to match the night sky.

"No!" came a shout from the snack shack. Bruce bumbled forward, trying to make his way out to help Charlie, to help his friend, but the concession stand had torn away from the pier. The zeppelin was expanded to its full size, carrying the giant away into the night. Bruce's sorrowful shouts were still audible as Charlie watched him float away safely into the night sky, his unlikely ride silhouetted against a silvery moon.

"Bye, buddy," Charlie said. He felt light-headed, and one of his hands slipped from the timber. He tried to swing around to grab hold just as the damaged lumber splintered and released from what remained of the dock.

But someone grabbed him by his wrist before he could fall.

"Got you," said Tim, hoisting him back up onto the pier.

39

It was the middle of the night. Charlie sat at the shore end of what used to be the wooden dock, trying to shake the ache of his sore ribs and waning adrenaline. Tiger approached. She had one arm in a sling, but she still tousled his hair. It was a gesture Charlie usually hated because it made him feel like a little kid. But he didn't mind it right now.

A bark from down the beach made Charlie look up. There in the moonlight was Powder, plaster cast around her front left paw, but still managing to chase gulls on her three good legs. And sure enough, farther down the beach, he saw Hank on crutches, hobbling alongside his good friend Parran. They were getting the download from Tim and the Juice Man. The old man recognized Charlie and gave him a wave with his crutch. Charlie couldn't hear what they were saying, but Tim laughed a lot in his big horse-guffaw.

Tiger wasn't nearly as relaxed as the other giant smugglers. She stalked the sand along the edge of the water, searching its surface, smooth as glass and dark as a shadow. Charlie couldn't imagine any way the Stick could have survived the jolt he'd received, but he felt a measure of comfort knowing that the carny roughie wouldn't rest until she was sure trouble was gone for good.

Then Charlie saw the old man put two fingers in his mouth and whistle. Tiger joined the smugglers as Hank presented each of them with a package wrapped in plain brown paper. Even in the dim moonlight, Charlie knew what they were. Each package contained a handful of cylinders made of pure giant gold, enough to make each of the smugglers rich. Wertzie was stupid to have given up his share for a chance to grab it all for himself.

Juice Man approached with a bag of ice and presented it to the boy. No one had wanted to send Charlie home more than the Juice Man, but his fat-lipped smile, collateral damage from his fight with the Stick, communicated a newfound respect. Charlie took the bag and put it under his shirt, feeling the sting at first but then a numbing cold.

"Where's Wertzie?"

Juice Man laughed and jerked his thumb back in the direction of the carnival. "Hank says to keep him spinning for a while longer."

"He's still in the Gravitron?"

"It's only been a couple of hours," said Juice Man with a shrug.

"Are you going to call the cops?"

"I don't think so. He knows too much. Tiger will have a chat with him."

Charlie imagined the different ways Tiger could make

Wertzie sorry for what he'd done, things that would make losing a measly index finger seem like a slap on the wrist. The guy would probably be better off in jail.

"Going back up to the carnival," said Juice Man. "Anything else you need?"

"I'm good."

"I figured you wrong, kid." He nudged Charlie's shoulder and patted his jacket, fat with gold. "You showed me something." Then the bald man headed back to his truck.

Charlie allowed himself a smile. The smugglers, especially his brother, deserved their rewards. They had all been there when it counted. And in the end, Charlie had helped his friend, even if it was not at all in the way he'd planned it.

He stared up into the heavens. The blimp, so monstrous and imposing when it yanked free from the dock, was long gone. He'd watched it spirit his friend silently across the sky, swift and subtle, until it appeared to be nothing but a dot. Then it disappeared.

The whole thing felt like a dream now. Meeting Bruce, hopping the train, fighting off a giant bully and the professional thug who'd tried to stop Charlie and the other giant smugglers. He tried to imagine telling his mom, or anyone else for that matter, what had happened to him over the past few days. No one would believe him, ever. Except Adele.

He wondered if Bruce was angry with him. Charlie had gone back on their deal, after all. Leaving him alone in the shack hadn't been easy, and he didn't like the feeling.

"You really believed Wertzie when he said I called DJ?" Charlie looked up to see his brother grinning that dumb grin of his. "Come on, man. DJ?"

Charlie smiled. "I didn't want to go home."

"When you told me what Wertzie said, I thought he might be up to something," explained Tim. "So I stashed the gold and called his bluff. 'Course, I had no way of knowing he'd hooked up with Mr. Stick. Speaking of which." He reached inside his own stash and held out a stick of gold to Charlie.

He just stared at it. "No way."

"It's a college education. Or something good. You decide."

Charlie took the gold and once again felt its cool weight in his hand. He felt weird accepting the reward; he'd never been in it for the money. Maybe he'd give it to his mom as a peace offering. He figured he had some time to figure out the right thing to do with it.

"Want a ride?" asked Tim.

"Where we going?"

"Home. You got school this week, and Mom's already plenty mad at me about the whole thing. Plus, I'm thinking about staying in Richland Center for a while."

"For real?"

Tim reached down and helped Charlie to his feet. "Carnival life is tough, Charlie. Greasy food all the time, weirdos, never seeing your family. Most guys don't do it for more than a few seasons. Besides, I finished what I signed up for. With your help, of course."

Charlie nodded. But he couldn't quite bring himself to leave the beach. He watched Parran and Tiger helping Hank into one of the SUVs. Soon the shore would be deserted again. "Bruce will be okay, right? Wherever we sent him off to?"

"Heck to the yeah! From what I understand, the place is a freaking paradise. Everything a giant could want." He saw the look on Charlie's face. "Well, you know. Almost everything."

Tim pointed just up the beach, where his truck was waiting. The two of them walked across the sand in silence. Charlie took one last look out at the gulf, breathed in warm salty air, then swung the heavy metal door open and climbed inside the truck. It smelled like elephant ears. Tim turned the key and the engine started with a loud bang. Charlie laughed. There was no way Tim's rusty old ride could make it all the way to Wisconsin, but what was one more adventure at this point?

The truck snaked its way through the quiet streets of Grand Isle, then onto a lonely stretch of highway headed north. Charlie stared out the window.

"You think I'll see him again sometime?"

Tim didn't answer right away. "No. I don't think so."

Charlie nodded. It was the answer he expected.

Tim turned on the radio and found a station that blasted the kind of weird rock he liked. Charlie leaned his head against the cool glass of the passenger window, watching the strange Louisiana terrain, lush and otherworldly, fly past.

He was headed back to his old life in Richland Center, yes. But the past few days had taught him that the world was bigger than he'd ever thought possible. And he knew he still had a lot more to see.

ACKNOWLEDGMENTS

Collectively, Matt & Chris would like to thank: Victoria Skurnick and everyone at Levine/Greenberg/Rostan Agency, Liz Szabla & Anna Roberto at Feiwel and Friends, Drew Niles, Amanda Veith, Joe Garden, Jeff Perry, John Urban, Frugal Muse Books & *The Onion*.

Chris would like to thank: Heather Sabin, Todd & Heather Pauls, Carter & Jackson, Camilla, Dennis, Linda, Andy, Megan, Doug, & Kathy Smith, Joe, Jan, & Kira Sabin, Matt & Shandra Fink, Alex & Kyonghui Wilson, Jerard & Calli Adler, Blake Engeldorf, Tom & Meghan Hendricks, Chris Briquelet, Ryan & Katy Pettersen, Mark & Keri Brathwaite, Rich & Kerri Modjeski, Dan & Amy Turner, Marc Schwarting, Rob & Max Wheat, Angela Keelan Martinez and Jesus, Brooke, & Shelly Dobbs, Tori Dobbs, Jym Britton, Win Sager, Dave Danielson, Adam Goodberg, Chris & Becky Henkel, Mark Murray, Mark & Karen Kampa, Shawn & Allison Quinn, Anita Serwacki, Joe Nosek, Doug Moe, Jim Johnson, Neil Spath, Tom & Lena Oberwetter, Rich Hamby, Kirk & Gabriela Bosben, Bill Jackson, Cracked.com, and as always—everybody at the Village Bar.

Matt sends giant hugs to Katy, Jake, Ben, and Sammi. Sky-high fives to Joe and Greeg, Judy Santacaterina and Matt Swan, the Prom Committee and all alums of Madison CSz, Jay, Yi, and Tha, Ken, Jill, Roo, and #2, Julie, Ted, and Jack, Colleen, Maddie, and Emma, Michele Laux, the Nygores, Kate Kollman, Patricia Ohanian Lundstrom, Halsted Mencotti Bernard, Paul and Meghan, John Roach, the Mothership Connection, and childhood friends everywhere.

THANK YOU FOR READING THIS FEIWEL AND FRIENDS BOOK.